CANYON CAVES –
SECRETS OF THE
EARTHBORN

GLENN M. FUNKHOUSER

WESTBOW
PRESS®
A DIVISION OF THOMAS NELSON
& ZONDERVAN

WestBow Press books may be ordered through booksellers or by contacting:

WestBow Press
A Division of Thomas Nelson & Zondervan
1663 Liberty Drive
Bloomington, IN 47403
www.westbowpress.com
844-714-3454

Scripture quotations are taken from the New King James Version. Copyright © 1982 by Thomas Nelson, Inc. Used by permission. All rights reserved.

ISBN: 978-1-9736-9899-9 (sc)
ISBN: 978-1-9736-9900-2 (e)

Library of Congress Control Number: 2023909641

Print information available on the last page.

WestBow Press rev. date: 6/29/2023

CONTENTS

DEDICATION

This book is dedicated to readers of all ages, genders and ethnicities. To those who love fiction, adventure, young love and who believe in the metaphysical world.

ACKNOWLEDGEMENTS

Primarily I want to give glory to God for blessing me with
the desire to write, and for spurring me on even when I wasn't
particularly inspired. I'd also like to acknowledge the invaluable
assistance of my sons-in-law Chris and Matthew for being willing
to format my books to conform to the publishers' requirements.
Additionally I'd like to acknowledge my wife, our four children,
the rest of my in-laws and twelve grandchildren; all of whom
have traveled this sometimes-troublesome life with grace,
conviction, and determination, they inspire me every day.

1

The offer x 2/ The itinerary is set.

P rofessor Marvin Jennings had just fixed his morning cup of coffee and picked up his newspaper when there was a knock at the door of his apartment. His was a modest apartment, consisting of only the bare necessities, inexpensive furniture, a small TV his parents had given him years before, a small kitchen table and a bookcase filled with thick reference books with worn bindings that only a very few would find interesting.

Jennings grew up in a middleclass household and like most boys of his generation he was fascinated with the idea of superheroes then in early adolescence with cars and girls, pretty much in that order. But his real and enduring fascination had always been with the past and the mysteries it held.

As far as his finances were concerned he really only ever spent much money on his wardrobe. His father's favorite saying was, "The clothes make the man," while his mother stressed staying in shape, hence her favorite saying was just the opposite, "The man makes the clothes."

He always tried to stay in shape, dress well and hold himself to a standard his parents would appreciate and held all things old in high regard, especially where all things ancient were concerned.

Jennings was the Professor of Archaeology at Montclair College, a small college in the township of Montclair Massachusetts. He chose that particular college because for one it was close to home, but mainly he chose it because in a roundabout way it had chosen him. The college was looking for a professor familiar with artifacts, antiquities, old bones and someone who could pass on that knowledge to others easily. Also they were in desperate need of someone who had a good head for figures. The math tutor they'd had for years was recently retired.

Just the day before he'd been speaking with an old colleague of his who was telling him about an ancient artifact. A stone tablet complete with strange symbols and hieroglyphics he'd found while at a dig site in British Columbia. He'd gone on more than a few expeditions with that particular colleague during which important discoveries were made, even if they were only important to them. But, on occasion some of the finds were of importance to the powers that be in the world of archaeology. Jennings was mulling over his discussion with said colleague when he answered the door.

It was Jack McKinney, a student in his third period class. Jack was smart, handsome and personable. However, he needed the professor's help. Jennings had multiple degrees not the least of which was one in advanced mathematics and he'd agreed to tutor Jack and his girlfriend, Lila Harper at the beginning of the year. Lila had a 145 IQ and would have been on the Dean's list every semester had it not been for one subject. She was on the modest side of good looking but had a personality that drew everyone to her. For both of them though, advanced mathematics was their Achilles heel, hence they were in desperate need of Jennings' help.

"Hey Professor, Lila and I wanted to change the day you tutor us from Tuesdays to Thursdays, if that's okay? Lila has a job babysitting her neighbor's kids on Tuesdays and Wednesdays to make extra money while she's taking classes. She said that the kids are a handful but that their parents pay well."

Jennings smiled and asked them to come in. After they were seated he assured them that the change was fine and began sipping on his now lukewarm cup of coffee. The three of them chatted for a while between the Professor's sips and Jack could tell that he was preoccupied with something. He took his eyes off the professor momentarily and happened to glance at a piece of paper on Jennings's kitchen table and said, "Uhm, Arabic hieroglyphics. Strange looking symbols too. Have you translated them yet, Professor?"

Jennings gave him a questioning look and commented, "You know the Arabic language, Jack?"

"Yeah, my grandpa Jack was an amateur archaeologist and taught me from the time I was six years old. He always said God gives each of us a gift and he said mine was learning languages and understanding and translating symbols. He was surprised at how good I was. I'd figure out a symbol, he would research it and find out that I was what he called, spot on."

Jennings was not only intrigued but somewhat perplexed too. He'd known Jack long before he'd had him for a student. "You mean to say you've been in two of my classes now and I never knew this about you? What else have you been keeping a secret? You're not some kind of an alien are you?"

He grinned as he turned around and said, "No, take a look, no implant in my neck, no antennas protruding from my head, just a regular guy. To answer your other question; I never had to use what I knew in class and the subject never came up."

Jennings smiled as he looked at Jack and thought to himself, this young man might be useful to me. How to approach him though, that was the question? He'd figure something out.

Meanwhile Lila wasn't paying much attention to their conversation she just sat there looking at Jack with adoring eyes, almost in a trance-like pose; seemingly unable to snap out of it.

Jennings squinted his eyes as he looked at her, then said, "What about you Lila, what's your story; do you have a passion?"

"Yes I do, Professor Jennings, right now I'm looking at my passion."

He chuckled at the comment and they both laughed. "Well Jack, I'm going to have a copy of the stone tablet my friend found at the dig site sent to me. How about you and I look at it together, say Thursday afternoon after I tutor you and Lila? I think you just might be a big help; what do you say?"

"Great," Jack replied, "sounds like a hoot." He grinned and said, "Sorry, an old-timers expression I picked up from my grandpa on my dad's side. My mom's parents died awhile back."

Jennings looked at the two of them, smiled, tapped his finger on the table and said, "That settles it then, we're all set. For now though, how about I give you two a lift to the college?"

All the way there Jennings thought to himself that this might just be what he needed to get out of the doldrums he was in. He'd been thinking for the last year that his life was going nowhere fast. He had a comfortable lifestyle but no lady friend and no prospects in that area either. And if he were being honest with himself, he'd lost the passion he'd once had to teach archaeology, he'd rather be on the hunt in some far away location discovering a culturally significant relic or artifact.

After they arrived Jack and Lila thanked him again for agreeing to the change and disappeared down the hallway. Jennings turned right, walked past the Dean's office and into the professor's lounge. He wasn't what one would call an extremely sociable person, but he did enjoy the occasional funny story told on some of the students by their professors, and the coffee was unusually good. The professor of linguistics had recently purchased a coffee maker with all the bells and whistles, which not surprisingly drew more of the faculty into the professor's lounge than ever before.

All the usual faces were there that particular morning. The lounge was the place where the morning weary professors could relax and enjoy their first and possibly second cup of coffee before they began their day dealing with some compliant but more often than not, non-compliant students. To be fair though he hadn't been a model student back in the day either.

After the small crowd cleared away from the coffee machine he could see that there was a new face that morning. She was tall, attractive, well-dressed, and talking with Jane Myers, the advanced mathematics professor. It surprised him that there weren't more men huddled around chatting up the new professor.

Jane's presence did tend to repel the more masculine of the species. She was a no-nonsense type of person; just the kind you'd expect to be teaching advanced mathematics. She could have been more attractive had she not generally fashioned her attire after Ms. Hathaway, a character on the Beverly Hillbillies TV series. But she was friendly enough and more than a little thankful that Jennings was willing to take some of the tutoring load off of her. She looked in his direction and motioned for him to come over.

She said, "Marvin, this is Angela Drake, the new girls health and physical education professor. She was just telling me how much she was looking forward to teaching here and hoped she could become acquainted with more of the faculty sooner rather than later."

Jennings extended his hand, smiled, and said, "It's nice to see a new face, especially one as pretty as yours; pleased to meet you, Angela."

Jane nudged him to draw his attention back to her and said, "Tell me again why your majors in college were archaeology and advanced mathematics?" She gave a slight chuckle after the question.

He smiled and replied, "My love and passion is studying the past, discovering artifacts, translating writings, etc., but I'm somewhat of a genius when it comes to mathematics."

Jane tilted her head slightly and said, "Jennings here takes a huge amount of the load off me by tutoring many of my students, a favor for which I'm most appreciative. How many are you tutoring presently, Marvin?"

"About ten I'd say. And yes, it helps me keep my mind sharp and I enjoy the one-on-one interaction with the students. It's not like archaeology where you're basically just lecturing or giving them the occasional antidotal field story here and there. Some of my student see archaeology as an adventure into the unknown, not unlike the way Hollywood presents it."

"Oh," Angela remarked, "I love archaeology. The study of the past fascinates me. I was just a young girl when Raiders of the Lost

Ark came out. I must admit I developed quite a crush on Harrison Ford, who played the lead character. He was the perfect combination of ruggedly handsome and intellectually stimulating."

"Yes," Jennings replied, "you and almost every other teenage girl at the time I expect."

Jane raised her hand and said, "I can relate, my best friend and I must have seen the movie 10 times if we saw it once; Harrison was so dreamy in that movie."

Angela nodded in agreement, pulled her hair around the back of her ear and asked Jennings, "When's your first class today, Professor? If I can, I'd like to sit in on it. I only have three classes today myself."

He looked at the clock on the wall, and replied, "My first class is in 10 minutes on the second floor in room 210."

"Fantastic," my first class doesn't start for another hour and a half; would you mind if I sit in on yours?"

"No, not at all, I'd welcome having someone in my class who's actually passionate about archaeology and mature enough to pay attention. I can't help but think that more than a few of my students took my class because they thought it would be an easy A, not because they're particularly interested in the subject."

"Oh, I'm sure that's not the case Professor Jennings, I'm sure there are at least a few who are interested." She checked her watch and said, "I'll see you in 8 minutes then."

Marvin's classroom was what one would expect for a class in archaeology. Photos of skulls and completed skeletons, photos of dig sites; and there was even a mockup of a skeleton postured vertically on a pole and hanging on a metal arm which hooked the bottom back of the skull that near the entrance door. Each time the door was closed the skeleton moved slightly causing no small amount of snickering and chuckles from many of the students.

Angela entered after all the students were seated. Marvin motioned for her to have a seat in the front row in the desk which he purposefully instructed his students to not sit in. Of course, there were two of his admiring female students who tried to occupy it until he said politely, "I'm saving that for another professor this morning, Simone, Bridget."

He began with, "For those of you who've been in my introductory class or have heard of my teaching methods you're already aware of my archaeological philosophy so to speak. However, there are some new faces who have transferred here, and of course my guest this morning, Professor Angela Drake."

She stood, turned to the class, and gave a slight wave and sat back down.

"So, to bring everyone up to speed, my take on archaeology is really rather simple." He paused as he took a minute to peruse the room. "Archaeology is basically meant as a means to study the past which in my mind encompasses all of the past. Meaning," as he turned to the board and wrote: "Our physical past, environmental past, our various cultural pasts and our spiritual or religious past."

One of the new students raised her hand. "Yes Amy, you have a question?"

"How is our spiritual and religious past relevant to archaeology?"

He smiled, looked around at the other students and asked, "Any of my introductory students care to answer that question for Amy?"

Brent stood up. "Go ahead Brent."

"Well, archaeology isn't just about bones, it includes artifacts of every kind and description not the least of which are religious ones designed for ritualistic ceremonies and worship. And because there are so many religions each of them have an accompanying unique spiritual component.

"Precisely put, Brent. So, there is no separation in this class between religion and the past." Amy seemed satisfied with the answer and nodded. "Now that we've established the relevancy of religion as it relates to archaeology let me draw your attention to some bones found in the area of Mesopotamia within the last two years. I believe all of you have a copy."

Angela held her hand up. "Oh yes, I forgot our guest and my colleague." He handed her a copy. "As you can see we have partial pieces of dinosaur bones, a few intact pieces, and some skulls of various sizes and shapes. One is of particular interest to me, it's not only large but unusually oblong in shape. The size is similar to one found about 200 miles west of there, which suggests if you accept that the body length is customarily 7 to 8 times the skull length then the head would have rested on a 7 foot or 7'6" body making the overall height to be 8 feet to 8'6".

Amy raised her hand again. "So, Professor, are you really expecting us to believe that giants actually existed? Is there any proof that they ever existed beyond the myths and legends passed down from generation to generation, and specifically those mentioned in the Bible?"

"Yes, there are actual photos of individuals taken not that long ago and even more recently. And since you brought up the Bible, let's use the measurements of their day to see just how tall a fellow by the name of Goliath was. It says in the book of Kings that he stood six cubits and a span. The cubit then equaled 18 inches and the span was half that which would've been 9 inches. So the shortest Goliath would be is 9'9" tall and according to the Bible he had four brothers equally as large."

He pulled down the white screen just behind him, depressed the clicker in his hand showing at least a dozen individuals in various areas on the European continent wearing their traditional garb who were head and shoulders taller than their fellow tribesmen standing next to them.

Angela raised her hand. "Could these photos have been doctored in some way?"

Marvin shook his head side to side, smiled and replied, "No, they've actually been tested and they're quite genuine. These and other individuals I believe are descendants of what the Bible calls the Rephaim or Anakin which is translated long necked ones. They're more commonly referred to as Nephilim."

"Which are?" Angela questioned.

"The hybrid offspring of the Bene Ha Elohim or sons of God and the daughters of men as stated in the sixth chapter of Genesis."

"So," Angela said, "you're basically a creationist?"

"Yes, to the extent that everyone and everything we know from the past and everything we see now screams design, which, if looked at logically means there was and is a designer. Therefore, the whole of archaeology from a realistic standpoint is derived from the study of the remnants of the creation unearthed which is inclusive of everyone and everything we find which originated in our near or ancient past."

The clock on the wall chimed which prompted an immediate ejection of all the students from their seats. And as usual it created a flood of bodies bumping into each other and squeezing through the doorway spilling out into the hallway accompanied by a seemingly endless chatter that refused to subside until the next bell rang.

Angela stayed behind and engaged the professor in an after-class conversation. "I have a few minutes before I have to go to my first class so I was just wondering if we might talk some more about this subject over lunch, maybe… possibly?" She said with a hopeful look on her face.

Marvin smiled at the way she asked the question and replied, "Sure, I'd like that. I'm always hesitant to ask a person's religious stance but from your demeanor in the classroom I gather you're on the fence in some fashion in that regards?"

"Let's just say I was raised to believe in a very mundane and non-fantastical version of the Bible. My parents did their best to demystify my life in totality, so to speak. You know, no Santa Claus, Easter bunny, Tooth fairy, and no giants."

"Yes Angela, I guess I can relate to that to a certain degree, but I'd hardly equate the contents of the Bible with a magical gift giver, a magical bunny and a magical tooth fairy. I do know however there are many people who see them as the same, unfortunately. Shall we meet in the cafeteria or meet somewhere else?"

"Well, there is a little diner only a few miles from here. It's a mom-and-pop restaurant called, The Country Nook."

"Yes, I've eaten there many times. How about 12:30." "Sounds good, Professor, see you then."

As she walked out the door Marvin couldn't help but wonder if things may be looking up for him on yet another front. It had been awhile since anyone as attractive as Angela or any female for that matter had showed any interest in him.

The sky was overcast, and it was a bit drizzly when Marvin and Angela met for lunch. They each had to park some ways off yet somehow managed to reach the door of the restaurant at the same time. He held the door for her, smiled and started to say ladies first but before he could she said, "Don't say it."

He chuckled and said, "You know what I was going to say?"

She nodded, "Let's see, it was either ladies first or beauty before age, am I close?"

He nodded, "Well, yes, the former, why, too predictable, too chauvinistic, what, old-school, maybe?"

Once they were seated she said, "It's just that everyone says, oh, you'll end up marrying someone like your father for sure." She paused. "My father would have said one of those, most likely the former; that's why I stopped you, I don't want those voices to be right. My dad's a great guy, don't get me wrong, I just don't want them to be right, okay?"

He grinned. "I see, well Angela, we've only just met so why was that even on your mind?"

"You seem nice, certainly handsome enough, obviously well-educated; it's just me being me, calculating that is. I hope you don't think I'm being too forward."

"No, honesty is good." After they ordered he said, "In the interest of full disclosure I'm not your typical archaeologist. To me Darwin was way off. He was right about a few things. The fittest do survive and humans and animals do tend to adapt to their environment, but one thing has never turned into another. There is no missing link and we're not the result of some cosmic anomaly, slime, fish or ape which evolved over time."

"Well, Professor, tell me how you really feel. I guess I wasn't clear when I spoke about my upbringing. I was raised to believe in the Bible just a less fantastical version than you. Creation makes sense in so many ways evolution doesn't. The fact that we and many animals are designed the way we are totally speaks against randomness or chance. Some say that that's just the way God chose to do it but that's not what His word says."

They continued talking as they ate, and the time seemed to fly by. They didn't have to check their watch, the restaurant's decor was old world Italian, complete with turn-of-the-century wallpaper, lanterns set on large sconce-like decorations on the wall and a huge cuckoo clock that had just struck 1 o'clock.

They looked at each other and as they were getting up said almost simultaneously, "Guess we'd better go."

Before they reached the door Jennings said, "I don't want to sound too forward Angela, but I'm going to the Grand Canyon this summer to check out some of their caves and I was wondering if you have plans, say, for the end of June through the middle of July?"

She turned her head to the side and tilted it slightly, hesitated then replied, "Well, Mr. Jennings, we've only just met as you said and yes that is a little forward of you, but hey, I don't mind forward so much."

He interrupted, "Oh, no." He stopped and chuckled at her response then continued. "I have permission to do some exploring in the canyon caves. I'm good friends with one of the park's administrators and he's given me a special permit. We'd have separate rooms of course and since you said it was a passion of sorts I thought you might be interested, that's all."

Once they were out on the sidewalk she responded, "You know, it really sounds like fun, but my parent's anniversary is this summer, I'll have to let you know, if that's okay."

He nodded in the affirmative and before they had gotten too far apart she turned and said, "Marvin, thanks so much for asking me, it could be a really unique experience; I hope it works out that I can come."

He nodded and went on. The next few days they chatted in the professor's lounge, but the summer trip subject never came up. Tuesday and Wednesday came and went and the day change for tutoring Jack and Lila had slipped Marvin's mind until he happened to bump into Lila in the hall.

"Hey Professor, we're still on for the tutoring session after school, aren't we?"

His mind was on something else entirely when she spoke, and he acted a little startled like he'd been totally immersed in thought.

"Sorry Lila, I was just thinking about the copies my friend sent me of the stone tablets I told you and Jack about. Yes, yes of course, I'll see you and Jack this afternoon."

Before they arrived that afternoon Marvin had not only laid out the material he needed to tutor them in mathematics but all the images he had of the stone tablets. He wanted to take advantage of Jack's obvious gifting to help him decipher the symbols which were extensive and seemed to be unlike any he'd ever seen before.

Marvin had just finished setting up a whiteboard to flesh out the symbols when he heard the doorbell chime. "Come on in," he yelled. They were all smiles when they came through the door. "So, you two look unusually happy, what's up?"

Jack was grinning and looking at Lila when he said, " We're engaged." Marvin looked surprised. He said, "Wow, congrats." Then he got a questioning look on his face and commented, "You guys are kind of young, aren't you?"

Lila smiled, "We're both 21." She shook her head and gave a not really expression, then continued with, "My mom had me when she was 20."

"Of course," Marvin replied, "certainly, you two are mature enough, but it does cost money to be a married couple in this day and time you know. The cost of living has doubled since I was your age.

"Oh," Jack quipped, "I should've clarified, we won't get married until we're out of college and have jobs, I'm thinking in two years maybe."

"I should have known," Marvin replied, "I always pegged you two as being levelheaded."

"Really," Jack said, "I always thought of myself as being somewhat spontaneous." He gave a slight chuckle and continued, "Nothing more boring than being predictable."

"You giving me that ring this morning certainly wasn't predictable, no way I saw that coming," Lila remarked.

Jack decided to get back on task and said, "So Professor, let's get to it?"

"Right, math first then the artifact."

Once the mind-bending and thought wrenching ordeal of advanced mathematics was finished for the day Marvin said, "Let's relocate to the living room, where I have a whiteboard and my computer set up, shall we?"

The two sat on the loveseat while Marvin placed the images on the board. He said, " I'll leave enough space at the bottom of each to label and hopefully identify them also, then we can check the ones on my computer, if we have time that is."

Jack stood up and walked over to the board totally focused on the first image at the top. "Oh my," he pointed to it and continued, "I'm fairly certain that symbol is for sons."

"Why the oh my," Marvin asked?"

"Well, unless I'm mistaken the symbols following sons translates to, "of the fallen." And look at this one Professor, there's a pause as if time has elapsed or possibly the symbol has been eroded over time. It reads, earthborn."

Marvin shook his head in disbelief. He said, "It's like you're a savant of some kind when it comes to ancient symbols. Of course, I picked out a word here and there but you're reading it like you wrote it. What about these symbols over here?"

Jack stared at them for a few minutes. It was as if he were pulling them from some part of his brain where they'd been stored just waiting to be accessed. "Are these in sequence Professor, because I'm sure these symbols should come before the ones I just translated?"

Once again Marvin was virtually stupefied. He put his hand on Jack's shoulder and asked, "What are your plans for the summer? I have a trip planned for this summer and I could use someone like you to assist.

"Working I guess, Professor, why? And what kind of trip exactly?"

"If I am able to get the grant I'm applying for to explore the canyon caves and to identify and catalog what I find then I'll pay you to come and work with me."

Jack looked at Lila then back at the professor and replied, "Only if Lila can come too." He looked puzzled and said, "Why do you want me to come anyway, I mean, you're the professor."

Jennings pointed his index finger at his brain then back at Jack. "I purposefully changed the sequence of the symbols Professor Grant sent me in order to gauge your abilities. How did you know this one," he pointed to the symbol, "should come before the first one you looked at?"

That's easy, Professor, this symbol clearly alludes to the watchers God sent to look over and guard His creation and the first one I translated is referring to the offspring or the giant hybrids born as a result of the union spoke about in Genesis Chapter 6 between the watchers and the daughters of men. The Bene Ha Elohim or sons of God and the daughters of men gave birth to the Nephilim or Anakin or whatever you want to call him. They were given a number of names, it all depended on what they looked like."

Marvin shook his head and smiled. "So, you have a knowledge of the Bible as well?" He nodded.

"You know that grandpa I told you about?"

"Yes."

"Well, he has PhD's in sociology, paleontology, and a Doctorate in Biblical Studies. He didn't just teach me about archaeology; he more or less combined it with everything he knows about the Bible."

"So, tell me more about these watchers, Jack, I'm not that familiar with them."

"Well, some scholars don't recognize them because they're primarily spoken of in the book of Enoch, which was never put in the original Biblical Canon. It does however refer to them in the book of Daniel chapter 4 verses 13 through 23. Basically, they were part of the heavenly host that sinned by leaving their former estate or spiritual form and took on the form of men to have relations with the daughters of Adam."

"Huh, I was taught that the sons of God referred to the natural men on the earth who were created by God."

"I can explain that Professor. It's because of incorrect translations that have been taught, but the original translation refers to direct creations of God. Anyone born of Adam is an indirect creation, it definitely refers to angels, no question about it. Not all of the watchers fell with Lucifer but those who did fall unfortunately still have a place in the heavenlies."

"The heavenlies, Jack?"

"That's right, Professor, Paul refers to them in Ephesians Chapter 6 verse 12 when he speaks openly about the principalities and powers and wickedness in the heavenly realm. And Daniel Chapter 10 verses 10 through 21 tells about the Angel Gabriel sent to answer Daniel's prayer and how he was delayed by one of these principalities and powers coming and going and needing the assistance of Michael the captain of God's army to run interference for the messenger. These entities still exist today and control dignitaries in cities and to some degree certain nations."

"Of course," Marvin remarked, " they're all invisible to the naked eye."

"Yes," Jack responded, "but their influence is all too visible. You only have to look at countries like North Korea, Iran, China, Russia, Saudi Arabia etc., and even the United States seat of power, Washington DC to realize that corruption is rampant in both political parties. My grandpa says that the rule of law in this country has long since been dead. He also said that there are people who are obviously guilty who've never been prosecuted because they have big money, the news media, crooked politicians, social media and the intelligence agency's running interference for them."

Marvin shook his head and thought that within only a few minutes he'd gained a great deal of respect for this young man, Jack McKinney. Naturally, he always knew that evil existed in the world, and he had a cursory knowledge of the Bible, but suddenly after listening to Jack for a brief period of time he received an overview of just how many of the world's leaders, no matter what party or regime they represented are influenced and to some degree even controlled by these evil entities.

"Well," Marvin said, "that explains a lot. But how did, what I mean to say is, did your grandpa ever figure out why God allows these principalities and powers to continue existing and wreaking havoc? Wouldn't it have been better, or to His advantage, and by the way to our advantage for Him to destroy them altogether?"

Jack sat back down beside Lila and paused before answering. "Yes, my grandpa said in order to understand that you first have to understand God. His two main characteristics are love and mercy. But his desire is for us to love Him not because there's no other choice, but that we choose to love Him in and of our own free will."

"Yes," Marvin replied, "but it's that free will that gets us into trouble. I'm reminded of a verse in one of the Christian songs I've heard quite often. We are free, freer than we ever should be. That's the real truth of it, isn't it? If only that free will in our lives could drive us to do good as opposed to do evil, it might all be worth it. Meanwhile we not only have the world and the flesh, but the devil as well to deal with."

Jack nodded in agreement. But then he said, "All you have to do is read the end of the book. Satan's day of reckoning is coming as well as those who fell with him. But it's in God's timing not ours.

"Marvin looked at Jack and said, "It seems as though your wise grandpa has begotten a wise grandson. Now, what about the other symbols; any thoughts?"

Jack stood back up and approached the whiteboard. He ran his finger over each one as if he were trying to slide interpretations of the image off the board and into his brain. His gift was obvious but his method and just how his brain worked was a mystery to the professor. It was like watching a sponge full, being slowly and methodically being rung out.

Marvin tempered his amazement as best he could and had decided it would only be after he was by himself that he would consult his friend Byron Hollingsworth as to the accuracy with which Jack was deciphering the symbols.

"As you can see the symbols here are repetitive, it's describing over and over again just how many of these daughters of men died giving birth to these hybrids and over here it goes into detail with what appears to be the names and descriptions of the ones who survived giving birth."

Marvin said, "Show me exactly what you're looking at."

Jack pointed to the section just below the one he'd described and said, "Look, this woman, and I can't make out her name; mainly because I wasn't taught to translate those specifically, but their physical attributes are in each case impressive. They were tall, strong, large in frame; what we'd referred to today as Amazons, very powerful warrior like women and apparently it was many of these women who nursed and helped to raise the hybrids whose mothers didn't survive."

"Wow, Jack, your blowing my mind here.

"Lila piped up "Yeah, me too," as she continued to gaze lovingly at her fiancé."

Jack smiled a Lila, looked at his watch and said, "We need to go; I told Lila's mother I'd have her back by 6 o'clock."

"Let me drive you and Lila, Jack, it's the least I can do. I'll even talk to your mom if you're late.

Lila smiled at Marvin. "No sweat Professor, the ride will suffice, I can handle my mom."

Just before they stopped at Lila's house Marvin said, "Don't forget to ask your parents about this summer. I'd love to have you two come with me."

"We will," they both replied. He looked at Jack and said, "Your gift could make all the difference in the trip's success, I really hope you can come."

Jack knew Lila's mom well enough to know getting her to agree to a trip would be tricky to say the least. Lila's dad was only moderately strict in comparison to her mom. Engagement or not, she'd need to know that they would be chaperoned 99.9% of the time and that the ones chaperoning were responsible and trustworthy adults.

When they walked in Mrs. Harper said, "Running a little late aren't we, no hanky-panky going on is there?"

Lila gave a nervous laugh that had just enough irritation in it to be noticeable. "We've been with Professor Jennings the whole time, Mom, and he just dropped us off."

Her dad came in, smiled, and asked, "Staying for dinner Jack, good eats tonight?"

"Sure Mr. Harper, my parents aren't expecting me until 7:30. I told them I might eat here."

"Good," he said, " always important to spend time with your prospective in-laws." He looked at his wife and said, "Right Barb?"

"Yes, I suppose so, plenty here for everyone." She said as she sat the last bowl of food on the table.

After they finished eating Jack decided he'd break the ice about the trip. After fidgeting in his seat, he said, "You know the professor's going on an exploratory expedition to the Grand Canyon this summer and asked Lila and I to go along. He wants me to help him with researching and deciphering any artifacts he finds and thought it would be nice if Lila came too. He also said that if the grant came through he was applying for he'd pay me for the time I was with him."

Lila's dad seemed intrigued. He was nodding in the affirmative and the expression on his face seemed to indicate he thought it would be a good experience. "Is this the professor we met at the science fair last year?"

"Yeah, he's a great guy and super interesting. Oh, and very responsible."

Lila's mom's head was down slightly, and her eyes were cocked in a way that said I'm not convinced. She waited until her husband finished and said, "Responsible or not, how is he going to conduct his business and watch you two at the same time, won't that be stretching him a little thin?"

Jack wasn't afraid of Lila's mom as such, but he didn't want to get on her bad side either. True to his leadership mentality though he spoke up. "I'll be with Jennings in the field all day and Lila too, hopefully. And I'm sure he and I would have a separate room from Lila. He knows we're engaged but as he would say, engaged ain't married."

"So, he uses slang does he?" Lila's mom remarked.

"No, I added that for effect, Mrs. Harper. But I know we'll have separate rooms for sure, no doubt."

"What month is he planning this expedition, did he say?"

"Yes, he said tentatively the end of June." Lila's parents looked at each other and her mom said, "We'll have to let you know, Jack, sounds like a good opportunity for you, especially since you have an interest in such things."

After they finished eating, Lila's mother looked at Jack and said, "We'll see, now, you should be going home, I know you both have studies to attend to."

He stood, smiled, and said good night. Lila got up, hugged him, and said, "See you tomorrow, Jack, I love you."

"Love you too, Lila; see you then."

While the engaged couple were jockeying for Lila's parent's favor Jennings was running some of Jack's revelations down then decided to Skype with Professor Byron Hollingsworth. Hollingsworth was a longtime friend of Jennings and an avid archaeologist. He'd gone on hundreds of digs and had had some amazing finds. He was also more adept at deciphering symbols than Jennings and might be able to either backup or refute Jack's translation.

As Jennings moved the phone screen over the images he could hear Hollingsworth say, "Yes, okay, that looks right." After he had shown him all the images Jack had looked at he turned the screen back on himself and said, "Well, what's your verdict, Byron?"

"In as near as I can tell your young friend is definitely on to something. It seems to be a record of sorts documenting certain events pertaining to the fallen ones and the earthborn."

"Okay," Jennings remarked, "so, the fallen ones meaning the angels that sinned and the earthborn are the offspring born to them by the daughters of men."

"Yes, well, it certainly doesn't tell the whole story or give any details about the fall or the day-to-day goings on of these earthborn creatures. But, I have to say your young friend, as you put it in your message must be some type of savant in this particular area. Amazing really, if you think about it, he said it was his grandpa who instructed him?"

"Apparently not just in archaeology but in the Bible as well. According to Jack his grandpa somehow managed to match the two, correlating passages in the Old and New Testament with various finds in archaeology as well as some of the mysterious mega structures around the world."

Hollingsworth went silent for several moments then said, "Are you still there Marvin?"

"Yes, I'm still here."

"I had to find a book I purchased about a year ago. The title is, "Ancient Gods and Giants." In this book it postulates that the watchers are a reference to part of the heavenly host."

"Yes, that's what Jack said too."

"Yes, they're direct creations of God created to help Him carry out His plans, His bidding if you will, and to consult together with Him in making decisions pertaining to his creation. It goes on to say that Lucifer persuaded a third of the heavenly host to side with him in an overthrow attempt to make himself equal with God."

Marvin was listening intently and decided to ask, "Do you remember if it gives any kind of a timeline?"

"No, it's unclear as to whether this occurred before or after the watcher's fall. These creatures are also referred to in the book of Enoch. Are there any more images on the stone tablet than the ones you showed me?"

"Yes, there are others. We, that is Jack and I haven't had time to look at the rest, but I've spoken with Oscar Talmage, the professor of ancient studies at the Marlin Institute and he's assured me there are whole walls in the Grand Canyon caves just recently discovered that no one to date has been able to decipher."

"Really," Hollingsworth said. "That's very interesting. Have you been given permission to explore the caves?"

"Yes, I'm going there the end of June. I'm hoping to take Jack and his fiancée with me, and I've also invited one of the new professors at the college to come."

Hollingsworth cleared his throat. "You know, my calendar is clear for that period of time through the end of July if you'd like another set of eyes."

"Absolutely," Marvin replied. "I'd welcome your expertise."

"Great, just let me know when you book the flight and I'll see if I can fly with you and your team."

"Yes, my team, I just hope my team as you call it can come. Jack and Lila are living at home and attending college and the professor I spoke of seems genuinely interested, so, I guess we'll see. I'll be in touch, Byron."

"Looking forward to it Marvin, take care."

A few months passed and during that time Marvin and Angela became closer; spending more than a few lunches each week at the Country Nook as well as having a number of dinner dates. Jack and Lila were finally successful in persuading her mother to let her go on the trip with a proviso that there be a female chaperone to match Marvin.

Her mother said, "Perhaps your single Aunt Matilda would be willing to go, you'll need someone to occupy your time while Jack and the professor are busy staring down hieroglyphics and digging up old dusty artifacts."

"I don't know mother; Aunt Matilda is such a fuss budget. She'll be complaining about how dirty the room is, constantly complaining about the hotel's help and basically making everybody's life miserable."

"That is my sister you're talking about. But I know she can be annoying sometimes. She's always saying how lonely she is, I just thought it might be a good experience for her. I should probably invite her over more often."

2

The flight/ The expedition begins.

As requested Marvin notified Hollingsworth once he'd purchased the necessary tickets. Fortunately for him there were 10 seats available when he called the airline.

Angela received word from her mother that she and her father had decided to postpone their anniversary get together until August. She was thrilled to be freed up so she would definitely be able to go on the expedition/summer vacation. She was so excited that she started making a list of the things she'd need to take as soon as she heard about the postponement.

She broke the news to Marvin during one of their dinner dates. She said, "I'm good to go, if you still want me."

Marvin looked up from his slightly bent over posture complete with elbows on the table and said, "I'm really glad to hear that," as he pulled two round-trip tickets to Arizona out of his briefcase.

He said, "I was betting it would work out; heaven forbid I should be stuck with Lila's spinster aunt."

"So," Angela replied, "one of those could've been for her?"

"Well, the ticket has your name on it. Although, it could have been changed at the last minute I suppose. It's the only way I'd be assured Jack and Lila could both come. To be honest I wasn't sure Jack would've been willing to come without her. He said he would, but young love is a powerful thing you know."

"So, you saying old love isn't?"

"You know what I mean, say, you're not saying you're in love with me or anything are you?"

"Would that be so terribly bad, Marvin?"

"No, not at all, I might be leaning in that direction myself I just don't want to put myself out there and get my feelings stomped on."

"Well," she said, "let's see how the trip goes, if what we have so far is any indication there may be hope for us."

He held his glass of sparkling water up and said, "Here's to hoping then."

The next day was Thursday and the last time the engaged couple were to be tutored. The final exams were only days away and Marvin had a flash card session lined up for Jack and Lila.

He called Jack to give him a heads up and said, "If you and Lila can get even two thirds of these right you'll ace the finals. Oh, do you think you have time to look at the rest of the images afterwards or would you prefer to wait until the end of the week?"

"Well, Professor, Lila and I have plans for the weekend, afterwards is fine. And just so you know Lila and I are good to go, that is if you were successful in finding someone of the female persuasion to go along."

"Good, we'll have a full house then. No need to worry about tickets, you two are already booked."

"Really, you were that confident, huh?"

"No, that hopeful. I paid a little extra just in case any of the tickets needed to be canceled or reissued. So, it'll be me, you and Lila, Angela Drake and Professor Hollingsworth. It should be a good summer trip and hopefully a productive one as well."

"Angela Drake, huh? She's the new girl's PE and Health professor isn't she? Lila loves her, says she's more like one of the students than a professor. I mean, you know, friendly, modern, up to date on all the new tech and fashions."

"Yeah, from what I've seen that's definitely her, Jack."

"Okay then, see you tomorrow Professor."

When Jack and Lila knocked on the door the following day

Marvin was just getting off a phone call with Hollingsworth. "Hey kids, come on in." He looked at Jack and Lila and asked, "You kids ready to tangle with some advanced mathematics?"

"Sure Professor, but I have some potentially bad news." "Okay, give it to me, Jack, maybe I can help."

Lila spoke up. "My mother wants to meet Angela before she signs off on the trip. She thought it was settled that my aunt would be going when Jack gave you the thumbs up. Sorry for the miscommunication."

"Sure, not to worry, I'm positive Angela would be more than happy to meet with your mother. Just give me a time and I'll see if she's okay with it."

"Wow, that's a relief Professor. Oh, and she's probably going to grill her to see if you two are an item. She basically said, "The he professor and the she professor better be having separate rooms or Lila will definitely not be going."

"Again, not a problem. We've only ever held hands, nothing more, now, let's get to the tutoring, shall we?"

The session lasted longer than usual and when they were done Jack stood up and approached the whiteboard. "So," he said, "these are the rest of the images, professor?"

"Yes, all that my colleague sent me. When he found the caves, he wasn't permitted to take pictures but since then the park administrator designated the caves a historical archaeological site, so we've been freed to not only explore the caves but document any artifacts and take all the photos we want. So, what do you think about the rest of the images, anything jump out at you?"

"Quite a lot actually." Once again he got up close and personal with the images and ran his fingers across each one. He took a pen from his pocket and put a small black dot on one of the symbols and moved several images down and said, "Huh, I guess this goes without saying."

Marvin gave Jack a questioning look again and said, " What goes without saying, exactly?"

"This is an actual passage as if someone were writing it, most probably one of the watchers."

"What's it say, Jack?"

"Well, Professor, I'll give you the non-adult version, seeing we're in mixed company. It basically says "We; again, I'm assuming the watchers, found it effortless to engage the daughters of Adam.""

"I guess their confidence is understandable given who they were." It says, "Our presence they could not resist." "That's it minus the graphic commentary."

"Okay then, thanks for watering it down. Of course, it makes perfect sense when you think about it. Compared to us earthly men, angels must be a gazillion times more charismatic."

"I don't know," Lila remarked, " I've always found Jack to be extremely irresistible."

Jack smiled. He nudged Lila's shoulder with his and said, "Thanks Lila, but I'm no angel."

Marvin chuckled at that and remarked, "I see what you did there, Jack, now, what about the rest?"

"Well, Professor, I put the dot where I did to keep my place and to see if it went with what I just read."

"Well, Jack?"

"It does. Again, this imagery tells a story. It roughly reads: "We, again referring to the watchers, are the fallen ones who've exhausted God's mercy by transgressing."

"And now, if we bypass the first thing that's translated we come to the daughters of Adam being in the family way as a result of them not being able to resist these beings, i.e., the fallen ones."

"Does it mention whether or not these earthborn had any interaction with their angelic fathers?"

"Not that I can see here, but there is almost always corroborating evidence. Possibly stone writings, wall paintings or symbolic images somewhere, it's just a matter of finding them, Professor."

"You mean there could be additional information elsewhere?"

"Yes, and it could be anywhere, not just in British Columbia. Because no matter where you go on this planet there are ancient legends surrounding these beings. They were flesh and blood with at least a portion of the power that their angelic fathers possessed."

"As I said before, Jack, I only have a cursory knowledge of the Bible. Were there any other characters in the Bible who possessed an inordinate amount of strength other than Sampson?"

"There were, according to my grandpa. There are two schools of thought when it comes to Sampson. One, he was a latter-day Nephilim therefore he didn't have the size of his ancestors. Or, because he was ordained by God to be a judge, God endowed him with supernatural strength. But here's where the smart money is. Sorry again, another of my grandpa's expressions. The Bible says the spirit of the Lord came on him and when it did he had the strength that only the angels possess."

"I recall someone telling me that at some point Sampson messed up, Jack."

Yes, Sampson let his flesh get the better of him with Delilah, however he was ultimately a force for good, whereas the Nephilim are only ever portrayed as evil or at the very least, not good. Of course the further along the generations go the more totally human they would become. In other words less evil."

"Right," Jennings replied, "I guess it goes without saying that if their fathers turned against God, then it follows the sons would most likely do the same. At least that's what seems to make the most sense. Okay, Jack, they're still 15 images left, care to venture a guess as to what they mean?"

"Sure Professor, give me a minute." After some time passed Jack got a serious look on his face. He mumbled something under his breath, then looked back at the professor.

"Is there a problem, Jack?"

"Yeah, well, if I'm reading this right, this passage is ominous."

"What do you think it says, Jack?"

"It's another dialogue of sorts. And I'm filling in the gaps. That is, I'm guessing at the symbols I don't recognize based on the ones I do recognize. It roughly translates to: "We, that is the watchers again, have transgressed the Almighty and have exhausted His mercy. Our seed has covered the earth and will continue through the generations of offspring for a time. He will constrain us until the time of the end, then we will be resurrected for punishment in the last days."

"Wow, Jack, that does sound ominous."

"Yeah, Professor, hence my concerned look. Of course, we know from the book of Revelations that that's certainly a possibility. Oh no." He looked at his watch, then at Lila and said, "We need to go."

Jennings said, "Wait, Jack. Before you go I wanted to let you know I had a conversation with Byron Hollingsworth and apparently he thinks you're a prodigy of sorts just like I do."

Jack turned, smiled and replied, "God's gift often seems unusual to those looking in at them, but to me it's just a part of who I am, like my brown hair and brown eyes, nothing special."

Lila piped up and said, "They're special to me, Jack."

Jennings chuckled and remarked, "Okay Lila, you're impressed with his looks and I'm impressed with his ability. You two have a good evening. Good luck with your exam. Oh, and don't forget, you only have a week to pack; don't wait till the last minute."

"We won't, Professor," they said in unison as they walked out.

The following week Marvin touched base with Angela about the trip during their lounge time. The second conversation they had he asked her if she would be willing to talk to Lila's mother. "It seems that Mrs. Harper wants some assurance that were not an item, hence her insistence on meeting you."

"Well, were not, not yet at least, Professor."

He smiled and elaborated. "Specifically, whether or not we have rounded home plate, so to speak."

"Oh, okay, I think I can certainly assure her that we have not. When does she want to meet?"

"Let me check with Lila, she should be in or around the lunchroom this time of the day." Lila answered right away.

"What's up, Professor Jennings?" "I need to give Angela a time for her to meet your mother, has she said?"

"Yes, as a matter fact I was going to talk to her in class today, now is good though. Ask her if 7:30 tonight is okay."

Jennings covered the phone with his hand and asked, "Tonight, 7:30?" She nodded in the affirmative then pulled up the notes section on her phone, showed it to the professor and pointed to it.

"Oh, hey Lila, your parents address, please?"

"Sure, it's 724, Bainbridge Circle."

Jennings repeated the address and Angela put it on her phone. "Okay Lila,, she'll be there."

"Great, Professor, see you later."

"I wonder if I should be worried," she said as she looked at Jennings.

"You'll be fine, Angela, Lila's mom is just one of those mothers who has to have a say in everything, even though her little girl is an adult now."

"Yeah, well, it'll be good to meet her mother I guess. I wish I could interact with all my students moms."

"You're braver than me, Angela, not something I'd see as a positive thing to do. Some of my students are really out there if you get my meaning. And you know what they say about the apple and the tree. Good luck with the interview, or possibly, the Inquisition."

"Thanks for being positive, Professor. I'll let you know tomorrow how it went."

Jennings checked the clock on the wall and said, "Lounge time's over for me."

"For me too, see you tomorrow, Marvin."

Jennings was never one to wait till the last minute so that evening he decided to start packing his suitcase. Not one to spend time ironing either, all of the clothes he bought were wash and wear and he usually packed one outfit for every two days he planned to be away. In this case seven outfits equals two weeks,' one large suitcase and one toiletries bag. He hoped the rest of his crew would be as frugal with their packing.

Before he finished his friend from his archaeological society called. "Hey Marv, how are ya' mate? I got some good news. The societies funding committee gave me the go-ahead to transfer 10 grand into your account. So, the grant's granted."

"Great news Howard, I only wish you were going, we had a blast the last dig we were on."

"Yeah, blast is right. Hey, I hear you got a sheila going along mate, good on ya."

"Yeah, that sheila's name is Angela. I'm hoping it'll be good; she seems really nice, definitely attractive."

"Well mate, good luck on the dig and with the sheila, talk soon."

"Yeah, thanks Howard, you're the best."

"Any time Marv, take care now."

Marvin always enjoyed talking with Howard. He was a real man's man, and Australia born and raised. He moved to the states from down under with his parents when he was 10. His accent was overshadowed by his contagious smile and enthusiastic demeanor. He was a real pleasure to be around.

Because of Howard's good news he'd be able to pay Jack for his help and also give Lila and Angela something if they decided to assist with photographing and or documenting the trip for the societies' archives. Things seem to be coming together very well and he was hoping things would continue to be that way.

He chuckled to himself as he was thinking, if the Lord's willing and the creek don't rise it could be a fruitful trip. A favorite expression of one of Marvin's grandpas, his father's father. Apparently, old-timer expressions are fairly common. Something everyone's grandpas are famous for he thought. But his mother's mother saying was his favorite.

"What you don't have in your head, you have to have in your feet." Truer words were never spoken. He was always forgetting this or that and he would have to make three or four trips where one should have sufficed.

That evening as Angela walked to the front door of the Harper's residence, she thought to herself, "Whatever you do, be nice, be respectful and don't react negatively to any provoking comments that may come from Lila's mother."

Knock, knock. Lila's mother answered the door, smiled, and said, "Well, you must be Angela, won't you come in." She motioned with her hand and said, "Let's go sit in the family room where we can talk privately, shall we."

Once they were seated Mrs. Harper said, "So, Lila tells me you're more like one of the students than a professor. I can see why, you're so young. How old are you if you don't mind my asking?"

"No, not at all, Mrs. Harper, I graduated from college six years ago and this is my first permanent position. So, I guess I am young compared to a lot of the professors. I believe the one I'm replacing was in her 50s."

"Yes, Mrs. Whitfield, I knew her well, a real Christian lady. How about you, are you a Christian?"

"Well, yes, I was raised in a Christian home. As a matter of fact, Professor Jennings and I had a conversation just the other day about that very subject."

"Really, and you two are dating?"

"Oh no, we've only just met. Of course, we have gone out to lunch and occasionally to dinner but we're just friends as it stands right now."

"And you're going on a trip together? Isn't that a little premature?"

"At the moment he and I as I said, are just friends, but we share an interest in archaeology; that's why he invited me to go with them."

"So, you knew there would be others going before you agreed to go with Professor Jennings?"

"Yes, he said Jack and Lila and a Professor Hollingsworth would be going I believe."

She looked questioningly at Angela and said, "And what will be the sleeping arrangements?"

"Oh, I'd have to ask Marvin, but I imagine he and Jack will share a room and Lila and I will share a room and I suppose Professor Hollingsworth will have already booked his own room by now. You should call Marvin to be sure though. I only know that he and I will not be sharing a room. As I said, we've only just met recently."

"Yes, so you've said several times. Well then, I'll hold Professor Jennings to the accommodations you've just stated. I'll call him tonight after you leave. I appreciate your coming over Angela and I hope you have a good evening."

Angela nodded, smiled, and said, "You as well, Mrs. Harper," as she walked out.

Marvin was minutes away from turning in for the evening when his phone vibrated. He always turned off his ringer before going to bed. His ring tone is extremely upbeat to put it mildly and after falling out of bed several times trying to answer a late caller he thought it best to put it on vibrate prior to turning in to prevent any future mishaps.

It was Lila's mother. " Hello, Professor Jennings?"

"Yes Mrs. Harper, how are you?"

"Fine, sorry for the late hour. I just wanted to confirm with you the conversation I had earlier with Angela Drake."

"Of course, Mrs. Harper, what did you want to confirm?"

"I need to be sure that everyone will have separate rooms and that you will give me your insurance that this is not a pleasure trip but as stated by my future son-in-law, Jack, a true expedition."

"Yes, Mrs. Harper, I understand your concern. Jack and I as well as Professor Hollingsworth will be sharing a room unless the professor wants his own and Angela and Lila will be sharing a room. And, as far as I'm aware there won't be any time that Angela and I or Jack and Lila will be alone during the trip."

"That's what I wanted to hear, Professor Jennings, always best to confirm everything beforehand."

"Yes Mrs. Harper. And... this is just from my own personal observation of course, but I think Jack and Lila are two of the most responsible levelheaded young adults I know."

"Well, while I appreciate your assessment Professor Jennings I know from past experience that the temptation to cross the line, especially where the engaged are concerned is sometimes overwhelming. I'm sorry as I said for the late hour and I thank you for your candor, good evening."

"A good evening to you too, Mrs. Harper."

"Well," he thought to himself as he jumped into bed; "I hope

Angela kept her cool with Lila's mother. She is definitely one intense lady."

The time remaining before the expedition was relatively short, but for all those involved it seemed to drag by exceedingly slow. So much so that each day as they viewed the markings on their calendars they hoped that one more day had passed than was actually the case.

Besides the anticipation of being allowed to go into the Grand Canyon caves there was the ongoing rush of the possibility that they may come across some earth shattering find that could put them on the map from an archaeological standpoint.

Each of the prospective travelers had their own personal reasons for wanting to go but collectively they knew even if they didn't make some new and amazing discovery that it could still possibly be an adventure of a lifetime.

Jennings reasons for going were obvious. He loved the thrill of discovery and being out in nature at its rawest. He also craved the excitement one gets sharing the adventure with others seeing it not just for himself but through the eyes of others. He saw himself as a bit more sophisticated than an Indiana Jones type, but he and the character obviously shared the same passion.

Hollingsworth would be the oldest one of the party but he felt that he still has some good years left and always dreamed of going out or rather ending his career with a bang. This expedition held that possibility if only in his own mind. Not to mention that he lived alone and craved companionship. He thought the two or three weeks of company with his good friend marvelous Marv and those he would bring with him should carry him along relationally speaking for another year at the very least.

Jack was the young adventurer who craved the thrill of exploring new places on the globe and finding ancient objects that had been buried by the sands of time or hidden for some mysterious reason, just lying there waiting to be discovered. And having his betrothed along to share in the adventure was just icing on the cake.

And Angela, she just wanted some new experience and to have that experience with a man who was obviously a good candidate for a husband. He was tall, handsome, personable and for sure her intellectual equal. She didn't see any downside to this adventure at all. A summer to remember, that was her hope.

Lila's reason wasn't complex and multifaceted like the others. She dearly loved Jack and to be with him in any capacity was all the incentive she needed. And she thought it would be nice to see the Grand Canyon up close and personal too.

The morning of the flight had arrived, and Marvin did a group text to everyone to make sure they were all on the same page. "We need to be at the airport at least one and a half hours before the flight takes off to check in, is everyone set and ready to go?"

Multiple dings bounced off his iPhone. Hollingsworth replied, "On my way now." Jack followed with, "My dad's bringing me now and Lila and her dad are on their way too. We should be there on time, see you there, Professor." Angela Drake responded, "Could you pick me up, I'm running a little behind?"

He texted her back, "Sure, I'm heading out the door now." When he got to her address she bolted out of her house, opened the back door of his car, put her suitcase in, closed the door and hopped into the front within a matter of seconds.

"Well," Jennings remarked, "that was both impressive and efficient."

Angela smiled and replied, "It comes natural to me. My father was in the service. We moved around a lot, so I had to get use to packing in a hurry, loading in a hurry, and quite often hurrying through the airport terminal."

After all of them had checked in and made it through security, Lila's phone vibrated then chimed like a doorbell. It was her mother giving her a whole list of last-minute instructions and things to look out for.

"Yes Mother, I'll keep your list on my phone the whole time I'm here. Yes, I love you too, tell dad I said goodbye."

They had only been seated in the waiting area a few minutes when the plane started boarding. Jack commented, "This tunnel going to the plane has more dips and bumps than an old cow path."

"Let me guess," Jennings said, as he looked back at Jack, "another of your grandpa's old-timey sayings?"

"You got it, Professor."

Lila's mother would not have approved of the seating arrangements. Marvin and Angela were seated next to each other as were Jack and Lila. Hollingsworth was the odd man out. He was seated just behind the other professors.

The direct flight from Massachusetts to Arizona was slightly more expensive than the one with a layover but definitely more convenient. The aerial journey took four hours and after the plane landed they hiked to the luggage carousel, did the bathroom stop and headed to the car rental desk.

Hollingsworth rented a separate car because he'd brought no small amount of streamlined artifact retrieval paraphernalia. He had slept for most of the four-hour flight so during the 40-minute drive to the hotel he was chatting with Marvin via his Bluetooth phone hookup.

"I was thinking Marvin, we should see about getting a guide. I hear it can be fairly tricky getting to the caves. I've taken the initiative of contacting three of them, but I was really impressed with Jacqueline Danvers. Her father was a guide to the Canyon caves for over 30 years and according to the website he never had one fatality."

"Well, that does sound encouraging Byron, not one, huh; she didn't happen to have a picture of herself on her website did she?"

"Yes, as a matter fact she did. She's rather striking too, I'd say."

"Send it to my phone, Byron."

"Sending it now." Ding. The photo transferred to Marvin's phone and came up within a matter of seconds.

Marvin asked Angela to check out the photo Byron sent. "Well, what do you think?"

"Well," Angela said, "very attractive for a guide. Who, by the way is only wearing a backpack, halter top, wide suspenders, and extremely short, shorts. She looks tall, I mean Amazonian tall"

She held it up so Marvin could see. He tapped his Bluetooth to call Byron back. "Hey, Byron, is she advertising her guiding abilities or her ability to pull off skimpy outfits?"

"Everyone's a critic," Byron remarked, "I'll have you know she comes highly recommended. Besides, I'll be paying for her services; you can find a guide of your own if you'd like."

"We'll give her a chance, Byron, we can always change her out if need be."

"Precisely," he responded. "Looks like we're here; nice digs."

"Absolutely," Marvin said. "It's a five-star hotel complete with racquetball, tennis courts, basketball, a swimming pool inside and out, culinary dining; basically, the works."

After parking in the hotel parking garage, they all stood in front of the building that seemingly went on forever in both directions and was at least 10 stories high. Before they made it all the way to the door the concierge squad surrounded them, took their luggage and the head concierge man motioned for them to follow him. Once they were checked in and settled Marvin texted everyone to meet in the restaurant's dining area.

He was anxious to have everyone give their input as to what their schedule should be. When he told the greeter at the dining entrance what he wanted the man said, "Oh, so, if you won't be ordering yet we have a lounge/conference room just through that doors over there." He pointed to a large double door just to the rear of the dining area.

"Fine, and yes, it will be at least another hour before we order. Okay team, let's go where the gentleman directed us, shall we?"

The room was long and spacious. There was a huge conference type table in the center of the room surrounded by 12 chairs, five on each side and one on each end. Two of the walls were floor to ceiling framed in glass panels, tinted presumably to make for a cooler room temperature.

"Let's sit down and try to plan the itinerary for the next two weeks." He pointed to Hollingsworth first. When Hollingsworth wanted to sound important, he donned a British accent.

"Well, dear boy," he said in his best Thurston Howell the third, impersonation, "I plan on spending every day with my own personal guide. We may even go to the caves occasionally."

Everyone burst into laughter. "Okay," Mavin said, "so we know you're a big fan of Gilligan's Island, Byron, but really?"

"Just joking my dear boy, still mimicking Howell, "I defer to your ideas on the matter."

Jennings looked at the others. "Is that your opinion too?" Jack and Lila agreed as did Angela. "Very well then, let's meet with Byron's guide and see when she'll be available and take it from there. Personally though, I would like to spend at least nine of the 14 days we're here exploring the caves, if possible."

Marvin looked at Byron who was still smiling from his impersonation and asked, "How soon can we meet this guide of yours?" He checked the text message on his phone and replied, "She should be here, I texted her before we came down in the elevator."

He'd no sooner said that than there was a knock on the door of the lounge. Byron could see her through the door window and motioned for her to enter. She came in and introduced herself, shook everyone's hand and sat down in the chair at the furthest end of the table.

"Okay," she asked, "what did you folks have in mind? I have two other clients who called after you and I need to let them know when I'll be available to guide them."

Jennings nodded and replied, "We plan to do some extensive exploring of the canyon caves, Ms. Danvers. I'd say for at least nine of the 14 days we'll be here."

"That's fine," she replied, "there are still regulations you'll have to follow even though you have the proper permission, so once I guide you to the caves each day I'll have my protégé stay with you while you're in the caves. That will free me up to be with my other clients. My protégé is Noel Danvers, my little sister. She's gone through the same training as me and has been with me a number of years. I'll introduce you to her the first day we go out, which I'm assuming will be tomorrow?"

"Yes," Jennings replied, "the earlier the better, I'd like to be able to make the most of each day we're here."

"Good, then I'll meet you folks out in front of the hotel in the morning, say 7:30?"

"Sounds good," Hollingsworth remarked. Oh, by the way, do you and your sister look anything alike?"

"Not at all, she's six inches taller than me and looks more like our father."

"Oh, your father is quite handsome then is he?"

"She smiled and responded, "Yes, quite handsome."

Before she left the room she turned around and said, "You folks get some rest, you'll need it. Oh, and if you chafe easily you might want to buy some Vaseline for your backside, those saddles can be a mite uncomfortable if you're not used to them."

After she walked out Angela remarked, "She actually had on a rather nice outfit, I wonder how she finds clothes to fit her; she's so tall. Her website photo must be geared towards attracting more of a male clientele?"

Marvin nodded, "That would most likely be a yes. Now, how about we get something to eat, I'm famished?"

"Capital idea my dear boy," Hollingsworth replied, "simply capital."

They all gave him a smirky look but Angela walked up beside him and remarked, "I really like your British take on Thurston Howell the third, Byron."

He replied, "My dear lady, you're a tad young to remember that show, aren't you?" "Reruns, Byron, reruns."

"Ah, yes of course."

The dining area had a Western-style ambience and the waitresses' clothes all looked as if they'd been fashioned after Annie Oakley. The waiters and bus boys wore buckskin shirts complete with tassels. Their jeans were covered by suede chaps and they wore cowboy boots.

After they ordered their food they talked about what the plans were for each day. Jennings said, "These plans are tentative but

I believe if we can stick to it we should cover most of what we came for."

When the waitress returned Marvin asked the blessing over the food which had come surprisingly fast. Hollingsworth commented, "They must have had it prepared in advance, amazing really."

"Well," Marvin said, "I guess that's all a part of the five-star service, hardly any waiting time."

"Yeah," Jack quipped, "either that or they nuked everything in a microwave."

There was some lite conversation during dinner and after they were finished eating Angela said, "Well, I for one am tired and I think we should take Jacqueline's advice and turn in early." Everyone agreed with her but stayed there and chatted a bit longer then they all headed for the elevator.

Sleep was only found by a few that night but they were all up bright and early, ate breakfast then went outside to wait for the guide. They'd only been standing there for a few minutes when a hot pink minibus pulled up. On the side of the bus, it read: "CANYON CAVE GUIDES, JACKIE and NOEL DANVERS"

Jacqueline jumped down the steps with her sister right behind her. Noel was almost a whole head taller than Jacqueline as advertised. She had raven black hair, piercing blue eyes and dressed like the website photo, as was Jacqueline.

When they walked over to the group Marvin commented, "And here I thought you only dressed like that on your website to attract a certain clientele."

"No," Jacqueline replied, "we dress like this because it's hot as you know what in the canyon and there's not much air circulating. You all might be shedding some clothes before the day is over with. Hop in the bus so we can go to where the stables are."

A few of them were slow to move, so Jaqueline said, "Come on people, chop, chop."

It took them about 10 minutes to get to the stables. They were all surprised to see just how extensive the stables were. When everyone was out of the minibus Jennings looked at Noel and said, "Just how many mules are there?"

Noel answered, "Well, there are generally six separate parties going into the canyon daily with a maximum of 8 riders per party. Then we keep 10 backup mules just in case one goes lame or gets sick. So, I guess we have in the ballpark of between fifty-eight and sixty mules at any given time. We just acquired six new ones to replace the ones we had to put out to pasture."

Jennings remarked, "That's a lot of animals to feed. And I see there's some construction going on at the other end."

"Yes," Noel replied, "the stables are in the process of being upgraded, they're adding five more stalls to make room for more mules. We're anticipating a much larger tourist trade next year."

"So," Jack asked, "Do we get to choose our own mules, Noel?"

"If you'd like." She waved her arm and said, "Come over here everyone, and I'll introduce you to your Canyon transportation."

The mules smelled, well, like mules but Jacqueline assured them that they were hosed down every other day and checked regularly by a local veterinarian. She also said," All these animals are rider friendly but as I said before, Vaseline is a rider's best friend. If you have sores at the end of the day, don't say I didn't warn you."

She gave everyone a hearty handshake, smiled and continued her spiel. Now, I'll leave you good people in my sister's capable hands, if you have any questions or any problems that she can't answer she'll contact me. Have fun."

"Wait," Marvin said, "is there a limit to how long we can stay down in the caves?"

Jacqueline smiled and replied, "Best not to stay too long, it gets dark here around 6:30. There is a place you can stay at the bottom of the canyon, but it costs extra. It's your choice. But, if you want to get out of the canyon before it gets too dark you'll need to start back within four hours after getting there."

After she drove off Noel directed them to the stables and brought out six mules. "They're all saddled up and ready to go folks, get on and follow me."

Angela and Lila not only looked a little nervous but they were holding their nose to stave off the smell. Noel smiled, "You'll get use to the smell, even when they're clean their odor is fairly pungent, but like I said once we're out on the trail you'll hardly notice it."

When they were about halfway down Angela kicked her mule slightly so she could get up to where Noel was in the lead. Her mule didn't respond to the first kick, so she kicked it a little harder and the mule started to trot. She was bouncing up and down so hard she was afraid she'd fall off. "Whoa, whoa, stop!" She yelled.

Noel grabbed the reins as she went by to stop her and said, "Two light kicks gets them moving, one hard kick makes them trot."

Angela cocked her eyes at her and said, "Now you tell me."

"Sorry," Noel remarked, "my bad."

She held her arm up to stop everyone else and told them the protocol that the mules respond to and apologized for not telling them at the start. She said, "I'm an assumer, it's always been a problem with me."

Angela said, "I need to go to the little girl's room."

Noel yelled back at the rest of them loud enough for the other party coming down the trail one hundred yards back to hear her. "Porta potty's just around the bend. And there's a hitching post to tie off your mules while you do your business. Please don't forget to do it or the mules will wander off for sure."

After everyone had used the porta potty and mounted back up Noel said, "It's not much further now, let's move out folks."

It was almost noon when they reached the first cave, and everyone was super excited. Jennings and Jack helped Hollingsworth unload some of his equipment while Angela and Lila refilled the canteens at one of the watering stations and helped with getting the rest of the equipment unloaded.

Noel pointed the way. "This cave was discovered quite by accident. Afterwards some of the Park Rangers and maintenance workers looked around and found five more. There could be others. Let's go in."

There was pitch blackness all around until Noel flipped the

switch and the caves lit up instantly. The different rock colors and formations were almost blinding at first. So, it took a minute for their eyes to adjust. They were only a matter of forty feet into the cave when they saw all manner of paintings, carved images and symbols covering the cave walls top to bottom at a height which was curious and seemingly went on forever.

Jack looked at Noel and asked her how far back the cave went? "This one goes back half a mile. There are breaks in the symbols and paintings etc. but if these walls could talk I'm sure it would fill volumes."

Jennings looked at Jack and said, "We'll make them talk, won't we, Jack?"

"I'm hopeful, Professor, but if the daylight's a factor we should take as many photos as possible and study them once we get back, don't you think?"

"Absolutely. Lila, Angela, could you ladies document as many of the paintings etc. as possible and also how far in each section is in relation to what you're documenting? And you'll probably need to use the wi-fi booster."

They unfolded their portable canvas chairs, pulled out their cameras and laptop computers set up the booster and started photographing and documenting. Angela said, "We should download the images as we go along to match the sections of the cave walls, Lila."

"Gotcha Angela, I'm on it."

It took them almost 3 hours to get to the end and once everything was photographed and downloaded and documented they headed back to the entrance of the cave. About 10 minutes after they started back Jack stumbled over something. At first he thought it was just a rock then he shone his flashlight on it and exclaimed, "No way."

Everyone stopped. Jennings came over and said, "What, Jack?" He kneeled down for a closer look. "Look Professor, it's a jawbone. And a big one at that."

Noel came over to look. "It must belong to an animal."

"No, not an animal, it's human. Hey Professor, are we allowed to take anything out of these caves?"

Noel's the one who answered. "Yes, but if it's of historical significance it has to go to a museum unless authorized by the parks administrator."

"Oh, it's definitely of historical significance all right," Jack said.

Jennings motioned for Hollingsworth to bring over one of his tool sacks. He pulled out a small chipping hammer, hand brush and chisel. Within 10 minutes he had safely unearthed the entire skull. He pulled out his tape measure and handed it to Jack.

"Here Jack, you found it, you measure it." It measured 14 inches top to bottom. Jack did some quick calculations and said, "This guy was a nine-footer, people. I'd say nine feet four inches to be precise. "Eureka!" He exclaimed. The first day and we've already found a human skull, well, partly human anyway."

Noel said, I've been in this cave fifty times and never saw it. Hey, listen folks, we need to be getting to the entrance and heading back before it gets too dark."

Once they were back at the entrance they packed all their equipment away in their backpacks and started to walk out. All of a sudden they heard what sounded like an Indian war cry, it was faint but everyone heard it.

"What was that Noel, it sounded as if it could have been coming from halfway back into the cave?"

She gave him a look then replied, "Did you see anyone else besides us in the cave, Jack? Noel asked.

"No, but it definitely sounded like a war cry or a chant, maybe."

"It's most likely that only a rock fell and the sound echoed off the walls and ceiling. An echo does carry far you know."

"I suppose." Jack replied. "Noel insisted that it was probably nothing and that they'd better go ahead and start back.

On the way, the professor and Jack both tried to stay as close to Noel as possible. They were interested in picking her brains as to some of the canyon's history. Angela hadn't known Marvin long, but she'd seen enough to know his curiosity was aroused after Jack found the unusual skull.

Hers was as well so she kicked her mule gently twice to get it to go as close to Marvin's as possible. She didn't hear Marvin's initial question, but she did hear Noel's reply.

"Well Professor, legends abound around this Grand Canyon and even more so after the caves were discovered. I'm sure you noticed more than one of the caves paintings had stick figure drawings depicting groups of men and that there were a number of the stick figures which were almost twice the size of the others."

He nodded in the affirmative then said, "Yeah, it was hard to miss. So, what do the locals say about them? Are there any descendants of the original tribes in this area? I know that Buffalo Bill's journal makes references to the tribe of rather large Indians."

She smiled, flipped her long black hair back over her shoulders and said, "To answer your first question, where do you think I get this jet-black hair from? And as far as the second thing you said, yes, I read that particular journal myself from the copies of the original."

Jennings smiled. "It's good to know that you read what I was referring to, and yes, I guess I should've figured with your reddish-brown complexion, black hair and as tall as you are. Exactly how tall are you anyway?"

"I'm 5 inches shorter than my father who's 6'10" tall, and he's a direct descendent of Sitting Bull, the chief of the Sioux nation. He united all of the Sioux tribes against the white settlers. Of course, he was eventually shot and killed."

"Yeah, I'm really sorry that the history of this country is so riddled with events about how badly the Indians were treated as well as all the slavery that went on in this country."

"Well," Noel remarked, "my ancestors weren't blameless during that time either, sad to think about it - but man's inhumanity to man is well documented, all you have to do is read the book of the Bible to discover that."

"Your absolutely right, Noel. And tearing down statues and changing names isn't going to rewrite history. As much as they'd like it too. History, as bad as it was, should stay and stand just as a reminder of where we must never go again. It's unfortunate only half of the country understands that."

After they'd gone a little further Jennings said, "So, if you're a descendent you must have heard stories."

"Yes," she replied. "A few years back, as I just said moments ago I had the opportunity to read some passages from my great-great grandfather's journal and Buffalo Bill's. He was alive when Cody was around. In his journal he talks about how Cody was a friend of many of the chieftains in the Midwest. In this journal he goes into detail about an encounter he had with what he called a transparent spirit."

"Really," Jennings commented.

By then Jack and Angela were moving as close as they could so they wouldn't miss a word. "Yes, I still get goosebumps every time I tell the story. He writes, I had just passed my people's tribal burial grounds on my way to a neighboring village when I saw a transparent form of a mighty warrior riding a horse. I could see the land easily through the warrior and the horse."

By this time Hollingsworth had made his way close enough to hear as well.

Jack was on the edge of his saddle and said, "Is that all of the story, Noel?"

"No, not hardly. He went on to say that once he'd gotten over the initial shock he continued on to his father's brothers tribe. They never used the term uncle or aunt. Anyway, when he got there the whole village was in an uproar."

Professor Jennings started to say something, but Jack spoke up first. "So, what was the uproar about?"

"Well, it seems there were a number of others who'd seen this transparent warrior pass through one of the tents, jump back on his horse and ride off."

"Well," Jack quipped, "at least that proved that your great-great grandfather wasn't just seeing things, even though he was, actually seeing things, I mean."

"Yes, and it seems that approximately nine months later that his brother's previously barren sister gave birth to an unusually large infant child. Which isn't too unusual except for the fact that her husband had been killed in a raid on another village two years earlier."

Jack did a double take and said, "So you mean to say..."

She didn't give him time to finish the sentence. "I mean to say that the infant child Manito, grew up to become the strongest and most feared warrior in the entire Indian nation."

"Exactly how big was this warrior, Noel?" "The Journal says he was half again the size of a man.

Lila decided to get in on the conversation. "What happened to him, Noel?"

"As I read on further in the journal I discovered that this warrior became so violent and uncontrollable they decided he had to be killed. They chose the best warriors from five of their tribes who mounted an attack and unleashed an array of six arrows on him all at once. When they approached the body, they saw that 36 arrows had hit their mark."

"Wait," Jennings said, "I'm no math genius." He grinned a little and continued, "Wait a minute, I am actually, and six times five equals thirty, the last time I checked."

"That's right," Noel replied. "When the warriors realized there were six additional arrows they looked around and saw my great-great grandfather's uncle a little ways off in the distance. He was the one who'd put the additional six arrows into what would have been relationally speaking, his nephew."

Jack was shaking his head. "That's some strange story, Noel." "Yes, and according to his journal that happened more than once, and each time a transparent warrior was seen."

Jennings said, "So, before we get off the subject, let me see if I'm tracking correctly here. If the transparent warrior was a fallen angel then in the book of Genesis when it says that there were giants in the land then, and after that; it must have meant way after that." He kind of chuckled at his comment.

Noel shrugged her shoulders and replied, "All I know is what I read in the Journal, you can come to your own conclusions."

Jack wasn't finished with his inquisition. He said, "If what the Journal says is true about Manito's size, he must've been close to 8 feet tall, or taller."

"As I said before, you can draw your own conclusions; according to some of the last entries in the Journal; everyone was glad that this warrior was no longer living. Look, up ahead, the stables are just over the next hill." By then the sky was mostly a deep dark blue with streaks of lighter blues and lavender running through every section.

It was twilight by the time they returned to the hotel. After they'd eaten Jennings stood up and said, "It's been a productive first day and I just wanted to say how well everyone did. Tomorrow we'll get together in the conference room and process everything we've taken photos of and documented today. We'll explore the caves one day and process the next. I think that's the best way to proceed, at least for now."

Angela was nodding in agreement and said, "I don't know about everyone else but I'm exhausted, and sore. Traversing the canyon by mule turned out to be a lot more taxing on my body than I'd imagined."

Everyone else agreed and as they were getting on the elevator Noel approached Jennings and told him that the local sheriff as well as the state police had issued warrants for two men that were attempting to locate and steal anything they could find of value in the caves.

She said, "The next time we go my cousin is coming with us. He's here to visit us while he's on leave from his seal team."

Jack overheard the conversation and said, "Wow, your cousin is a seal, that's amazing."

"Yeah, some say he could be the poster boy for serving in the military."

Jack laughed, "It seems everyone has an old-timer saying, you don't hardly ever hear the words poster boy anymore."

Jennings looked a little concerned at Noel's comment but said,

"If you think that's warranted, I'll defer to your decision, Noel. Will he be carrying a weapon?"

"Most likely more than one, but he has a concealed weapons permit. Hopefully, we won't need him or his weapons, but it's always best to be safe."

"Sure, absolutely," Jennings remarked, "looking forward to meeting him, see you day after tomorrow, Noel."

Jennings and Jack had trouble getting to sleep that night, what with the excitement of finding the skull and Noel's last-minute information. However, everyone else it seemed from what they said at least slept like the proverbial log.

3

The caves the thing/ The earthborn.

The next morning, they joined two tables in the hotel's restaurant to have enough space for everyone to eat and go over the map designating where all the caves were located in the canyon. Jennings pointed to each one in the order they'd explore them, then said, "I'll give everyone some time to do a little sightseeing... he checked his watch and continued, "then we'll meet back in the conference room, let's say, at 10 o'clock."

When they finished their breakfast and were getting up from the table Angela looked at Jennings and said, "On our way in I noticed that there's a museum of the canyon we can go to, it might be informative."

"Okay, sounds good."

Jack and Lila were standing beside them and Jennings nudged Jack and said, "What about you guys? Care to join us?"

"Sure," we'll come."

Then Jennings look at Hollingsworth and said, "You can come too, old boy."

"Really," Hollingsworth quipped, "Old boy, indeed."

Once they were there and started to read some of the plaques revealing the supposed age of the canyons, claiming hundreds of millions of years it took to form them Jennings chuckled.

"What," Hollingsworth commented, "Are you one of those young earth people?"

"Young, no," he replied, "but when people start throwing out 65, 70, 100,165 million years I tend to be a little skeptical. For one thing carbon dating is a man-made determinant. And calculating how long it took for the river to carve out a canyon that size and corelating it with the different layers of rock to justify it, well, It's extraordinarily theoretical at best."

Hollingsworth raised his eyebrows, smirked a little then said, "So basically you just think they're making things up?"

"Oh no, not at all. Let's see, we were here 65 million years ago, and we know for a fact that all these numbers we're designating as gospel are totally accurate… Given that we or someone else came up with a way to gauge the Earth's age, like we couldn't possibly be wrong."

Angela grinned at Marvin and asked, "Exactly how old do you think the earth is, Professor?"

"Well, the earth could be older than mankind, to a degree at least. I've read that some theologians say that the difference between Genesis Chapter 1 verse one and Genesis Chapter 1 verse two could be hundreds of thousands of years. The correct interpretation of Genesis Chapter 1 verse two is, (paraphrased) The earth became without form and void, suggesting that it had some degree of form at one point in time. So, if that's true it could explain a lot."

Hollingsworth got a smirk on his face and said, "How so, my dear boy? Exactly what are you suggesting?"

"I'd be interested in knowing too," Angela added.

"Okay then, if there were a created earth complete with some type of inhabitants, animals and vegetation, it would explain the dinosaurs and the theory that the earth could be somewhat older than 10,000 years as intimated by the Bible. But suppose the dinosaurs were on the earth and there was massive amounts of vegetation and water; basically everything they needed to sustain their huge bodies. And let's say all this lasted for a sustained period of time until Lucifer was cast down with a third of the heavenly host." Hollingsworth grinned and said, "Continue."

"Well," Jennings remarked, "after I found out that Jack was such a Bible scholar I did some research of my own and according to what Jesus said, which is… (paraphrased) I saw Satan fall like lightning to the earth, could have caused such a cataclysmic event that the earth actually tilted on its axis, causing widespread flooding and eventually the Ice Age. Either of which could have easily killed those massive beast and caused chapter 1 verse two of Genesis where it says that the earth became without form and void and darkness was on the face of the deep, to happen rather quickly."

Jack nodded in agreement. "My grandpa was a believer in that theory. He said while there are indications that some dinosaurs still existed in the Old Testament times, the majority of them were wiped out by some catastrophic climate changing event. The flood would have wiped out most all sustainable vegetation necessary for the dinosaurs survival. He went on to say the ones that could have survived would have most likely been amphibious but others could have as well."

"Right," Jennings replied as he looked at his watch. "We've just enough time to go back to the hotel, gather everything we collected yesterday and make it to the conference room by 10 o'clock. I was only able to reserve it for two hours."

Angela got a questioning look on her face. She said, "Why for only two hours, Marvin, why not all day?"

"The other group staying at the hotel booked it for the entire afternoon, or so the hotel manager told me. I saw the man in charge of the group talking to the concierge. He reminded me of the only photograph I've ever seen of Jimmy Hoffa. A very sinister looking fellow to say the least."

After they were set up in the conference room Jennings stood at one end of the table. "Okay, folks, let's go over the first section of the cave walls and work our way to the back."

Lila stood up. "In the first section there are by my count six paintings, twenty carvings and six one-line sections of some type of hieroglyphics."

Jennings responded, "Very good. Now, were we able to detect any patterns, Angela?"

"Yes, there are six sections with the identical amount of paintings and line sections in each."

"So," what should we deduce from that, Byron?"

"Well, my dear boy, I should say that the same individual or group of individuals are responsible for them all."

Jack raised his hand. Jennings chuckled a bit and said, "Yes, Jack, this is not a classroom, no need to raise your hand; go ahead."

"Well, did any of you happen to notice how high up these marking/paintings were? Any one of us would have to use a stepladder to even begin to make them. So unless the caves floor somehow receded over the years whose ever handywork it was must have been considerably taller than any of us."

"Good point, dear boy," Hollingsworth remarked. "I suppose; that is, if you assume the cave floor was higher at the time they were done, which doesn't sound very feasible to me."

Marvin shook his head. "Jack's right of course, they were very likely done in the last 400 years. These caves were most probably formed thousands of years ago so it stands to reason that the images were done after that; the question remains just how long? The surface level in the cave probably remained the same for the last 4 to 500 years."

Hollingsworth cleared his throat. "Well marvelous Marv, you're the math genius, how tall would someone have to be to comfortably deck those walls, so to speak?"

He pursed his lips, moved his head side to side then replied, "8 feet, 9 feet maybe, or there abouts. But, if they were done back in the day why are they so primitive? I mean, these were the offspring of powerful and intelligent beings. These images are something one would expect the locals of that day and time to do."

Jack started to raise his hand then lowered it quickly. "Maybe that's because they were half human, possibly raised by human women of the day. Why don't we try to decipher them before we dismiss them as primitive?"

Hollingsworth pointed to Jack and said, "Just so my boy, just so. Take a look and tell us what you see."

Jack walked over to the screen and studied the paintings first, ran his fingers over the hieroglyphics and symbols and said, "The stick figures by themselves are fairly easy. They represent several groups of natives, most probably in a hunting party of sorts. We see the feeble attempt at drawing a deer, a bear, a large deer, most likely an elk of some kind. I never noticed it while we were in there, but this very large stick figure looks to be pursuing a buffalo on foot."

"Angela commented, "I mean, I'm no hunter but wouldn't that be rather unfruitful, not to mention dangerous?"

Jack grinned, turned to her and said, "My grandpa was a lover of old books in general, not just the Bible. He said he had the privilege of reading one of the original journals of Buffalo Bill Cody's on microfiche. Of course, the actual book is in a museum. In it Cody wrote about a conversation he had with one of the Apache chiefs and his medicine man."

Hollingsworth laughed. "Really, my dear boy, a medicine man? Was he jumping up and down, shaking a rattle of some type and saying haya, haya, haya?"

"No, Professor Hollingsworth, while they were talking a young Indian brave brought in a bone and gave it to the chief. The medicine man and the doctor riding with Bill Cody both confirmed it was a man's thigh bone."

"So," Hollingsworth said, "the young fellow found a bone, so what?"

"Yes, well, here's the catch, the bone was two times the size of a normal man's thigh bone and there was a story that went with it. The chief said his father's father had seen these giant warriors and they could chase down a buffalo and knock it over going full speed. So, it's not so far-fetched as one might think. Obviously, someone was documenting what they saw, no matter how primitive the depiction."

Jennings said, "I've heard similar stories, Jack. What about some of these strange hieroglyphics? If you can even call them that. I've never seen anything like them."

Hollingsworth got up and stood beside Jack and pointed at one of the symbols that looked like an arrow passing through a triangle and it repeats over and over. " What do you make of that, Jack?"

"Well, according to my grandpa the triangle shape generally represents some kind of evil or a controlling force, much the same way that the pyramid shape does. The arrow depicted penetrates the pyramid shape but doesn't appear to have any affect. In other words, if it did have an affect the next symbol would show the pyramid shape fractured or damaged in some way."

"I agree," Professor Hollingsworth said. "And, if you look closely the pyramid shape has a line around it inside the perimeter. In Egyptian symbols that represents transparency of some kind, don't you agree?"

"Yes it does, Professor. You know, I wish you and my grandpa could meet sometime. You two would have some interesting conversations."

The professor smiled at Jack and replied, "No doubt you're right. So, does the transparent shape mean what I think it means, Jack?"

Jack nodded. "Yes, I'm afraid it does. It most likely represents a spirit of some kind and a futile attempt by someone at killing it."

He and the professor went over to the line text and studied it momentarily. Jack turned and looked at everyone else and said, "This proves what we've been saying. The first line text reads: The spirit transgressed my tent. My arrows flew as swift as the eagle but passed through with no resistance. The second line text reads: My squaw's life was taken in childbirth. The male child fought to escape and prevailed. The third line text reads: The male child grew to be a mighty warrior and became uncontrollable. Because of this we gathered many braves together to take his life from him."

All the others were fairly on the edge of their seats by then. Jennings asked, "What about the last three-line section?"

Jennings looked shocked at Jack's interpretation and said, "Oh, okay, I guess that makes sense. What about the last three-line sections; are they dark too?"

Jack had been glancing at the other three sporadically as he was deciphering the first three. He said, "No, actually it looks as though once the third and fourth generations were born to these women the uncontrollable urge to do evil stopped. The offspring were large and strong alpha males, otherwise normal in every way because now they were more human than not."

"Thank goodness for that," Hollingsworth quipped. "And may I say, Jack, you're every bit as impressive as marvelous Marv said you were. It undoubtedly would have taken me hours of research and days of processing what I'd learned, well done."

"Okay," Jennings said, "that's a good start." He looked at the clock on the conference room wall. It seems our time here is up; however, we could take this back to one of our hotel rooms."

"Or" Angela offered, "we could eat some lunch first, then continue."

"Of course," Marvin replied, "I'm sure everyone's hungry. Let's get something to eat then meet back at mine and Jack's room." After asking the restaurants hostess if they could combine two tables they all ordered and chatted while they waited for the food.

Jennings said, "We really should stay focused on our main objective. A large skull my colleague found in British Columbia got me to thinking. Every place on the earth that you could name has legends of giants, of hybrid beings and even hybrid animals. My vision for this expedition is to find tangible proof, some thing or things that would prove beyond the shadow of a doubt that those entities in fact existed."

Jack nodded. "I agree Professor. The suppression of these skeletons is well documented. Individuals and organizations have been responsible for keeping this information and physical evidence from the population at large for millennia. There've been quite a few secular books written trying to disprove the deity of Christ but the spirit and the organizations behind them have been guarded for millennia also. In other words they conduct their business and do everything they can by any means to convince the masses that there's nothing to see here."

There was silence for a few minutes then Jack continued. "When the dinosaurs roamed the earth in this part of the world their existence was well documented because it fits the evolutionary narrative. However, the hybrid offspring stories fit the biblical narrative so those are the ones that these people try to squelch. There wouldn't be any remains of the watchers as such because we know that they were immortal, at least until God passes judgment on them at the end of the age."

Hollingsworth replied by saying, "I think it's worth noting that we haven't really found out much that's new about these watcher creatures or how they fit in with what went on before or possibly after God created the earth. I mean, did God really have to have these fellows watch over large plant eating lizard types?"

Jack chuckled. "It's just another way that you and my grandpa are alike. His theory was that the watchers weren't dispatched until the second creation when God created mankind. We were created in His image so He naturally felt more invested in us."

Lila had been silent up until then. She had just sat back and took it all in. Then when the dinosaurs were brought up she said, "I mean, really, what purpose did they serve? It's not like you could build a shelter big enough for them or domesticate them."

They were all nodding in agreement then Hollingsworth looked at Jack and asked, "Well, dear boy, I'm sure you're grandpa had a theory about that too, didn't he? And if so, I for one would like to hear it."

Jack hesitated then said, "Actually, he did."

Evidently there was too much of a pause for some so after a moment went by Jennings brought both of his hands up halfway and out to the side as if to say, "Okay, what?"

"Well, and this can sound a little out there but what my grandpa said was that… You know how a lot of people when they first do something they want to do it in a big way, just to see if they can?" Everyone nodded.

"Well, that's it, that's what he thought. God didn't want to create small unimpressive creatures, so, he went for it, in other words, he went all out, the whole enchilada."

Jennings and Hollingsworth looked at each other, smiled and said almost simultaneously, "Yeah, that makes as much sense as anything I could have come up with."

Angela remarked, I can see that; a big God, big creatures, and they were very impressive, no doubt."

By then their food had arrived and everyone was silent while they enjoyed the meal and when they were finished Jennings stood up and asked, "Are we ready to resume? We do have five more sections of cave to cover."

"Yes, Hollingsworth replied, "we might have time for one or two today, maybe they'll reveal more information as to the actual character of the so-called, watchers."

"One can only hope, Byron," Jennings remarked.

Once they'd regrouped in the hotel room it seemed everyone was eager to continue except Angela. She was noticeably quiet. After Jennings set up his whiteboard he looked over at Angela and could see that her head was lowered.

"Angela," Jennings said, "are you all right?"

She looked up slowly and replied, "Yes, I guess. It's just that when I was coming out of the ladies' room I saw the union leader you spoke about and another man giving me the evil eye. I mean, they had to be looking at me, I was the only one standing there. It really unnerved me."

Professor Jennings' eyebrows furrowed and he got a concerned look on his face. He said, "Maybe I should have a talk with him, or possibly the hotel's security."

"No, no, let's continue with what we've been working on."

"Are you sure, Angela?" "Yes, maybe we can check with him tomorrow and see if he knows anything."

"Okay, if you're sure?"

"Yes, I'll be fine. Although, I'd probably feel safer if I could sleep in yours and Jack's room tonight. I'll ask management for a cot." "Absolutely," Jennings replied.

Angela called the hotel desk and asked them to bring a cot to room 315 while Jack and the professor hooked the camera up to the computer. Jennings said, "Now we'll use the whiteboard to put up photos we've printed off the computer, then put them in order and take it from there."

"We've already successfully interpreted the first section, at least I believe we have." He looked at Hollingsworth who gave him a nod.

"Yes Marv, I'm fairly certain you're young protégé and I have successfully deciphered that section. I'm wondering though, if we shouldn't have started at the end of the cave and worked our way back to the entrance. It's hard to know where they started."

Jack gave Hollingsworth a, "Yeah, back to front; that could work." Then Jennings remarked, "No reason why we couldn't, let's give it a try."

Angela filtered through the first section of photos taken at the end of the cave. "Okay," Jennings quipped, let's see what we can see. Jack we'll follow your lead."

Once he looked over the bulk of them he turned to Professor Hollingsworth and said, "It looks like you saved us some time, professor."

"How so, dear boy?"

"You were right, whoever did these started here at the end and worked their way back toward the entrance. And if I'm not mistaken this section predates the last one by at least 350 years or so."

"That's hard to believe," Angela commented. "What about the other caves?"

"Exactly, Ms. Drake."

"Call me Angela, Jack, I'm not that much older than you. And "exactly what?"

"Well, we might want to look at all the caves before we attempt to decipher them. This one starts a little over 500 years ago and ends approximately150 years ago by my calculations."

Jennings looked confounded. He said, "What are you using to base your timeline on, Jack?"

"Did you notice the last two symbols just below the last line section on the wall,?"

"Yes, I thought it was something someone started but never finished. You didn't say anything about it so I assumed it wasn't relevant to the rest."

"You're right, in a way Professor. It wasn't related to the rest of the symbols per se, it did however date the approximate time the wall was worked on."

"How so, dear boy?"

"My grandpa showed me photos he'd taken of drawings on the inside of an old Apache tent. He actually spoke to a descendent of White Cloud, an Apache Chieftain. The symbols are for pony soldiers, i.e., the Calvary, and the rectangle shape has 20 notches inside representing 20 states. This flag was first used in the late 1800s."

Lila was semi-oblivious to what was being said, dividing her gaze between the images and Jack but when 350 years and 150 years came up it peaked her interest.

After Jack finished talking she asked, "How exactly do you know the cave images started around 500 years ago?"

"The last symbol on the cave wall at the end had an elementary image of a ship then below it the shape of a rectangle with a cross having a line side to side and a line top to bottom. That's the image of the flag that Christopher Columbus sailed under for Queen Isabella just over 500 years ago. That means some of the earthborn were either present when Columbus landed or interacted with some natives who had."

"That's brilliant, dear boy," Hollingsworth said. "How on earth did you make the connection?"

"I wouldn't have if my grandpa hadn't drilled a gazillion symbols into my head while I was growing up."

Jennings was upset he totally missed the symbols but not being one to be jealous of another he said, "I knew I was right to ask you to come, Jack. I guess now we really should check out the other caves so we can attempt to translate the walls in chronological order."

"Yeah, Professor, and if the last one starts at Christopher Columbus then the first could conceivably go back 10,000 years; all the way back to the beginning of civilization or even humankind."

Hollingsworth cleared his throat. "I do believe we've strained our brains enough for one day, Marv. If we're to photograph and document the remaining five caves, then translate/decipher what we've found we should probably have some dinner and retire for the evening. Best to start out early tomorrow if we're to study as many of the caves as we can."

Jennings nodded in agreement. "Right, Byron, but before that I'm going to talk to hotel security and the concierge. I'm not going to shrug this off, it's best to find out what the deal is and either handle it ourselves or make sure someone else does."

"I'm coming with you, Marvin." "Very well, Angela. Probably better for you to tell what you saw and how it made you feel."

Jack asked, "Should we go ahead and eat, Professor?" "Yes of course, Jack, you three go ahead and don't wait for us, it may take a while."

"Okay Professor, see you two later." As they were headed for the restaurant Lila asked, "Has something changed with the sleeping arrangements, Jack?"

"Well, Angela said she would feel safer if she could stay with the professor and me tonight because of that union leader she told us about."

"Oh, so I'll be all by myself and if whoever was after her decides to come and do something how will they know she's not in the room."

"Yeah, I never thought about that, Lila. I guess we'll just have to wait and see what the professor finds out from hotel security and the concierge."

Hollingsworth was listening to them the whole time and remarked, "You do know they have locks on all the doors, dear boy? But if you don't trust the locks simply wedge a chair under the doorknob, simple."

While Jack, Lila and Hollingsworth were ordering their food Jennings and Angela had caught up to the concierge. He gave Angela a look and tried to walk off.

"Boy," Jennings said rather abruptly. "My friend here was unnerved by the union leader you were talking to today. What were you discussing at the time?"

The concierge looked at Jennings then back at Angela. "Well, I could say it doesn't concern you but the truth is he was asking about your group's business here. I told him all I knew was that you folks were exploring the caves and when he saw Ms. Drake he got a nasty look on his face and took off."

"What union is he a leader of anyway?" Jennings asked.

"They're scientists of some sort. I think they're into geology and astronomy. Don't ask me how those two disciplines are related. In my opinion the whole group acts a little wacky."

"Thanks, Greg, is it?"

"Yes Sir, my name's Greg."

"Okay, Greg, we need to talk to the head of security in this hotel, where's he or she located?" He pointed to the hall next to the gift shop. Go down to the end of the hallway, you can't miss it."

When they knocked on the door a voice inside said, "Enter." The man behind the desk stood up to shake hands and said, "What can I do for you folks?"

Angela told her story and the conversation they had with the concierge. "I see, so you felt threatened by this man?"

"Yes, very threatened as a matter of fact. I even thought about staying with my friends here, tonight."

"No need for that Ms. Drake. The locks on our doors are tamperproof and we have six security officers who patrol the halls all night. They're totally separate from our daytime security. You'll be perfectly safe I assure you. Now, is there anything else I can do for you?"

"I suppose not, if you're sure the men are trustworthy?"

"Yes, very trustworthy Ms. Drake. And as I look at the room numbers I can see Mr. Jennings is right across the way, so he's close by too. Now, if you'll excuse me I have a conference call with the manager and part of the staff."

As they were making their way to the restaurant Angela said, "I guess I won't need to sleep in your room tonight after all."

Jennings laughed. "It's probably for the best anyway; Lila's mother would have a veritable fit if she found out. Plus, we would have to confess to her, either that or be deceitful and not tell her."

"Right," Angela replied.

They were entering the restaurant just as the others were getting up to leave. Lila asked, " What did you find out?"

"Well, the concierge wasn't much help and the hotel security man said not to worry. He said to trust the locks and the six security guards patrolling the halls at night. He assured us we'd be safe and that it wouldn't be necessary to share rooms."

Hollingsworth commented, "Glad to hear it Marv, Angela. Look, I'm heading up for some much-needed rest."

"Yeah Professor," Jack said, Lila and I are…." He stopped in his tracks.

"Oh, that's right, we're not supposed to be alone so I guess we're staying while you lovely people order and eat."

"Great," Angela quipped, "no quiet dinner for two, then."

"Sorry," Lila said as she gave an apologetic smile. "My mother is sure to ask. But hey, it's good that we won't have to share a room and sleep on a cot tonight, right?"

"Yes, that's right Lila." She looked across the room then continued with, "Maybe you and Jack could sit at the bar for a while."

"Yeah," Jack replied with a nod. He looked at Lila and said, "let's go pick the bar tender's brain, maybe he knows something."

While Marvin and Angela were enjoying their dinner, Jack was making nice with the bartender. Jack checked out the name tag on his shirt. "So, how long have you been working here, Frank?"

"Five years yesterday, and believe me when I say, I've seen it all." "Really, what about those union guys, have they been here before?"

"Yeah man, and those so-called scientists act more like the Mafia than anything else."

"How so?" Jack asked casually. "They have upper East side Chicago accents, they're rude, inconsiderate and they're lousy tippers. And there're all packing heat. I got a clear view of one of their shoulder holsters complete with a snub nosed 38 the other day."

"Have you ever seen any of their literature?"

"Yeah, typical evolutionary propaganda. Geologists and astronomers my patooky, they're no more scientists than I am. They're a part of the evolutionary propaganda machine if you ask me, real mind twisting manipulators, the bunch of em."

"Good to know, Frank; thanks for the information." Jack nodded, "Have a good evening."

Jack and Lila joined Marvin and Angela on the elevator ride. "I think I may have found a reason for the odd and sinister looks, Angela."

"Really?" The union label is a front for an evolutionary group, sworn enemies of anything and everything related to the Bible. The barkeep said they're a nasty bunch too. So, my suggestion is to steer clear of them, if possible."

"Well," Jennings replied, "sounds plausible. They hear a group of Christians are studying the caves and it gets their anti-theological pants in a bunch, hence the dirty looks."

As they were exiting the elevator Angela remarked, "As long as it doesn't go any further than looks."

The two men told the two ladies good night and just before they entered their room Jennings said, "Call me if there's trouble, Angela."

"I will marvelous Marv." "Cute, Angela, very cute."

Since they'd decided to change their day in the caves; one day in and one day out; Marvin contacted Noel first thing the next morning.

She was in the process of getting last-minute instructions from

Jacqueline pertaining to a conference group coming to visit the Canyon the following month when he called.

"Hey Noel, is it okay to book 5 consecutive days to go down into the caves? Also, we need to start at the oldest and work our way back if that's possible."

"Sure, it's going to cost extra though. I'll have to call in my reserves to cover for the days that I'd be working for another group. One hundred bucks more for each day that's changed."

Jennings replied, "It's a deal, how about today, can we count on you for the day?"

"Yeah, meet me at the same place in 30 minutes, be ready though, the later into the year it gets the quicker the sun goes down."

After what they'd collected the day before everyone was super excited to see what else they'd find. Using the new method of back to front the hope was that they'd have a more linear recording of the caves history. Which would obviously be more advantageous and also more acceptable to the society they'd be reporting to.

4

Secrets of the earthborn/ The journal.

Once again they started the descent into the canyon. It seemed that the colors of the canyon changed from day to day. They each commented on as much and were oohing and aweing over the rainbow-like colors that seemingly changed with each step they took into the canyon.

Noel had the same guide outfit on with the exception of a small bulge pushing the lower middle part of her shirt out in the back. Marvin noticed it and assumed it was a firearm of some sort possibly for scaring away any varmints of the furry or two-legged variety that they may encounter.

They passed the cave they'd already studied and proceeded for another half mile passing cave after cave till they were at the sixth one. Noel dismounted, looked at the group and said, "According to the experts this is the oldest one and most likely the first to have markings. I guess you'll be the judge of that, though. I'll be back in two hours. I'm going to help one of the other guides; just give me a call if you need me before that."

All of the caves were equipped with lighting but these lights were up higher than the rest which interacted with the rocks differently than the one they were originally in. The angle of the lighting gave a luminescent luster to the rocks that was almost blinding at first, even more so than the initial effect from the first cave. Once they were in they moved to the back immediately and started photographing and documenting.

"No flag symbols here, Jack," Jennings quipped.

"Right Professor, give me some time though and I just might find something to indicate when they were made."

So, while the others were busy with the camera and the computer, Jack used his huge Sherlock Holmes type magnifying glass and studied the wall practically inch by inch.

Hollingsworth was peering over Jack's shoulder while he was scrutinizing the walls. Jack flinched a little when Hollingsworth said, "What's the prevailing theory for how the Native Americans got here, dear boy?"

"Don't you know, Professor?" "I know what I've read, what have you heard?"

"That their ancestors came here when the landmasses were still connected, it's the only logical explanation. The time period is anyone's guess. I can say one thing for certain though, the symbols in the top left-hand corner of this wall depicts flying entities of some kind coming down and being worshiped by the inhabitants." Jack pointed to one drawing in particular.

"Yes, yes, I see what you mean, dear boy. They're depicted with wings. Of course, we're fairly certain that's a myth, angels don't need wings to fly, they're like software in a computer, massless, aren't they?"

"I've never seen one, Professor Hollingsworth so I couldn't really say but it seems logical to assume they're wingless and massless as you put it. Look at the next grouping, Professor."

"Yes, a bit graphic isn't it?"

"Yes," Jack replied, "but it does square with the Genesis account. I think I'd be safe in assuming these depictions predate the flood. People's lifespans were considerably longer in the first 1000 to 1500 years and even after that it was 7 to 8 times the present-day lifespan."

Jennings was freed up enough by then to listen in on the conversation. "Predating the flood, is that what you said?"

"Yes," Jack replied, "just how much I couldn't say, but if the flood was approximately 4500 years ago then we could be looking at anywhere from 5000 to 7000 years ago for these particular cave markings."

Hollingsworth wasn't quite as biblically proficient as Jack so he asked, "I don't recall, exactly what was God's purpose for destroying the earth, again?" Jack was fairly amazed at Hollingsworth's question but answered anyway.

"Genesis talks about all flesh being corrupted by these godlike beings. That's why God decided to destroy all the inhabitants but eight. Given the fact that Noah and his wife could still procreate and his three sons and their wives certainly could, it wouldn't take long to get the ball rolling again. Some of these men in the Bible times had as many as 70 sons and daughters. A really good reason for monogamy if there ever was one, I'd say."

"Hollingsworth chuckled, and pointed to Jack while saying, "Right you are, dear boy, multiple partners, multiplies the sons and daughters exponentially."

Angela checked with Marvin and Jack to see if they wanted her to input an approximate age of the cave drawings into the computer. Jennings replied, " Yes, for the time being put it at 5000 years then put a question mark next to it. We may have to change things as we go along, but for now keep it at five millennia."

They finished the first section, then the second, then the third, and when they got to the fourth they heard an unfamiliar voice say, "Hello, hello."

At first they thought they were hearing things then Jennings said, "Yes."

An indistinguishable figure appeared from the darkness. The twist and turns in the cave sometimes blocked the light almost completely in some areas making it virtually impossible to make out someone only 15 or 20 feet away.

After the figure came within 5 feet of them they were able to see it was a middle-aged woman wearing a camo suit and hiking boots. She smiled and said, "I'm sorry for the intrusion but I was wondering if I could join your group? I spoke with Noel and she said it would be up to a Professor Jennings since he's the one heading up the group."

Jennings extended his hand and introduced himself then the others. "This is Professor Angela Drake, Professor Byron Hollingsworth, Jack Evans and Lila Harper. And you are?"

"Oh, yes of course, I'm Melanie Jones, Professor of Anthropology at the Birmingham Institute."

"Well," Jennings said, "anthropology is a discipline close to my own heart. So, why the interest in the caves?" "The same as you and your group I imagine, although I tend to view most of what I find from a strictly evolutionary viewpoint."

Raised eyebrows amongst the rest of the group abounded after her statement. "Then creation is totally off the table?" Jennings commented.

"Yes, well, I mean I never really considered the whole creator angle, really. Too much faith involved and not enough fact."

Jennings' dander was beginning to get up but he was able to keep his cool and answered. "Really, well it seems our interest and yours are at cross purposes then. Given the fact that there are no facts substantiating evolution whatsoever I feel it best if you don't join our group, Professor Jones."

"Oh." She momentarily gazed at a section on the wall just above them and posited, "I see a large dinosaur type looking creature in some of the depictions and what looks like tiny humanoid looking figures there. Exactly what do you creationist do with the dinosaurs?"

"We creationists never denied their existence and according to the Bible some may have even survived the flood but if the massive amounts of vegetation needed to support their survival was no longer there they would've simply died off. Besides, dinosaurs and their existence don't have anything to do with mankind. The bottom line involving any conversation about the earth's design is that design doesn't happen randomly or by accident, nor does it happen over thousands or millions of years. Design equals designer, period."

Angela was seeing a side of Jennings she hadn't seen before. Of course, the others had. You could tell by the look on her face she felt a little sorry for the woman even though she completely agreed with Marvin.

"Okay," Melanie replied, "I'll just been going then, you all be safe, these caves can be dangerous if you're not careful."

After she left Hollingsworth commented, "Is it just me or did her last words seem more like a threat than a friendly warning?"

Jack replied, "I guess it could've been taken either way." Then he looked at Professor Jennings and asked, "Should we finish with this cave and go on to the next, or head back?"

Jennings checked his watch. "I'll call Noel and see what she's thinking." When she answered he said, "Yes, Noel, how much time do we have before we need to leave?"

She paused for a second and replied, "We should probably leave in an hour, so finish up and lets meet at the cave's entrance."

"Gotcha, will do. Okay folks, we have three sections left so let's do them as quickly and thoroughly as we can and meet Noel at the entrance. She said to meet her in one hour."

They had a few minutes to spare before the time Noel designated so while they were sitting there on the bench just outside the entrance, Lila asked, "As Christians; how do we square dinosaurs with the creation story?"

Jack replied, "Logically, as I said before, for those massive beasts to just cease to exist there would've had to be a catastrophic event of some kind. Some intact carcasses of mammoths were found under the ice that still had undigested food in their bellies. Some were unearthed from under mounds of sedimentary rocks. Now, if you go with the Ice Age, that would've only ever happened slowly over time. That is, unless there were a sudden shift of the earth on its axis in which case the Ice Age could have happened more quickly. Or even if you subscribe to the flood; something had to have happened relatively quickly in order to trap those beast where some of their remains were found."

"Right you are, dear boy," Hollingsworth quipped, "beast of that size just don't go away for no reason." By then Noel had showed up and when she was questioned about Professor Jones she looked surprised and then concerned.

"No, I don't know anyone by that name."

Jennings shook his head in disbelief, then remarked, "Exactly how did she get down here unless she was with a group?"

Noel shrugged her shoulders then replied, "She couldn't, is the simplest answer. I suppose she could've been with my sisters group; they usually take a 10-minute break every two hours, especially if there's any elderly tourist in the group. I'll ask her this evening."

The trek back up the canyon's trail was slow that day but the group didn't mind. The panoramic vision of the adjacent canyon wall and the sky slowly preparing for sunset was breathtaking. There were streaks of turquoise green, blueish pinks and deep scarlet covering the horizon which were accented even more by the cool cobalt blue background. Then, just before they reached the top one of the parks tour helicopters pierced the sky a 100 feet or more above them taking a group on a twilight tour over the canyon.

Jack looked at Lila and said, "I'd like for us to take one of those before we leave." Jennings chuckled, looked back at Jack and said, "I hope you brought plenty of money then, I'm told that a short 20-minute flight cost $200 per person and if you want the special tour it can be up to $600 per person."

"Okay," Jack quipped, "I guess that'll have to wait until our honeymoon or for some other special occasion."

While they were taking their mules back to the stables, Noel said, "I contacted my sister and she said the lady matching the description you gave came back an hour ago. She was with another group and she's positive that she's a part of that union bunch at the hotel."

Jennings nodded in the affirmative. "I guess I should've known something was up. Her approaching us like that and all."

"Yeah," Jack remarked, "most likely checking us out to see if we're the creationist we're reported to be. Those anti-God heathens should get a grip."

Lila nudged Jack with her arm and said, "We shouldn't label

people like that, Jack. They have a right to their opinion, even if it is wrong."

"Of course they do, Lila, just as long as they don't try to silence my opinion or cancel out what the Bible says the way it's being attempted and quite successfully I might add along with every other aspect of our history."

"That's so true," Angela added, "within two generations the ones growing up then won't have a clue as to the real history of this country, or belief in the Bible; it'll all be cancelled out of existence."

"Well," Jennings replied, "It's unfortunate, but the powers that be are consumed with doing just that. However, we're not here to challenge them, we're here for a very different reason. So, I suggest we get back to the hotel, organize what we've found today, get something to eat and then get some rest."

Everyone's mind was reeling at some of their discoveries and the revelations brought about by the symbols and drawings already translated and the speculation of what else might be revealed.

The next day they were all up early, had eaten and made the short trip to the stables. When they arrived there were several local police and Park police vehicles only a few yards from where they usually mounted the mules.

Jacqueline and Noel were speaking with the officers. Jennings approached them while the others stayed next to the hotel shuttle.

"What's happened?" Jennings asked. Jacqueline continued to talk with the officers and Noel stepped to the side and stood next to Jennings.

"It seems someone opened a number of the enclosures and let 12 of the mules out and tried to set the stables on fire. I was about to contact you to let you know we'll have to postpone today's trip and go tomorrow. This is a crime scene now and they need to keep the area clear in order to investigate."

"Sure, of course, I understand, Noel. Was anyone hurt?" "No, it just looks as though someone or someone's tried to stop today's groups from entering the canyon, for reasons unknown. Even though I have my suspicions."

By then Jack was standing next to Jennings and decided to enter the conversation. He looked at Noel and said, "If I were you I'd impress on the officers over there the need to check out the caves. It's obvious this delay was orchestrated for a reason, perhaps to even destroy what we're endeavoring to document."

Noel got a surprised look on her face. "I never considered that, but it makes perfect sense. I have a good friend on the police force, if I can't convince him or anyone else on the force to go then maybe my sister will be able to."

Jennings remarked, "It could be dangerous if there is actually someone in the caves who are up to no good."

Noel got a grin on her face and said, "The friend I mentioned was with a Delta force commando unit for 10 years. I've had special weapons and tactical training in the military and don't even get me started on my sister Jacqueline."

Jennings said, "Let me guess, she's a ninja."

Noel laughed and replied, "No, but our first cousin Marko was a sniper stationed in the Middle East and a Desert Ranger before that and when he came back he taught her everything he knows and she won a gold medal at the 2012 Pan Am games in judo. She basically had the same training as all of the special force soldiers."

"No way," Jack said with a combination of surprise and awe in his voice. "I'd like to come with you if you do decide to go."

"No, Jack. And it's not if, but when. I got a gut feeling as soon as the words came out of your mouth that that's exactly why this was done. You folks go back to the hotel and do your thing. I'll get with Cal and Jacqueline and try to get started down the canyon trail as soon as we can."

Jennings nodded and said, "Okay, please let us know what you find out, if that's possible."

"Sure Professor, as long as Cal thinks it's okay; you folks have a good day."

"Be safe, Noel," Jack said. She nodded and walked away.

Jennings explained what had happened to the rest and also told them what Jack had said, and Noel's response. Angela remarked,

"That doesn't surprise me about her. There's just something about the way she carries herself, she just has a very calm demeanor about her."

"Yes," Hollingsworth added, "I daresay she could handle herself in any given situation. Well, back to the hotel and more deciphering of the symbols."

"Yes," Jennings said, "we certainly can't afford to waste the day, let's go." As Jennings and company were getting things set up in the hotel; Noel, Cal Parker and Jacqueline had already started down the trail leading to the canyon caves.

Cal Parker was six feet three inches of solid muscle; the phrase 'brick wall' would be an apt description. Noel and Jacqueline weren't as physically imposing but both were unquestionably fit and formidable themselves. Because they were experienced riders they moved quickly down the narrow trail. When they came around the last bend they could see four men at the entrance of the first cave. They dismounted then flattened their bodies up against the cave's outside wall to avoid detection.

One had a flame thrower; one was pulling a small portable generator and the other two were pulling an air compressor and what looked like a small jackhammer. They waited for the men to enter the cave before advancing. Once they reached the entrance Cal peeked in long enough to see that one of the men hadn't gone far. He came up behind him, put him in a chokehold so he couldn't yell and held it until the man passed out.

Noel zip tied his hands and feet, gagged him after which they proceeded to go further into the cave. When they didn't see the other three men they determined that they must have gone to the end of the cave and were planning to wreak their destruction as they moved back towards the entrance.

They used the bends and the blind spots for cover as they slowly and quietly moved toward the last section of the cave. With each step the whooshing sound grew louder and when they were close enough to hear the other men Cal made some noise and waited.

One of the men said, "Spike, is that you?"

Cal mumbled a, "Yeah." "Well, come on then," one of the other men yelled, "let's get this party started."

Fortunately for Cal and the women the demolition crew hadn't brought much in the way of lighting except for the small lights attached to their head bands. So, using the lack of light to his advantage Cal made his move, followed by Noel and Jacqueline.

Once they subdued and secured the other three men Cal ran to the entrance of the cave and called his captain and also gave a heads up to the state police. In the daylight they could see that one of the men was the so-called Union leader.

"Well," Cal said, "attempted destruction of Park property and potential historical artifacts holds a considerable fine and jail time."

He looked at the man who was obviously the leader and said, "Who else is involved?"

"Were not saying a word, so save it."

"Suit yourself, have a nice time in prison fellows."

It took about 15 minutes for the police helicopter to get there and Cal's captain gave him a stern look and said, "You'll be facing a formal review for going out on your own like this and a reprimand on top of that. And what were you thinking taking two civilians with you?"

"Really," Cal replied, "these two ladies could probably take on any man in our unit."

"Still, you should have trusted your captain enough to give me a heads up. I'll see you up top, Cal. Oh, and even though this wasn't sanctioned, you'll still have to fill out a report."

"Yes sir, I know the drill." His captain grinned, gave him a wink and said, "Just between you and me Cal, good work, you too ladies."

Noel and Jacqueline smiled at the captain and gave him a two-finger salute.

"Okay ladies, let's move out, daylights fading fast." Once they were out of the canyon Cal went to work on the report. Jacqueline checked to make sure everything was secure at the stables and Noel called Jennings.

"Hey Professor Jennings, I just called to let you know we were successful in taking down Mr. Union leader and his crew. We caught them red-handed trying to vandalize the first cave. They had a flamethrower, a generator, an air compressor and a jackhammer. They're in police custody as we speak. Tell your young friend Jack we owe him one."

"I will, and Noel, thanks for not only taking care of them but preserving the caves so we can continue our work." "No problem, Professor, see you and your group tomorrow."

While Noel, Cal and Jacqueline were engrossed in their adventure apprehending the bad guys Jennings and his company were evaluating some of what they'd found from the day before.

Besides the images of what had to be the watchers/angels they translated more of the line sections. Jack said, "The markings on the second line section seem to mimic the first.

Hollingsworth was looking at the image with Jack. He said, "They appear to be a contradiction, dear boy, wouldn't you say?"

"You'd think so wouldn't you?" Hollingsworth moved in a little closer. "I can only make out a few words, Jack. The word left, defiled, ravaged, tent and more."

"Yes, Professor, I think I can fill in the blanks. The first line appears to be an eyewitness account of a Chieftain from the Arapahoe tribe. Apparently he saw one of these spirit beings transform from spirit into human form. He goes on to say the human form entered several of the tribes tents and then vanished. It translates: the spirit left, a man stood, passed through our tents, and was no more. The Great Spirit raged; the spirit man was vanquished; his seed remained to defile the earth."

All the professors sat there looking more than a little confused. Angela said, "I'm no Bible scholar but didn't I read somewhere that the angels who left their former abode and transgressed were chained up or something?"

The other two professors nodded in agreement.

Jack said, "Yes, you're right, Angela. The original watchers who sinned were chained up to await their final punishment. But in Genesis Chapter 6 it says that there were giants in the land in those days before the flood and after that. Goliath and his four brothers were giants and they existed a good 1,250 years after the flood."

Jennings remarked, "So you're saying that there were others who committed the same transgressions?"

"Yes, and I'll explain that a little later. The land of Canaan that was taken by Joshua and his army was inhabited by giants. The men who were originally sent to spy out the land came back and said, "We are as grasshoppers in their sight. Even using the short method of measurements at the time as I said before Goliath had to be at least 9'9" tall. Some try to say he was only marginally taller but the weight of his breastplate was 200 pounds and the tip of the spear weighed 12 pounds by their own measurements. So, he had to be super big."

"So, where did they come from, dear boy," Hollingsworth queried?"

"According to the book of Enoch after the watchers' debacle God divided up the nations according to the number of the sons of God, which was recorded as the number 70. They were comprised of lesser spiritual beings who also became corrupt."

"What," Lila blurted out? "I'm really confused, I thought angels were supposed to be good."

"Yes Lila, at first they were. Then, they were not. They became corrupt, solicited worship for themselves from humans because of their beauty and power, so eventually they succumbed to the same temptation as the watchers. This chain of events resulted in the same thing that was spoken of in Genesis Chapter 6. Where it talks about the mighty men of old, the men of renown, i.e. the gods spoken of in Greek mythology. We know them as Zeus, Apollo, Hercules, etc.."

Lila said, "If that's true, where did they go, and why don't we see any of these creatures around now, Jack?"

"The offspring of the Angels weren't immortal; so they died off, many died as a result of the flood. Then God relegated these spiritual beings to what we would call middle heaven. That's where the principalities and powers that the apostle Paul speaks about exist to this day."

Hollingsworth smirked and said, "So, no more hanky-panky, then?"

"That's right, Professor, but just like in Daniel's day they can still block or delay prayers from being answered, influence the hierarchies of towns, cities, countries and nations. Basically wreak havoc in the spiritual realm. Satan's most successful weapon is now and always has been in convincing people that he and his minions don't exist. And believe me when I say that the pews are full of them. When you demystify the Bible you dilute it to the point of no affect."

Jennings was sitting and even after all he'd seen he was still amazed at the knowledge this young man possessed. He said, "Did you ever ask your grandpa why God kept making the same mistake?"

Jack smiled. "I believe I mentioned it before but he basically said it all boils down to free will."

"Ah, yes, Hollingsworth quipped, "the dreaded free will."

"Yes," Jack replied with a sigh, "it's a recipe for sin and degradation. To create a perfect world we would have to be like robots, programmed to do everything the same. Never veering from a prearranged program, where, like the ants that basically run-on instinct. They all look alike and perform tasks without question. So, in order for God to not create us that way He basically had to live with the ungodly behavior we'd inevitably undertake."

"Still," Jennings remarked, "Wouldn't it be good to live a life free from sin and disobedience?"

"Well," Jack replied, "only one did that Professor, and he had God as His actual father and the Holy Spirit as His quote unquote, biological Father. He was tempted like as we, yet without sin. Some say he had an advantage. Some say we have that same ability, but what we don't have that Jesus had is an inexhaustibly infinite desire to please God, therefore, we sin."

Angela had been quiet for a while then she decided to say, "How exactly are we supposed to succeed when even some of the angels couldn't?"

"Exactly, Angela," Jack replied, "and… that's why we need a what…?"

"A Savior," Lila blurted out. Jack touched his nose with his index finger and then pointed at Lila and responded, "Precisely, Lila, precisely. He's the only way that we'll ever make it into heaven, it's the blood of Jesus plus nothing."

"There's still something I'm not clear on, Jack," Angela said. "Why did God need part of His heavenly host to watch those on the earth, isn't He supposed to be omnipresent? Why delegate when you can do it all yourself?"

"That's a good question, Angela, a very astute question as a matter of fact. My grandpa would've answered that question with a question. He would use an analogy; something like why do contractors hire carpenters, plumbers, electricians, heavy equipment operators, and concrete workers, etc., when most contractors are more than capable of doing all those things themselves? It's a matter of expediency."

"Wait a minute," Hollingsworth said. "Most of the contractors I've ever dealt with don't know anything, dear boy."

"Granted, Professor Hollingsworth, not all contractors do know how. My point is angels are for all intents and purposes an extension of God, Himself. So in that regard He is actually doing it all. They're not only his spiritual family but his subcontractors so to speak. Does He need the heavenly host? No, he really doesn't, just like we don't need a spouse or children or friends, we choose to have those in our lives because whose image bearers are we? God's of course, even imperfect as we are."

"Imperfect is right, Jack," Jennings remarked.

"Yes, but most earthly fathers love their children even though they fail them miserably sometimes. The Scriptures bare it out. Jesus said, (paraphrased) If you being evil know how to give good gifts to your children how much more does God want to give us good things."

"Still," Hollingsworth said, "Things would be a lot simpler if we could understand God fully."

Jack nodded, "Yeah, If we could fully understand God it would be possible for ants to fully understand us. The gap is too great, we see through a glass darkly. It would be nice to be able to call God on the phone and ask Him to explain all the mysteries that befuddle us. That just ain't the way it works as my grandpa would say."

Jennings chuckled a bit at what was yet another one of Jack's grandpa's old timey sayings. Then he said, "So, do we know what these last few symbols here represent? I see a few I think I recognize but I'm afraid it's not enough to be of much help. I see peril, I see continually and possibly destruction."

"Right, Professor Jennings, and as much as I want these caves to reveal the nature of who these so-called earthborn creatures are, so far all we're seeing is an overview of what some of them did and the resulting aftermath. Maybe the other caves will go into more detail. What we really need is someone who had a relationship with one of these earthborn creatures to have a better understanding of them."

Angela gave a slight nod and said, "That might be too tall of an order."

"I don't know," Jack replied, "there may have been someone who was successful in being a friend to one of them, as far-fetched as that sounds. They can't all have been unapproachable. There has to have been someone, all we have to do is find him or her or something they left behind to explain it."

"Right you are," Hollingsworth added, "a confidant of sorts, they couldn't have all been psychopaths, certainly." He yawned and said, "I'm very tired. I say we get some food, call it a day, come back at it fresh in the morning. A new day, a new cave."

Everyone else agreed. And after they had joined two tables in the restaurant they joined hands to bless the meal. Jennings took the lead.

"Let's bow, shall we? "Father in heaven we thank You that You have hidden Your truths from the worldly wise and delivered it unto babes. We understand enough to know that You are sovereign and Your words are meant to guide us and not to reveal all, seeing if that were the case there would be no faith involved. We ask that You bless this food and bless this expedition, in Christ's name, Amen,"

When they finished blessing the food Angela noticed more than a few people staring. She said, "It would seem we had an audience as we prayed."

"No doubt," Hollingsworth remarked, "we're obviously surrounded by heathens."

Lila most certainly bore the milk of human kindness gene. She said, "We really shouldn't judge people Professor Hollingsworth. They are simply blinded by the world, the flesh and the devil; we should pray for them like Jesus said."

"Right you are young lady, my apologies. There was a time though when those who weren't Christians at least respected those who were, enough not to stare at any rate. Now, it seems we are all simply fodder for the masses."

Jennings nodded in agreement, "That's true, but I have to believe everything is working out according to God's plan."

When they finished everyone retired for the evening except Professor Jennings and Jack. They had texted the Grand Canyon Museum curator to ask him about the skull. The Curator texted Jennings back right away and asked if he and Jack could bring it to his office that evening. When they got there and handed the skull to him he looked as if he'd just won the lottery.

He said, "This proves what my wife has been telling me for years. She said there was a lost manuscript/journal her great-grandfather read to her as a little girl. In it these hybrids were described in detail and that her great-grandfather's father had befriended one or more of them. She said she hadn't seen it in years but she was sure he'd put it in a safe place before he died."

"That's unfortunate," Jennings commented. "I don't suppose she has any idea where that safe place might be?"

"No, but he taught her a riddle and the answer to it, unfortunately she no longer remembers the answer."

"Does she at least still remember the riddle?" Jennings asked. "Oh yes, my yes, but what good is it without the answer?"

"We may be able to solve it," Jennings said hopefully.

"Really, the curator said, "that would be marvelous if you could. The way my wife described it you'd think it held the secrets of the universe or something. I'm sure it was important to the one who kept the journal but secrets of the universe, I'm skeptical."

"Could we speak to your wife, perhaps tomorrow?"

"I don't see why not, she's retired. I'll give you our address and I'll tell her to look for you..."

"What time do you think?" Jennings looked at Jack. "How about tomorrow at... Wait, could your wife send us the riddle in an email, it would save us a considerable amount of time?"

"Yes, she's very computer savvy, I'll have her send it to you first thing in the morning, say 7 o'clock?"

"Sounds good," Jennings said, "here's my number."

The curator was smiling and still staring somewhat intently at the skull when he said, "I'll have this on display within the next two days. I need to clean it and get a plaque for it." He held it up next to his head and said, "Most definitely not your average human skull."

On the way back Jack said, "This riddle might just be the break we're looking for, Professor. Imagine, an up close and personal look at one of these hybrids. How many people over the centuries have wanted to discover the secrets of the earthborn and we might just be the first, or third after the curator's wife and her great grandpa."

"Let's hope you're as good at solving riddles as you are at everything else, Jack."

"Yes, let's hope so, Professor."

They told the others the next morning at breakfast about the riddle. Hollingsworth raised his eyebrows and commented, "Riddles have never been my forte, my brother on the other hand was quite good at them, if there were some context to go with the riddle. It should be quite interesting to find out just what the riddle is."

He looked at Jack and said, "Feeling confident, are we, dear boy?"

Jack smiled and replied, "Confident that if the Lord gives me insight as He has in the past I'll be successful in solving it."

As soon as they finished eating, Jennings's phone pinged. It was the riddle from the curator's wife. It read: From the humble who seek to find-Mysteries untold as yet to mankind-Out of the rock the penitent seek, to kneel you must or its secrets will keep-Third from the first and third from the last-To solve the riddle is to learn from the past.

"Well," Angela remarked, "Cryptic much?"

Lila shook her head and said, "No clue here."

Hollingsworth looked as if he were thinking and commented, "I'm afraid I have absolutely nothing jumping out at me, dear boy, pity."

Jennings said, "Well, let's assume it has something to do with the caves. I mean the caves have to figure in some way, don't they? Where else would be a perfect place to hide something?"

"Right," Jack said, as if a lightbulb had just lit up in his brain. "Of course, Professor, let's use what we already know. There are definitely keywords in the riddle. One, humble; and that certainly goes with kneeling. So wherever this book/journal is hidden it's most likely in a lower location. It's definitely referring to the book... Look at the use of the words mysteries, find, and mankind. We are mankind looking to solve a mystery. Another clue is rock, so it could be hidden underneath or behind a rock. Oh, yes. No, that doesn't line up at all."

"What?" Jennings asked.

"I was just thinking about the number of caves. But in order for three from the first and three from the last to be referring to the location there would have to be five caves and there are six, so...."

Noel happened to be walking by during Jack's last comment. She said, "The last cave was only recently discovered, if that helps. You were saying that the number makes a difference."

"Right," Jack said as he stood up. "At the time this was written there were only five caves that had been discovered. That means what we're looking for is in the third cave."

Hollingsworth grunted then remarked, "Could you put this all together so we can see the picture you obviously already see, master Jack?"

"Sure, somewhere in the third cave there's a rock, most likely along the base of the cave wall that's hiding the book/journal. That has to be it."

"Only one way to find out," Jennings said, "let's check out cave number three."

Noel had just come back from getting a granola bar and a bottle of juice. She said, "You folks ready to roll? "

"Yes," Jennings replied, "and would it be possible for us to explore cave three today?" "Sure, no problem, you guys hop in the shuttle and I'll meet you at stables."

Once they were all saddled up Noel road over to Jennings and asked, "Any particular reason you want to see the third cave?"

"Yes, we've come across a riddle of sorts that leads us to believe there may be something of significance in that particular cave. Jack thinks he has it figured out, why, is there something wrong?"

"Oh no, just curious. You've already found something I missed when you found the skull. Maybe you'll find something else. I must say you intrigue me, Professor Jennings. How old are you anyway if you don't mind my asking?"

"No, I don't mind." Just then Angela came along side of them. He answered her by saying, "Most likely old enough to have graduated from college before you were born."

Noel smiled and said, "Not a problem on my part, Professor." She kicked her mule twice and rode on.

Angela gave him a look and said, "What was that about, Marvin?"

"That was nothing, Angela."

"Oh, so she didn't just hit on you?"

"I suppose she did, but it was a hit and a miss. You're younger than me but I'll bet you've got at least 8 to 10 years on her. So, no need to worry, Angela."

By the time they reached the cave the sun had gone behind a massive grouping of white fluffy clouds. Hollingsworth grumbled, "It could have gone in a bit earlier, this heat is stifling." He rubbed his backside after he dismounted and continued with his subtle complaining as he looked at Noel.

"I should have listened to you and bought some Vaseline, my dear. This must be what a babies bottom feels like."

She wagged her finger at him and said, "I told you so, check with me when we get back to the stables and I'll give you the spare jar I have in my tool bag."

"Bless you, dear girl, I'll do just that."

As they entered the cave Noel flipped the light switch on and said, "Too bad these lights are only in the first section."

Jack said, "Yes, we're looking for something very specific today and the additional lighting would be helpful."

Noel replied, "I don't suppose you'd clue me in as to what you're looking for would you?"

"Sure," Jennings said, "we're not trying to be secretive. There's a journal that we think may have been hidden down here some time ago which could contain information about the Nahullo." (Indian's name for giants)

"Really," she said with a questioning look. "You know, it's extremely damp and humid in these caves... pretty much a perfect atmosphere for things to decay, Professor. Not much of a chance it'd still be in legible condition, is there?"

"Yes, well, if it's underneath or behind a rock it should have been protected to a certain degree, it's worth a look."

He glanced at Jack and said, "We're thinking it's along the base of the wall, are we?"

"Yes, that's my guess anyway. Everyone keep your flashlights fixed on the base of the wall. We should keep together and check behind one another. We'll check the base of the left wall first all the way back and then the right coming back towards the entrance."

Noel was shaking her head. "You folks really think there's something hidden down here?"

Jack replied, "Yes, we're using the educated guess equation factor," he said with a chuckle.

"Never heard of it."

"Well, you use your education to take what you do know, formulate an equation, factor in a little of what you think you know and mix it with a guess and you get an educated guess equation factor."

"If you say so," Noel quipped. "What exactly is it you're looking for?"

Jack was intently flashing his light along the base of the cave and replied, "A loose rock in the wall or possibly in the floor; anything large enough to hide a small journal."

"Well, this cave goes back as far as the others," Noel remarked, "so it's going to take a while."

"Only as long as it takes to find it," Jack quipped.

They completed the left side and were halfway back to the entrance when Angela said, "Wait, there's a rock there that looks like it could be loose, but there's not enough sticking out to get hold of it." Jennings knelt down and took out his pocketknife, then he asked Jack for his. "Let me see if I can put one on each side and wiggle it enough to work it out."

The knife slid in the right side easily but the left took a little longer. He put pressure on the knives and slowly worked the rock loose enough to pull it out. Once it was out he shown his light into the hole, looked up to the others and said, "Well, here goes."

Angela put her hand out as if to try to stop him. She said, "Wait, shouldn't you just be putting a stick or something back in there first in case there's a snake or scorpion or whatever else might be in the hole?"

Jack chuckled a bit then replied, "I don't think there's enough room on either side of that rock for anything to have gotten in there. No doubt there's been many years' worth of expanding and contracting that's gone on, so it's little wonder the rock is wedged in there tight."

So Jennings put his arm inside the hole all the way up to his elbow. "Wait," he said, "I feel something. Yes, it's wrapped in a flap of some kind. As he pulled it out he said, "It's some sort of musty smelling leather. He removed the leather wrappings and on the front it read... W.C. Coopersmith, and the year next to the name was 1868.

Everyone's excitement was at a fever pitch. As they hovered around Jennings; speculation as to what was in the Journal was darting around in everyone's head. Lila said, "My goodness, I wonder what's in there? And just think, it's most likely been hidden there for over a hundred and fifty years."

Hollingsworth almost fell over as he kneeled down to get a closer look at the Journal. "Astounding, I can't believe we actually found it, Marvin."

Jennings's looked over his shoulder at Hollingsworth and said, "You must be excited; you haven't called me Marvin since our college days. And I believe we have Jack's deductive reasoning to thank."

Noel's surprise was greater than when they'd found the skull. She said, "You people haven't even been here a week and you've already discovered a skull and a journal. Imagine if you had an entire year to search these caves."

Hollingsworth looked at Jack and snorted, "Well, we do have a master puzzle solver in our group. And a year would be nice but I fear we're sorely lacking the funds for that length of time."

Lila was as close to Jack and the professor as she could be and said anxiously, "Are we just going to stand around looking at it or are we going to look inside?"

"Patience," Jennings replied, "since we're down here we may as well photograph and document everything and look at the journal when we get back."

Angela gave him an annoyed look and quipped, "Well I for one am extremely curious as to what's inside the journal. It's of historical significance even if it only contains drivel."

Jennings smiled at her and said, "I'm confident that it contains more than that but you're more than welcome to read it while the rest of us study the cave, Angela."

"No, I guess I can wait. She handed Lila the laptop and said, "Let's get set up."

Everyone gathered up their equipment and moved to the back of the cave. They went through the motions of photographing and documenting the markings on the wall even though they were all extremely excited to see just what was in the old leather-bound journal.

After looking over a large portion of the wall Jack gave a sigh and said, "Most of what I'm seeing here is the day-to-day goings on of the tribe. Hunting for food, drying the animal skins for clothing and blankets etc."

Something caught his eye. He muttered something then said, "Wait a minute, this looks interesting. Check this out professors. This line section seems to say…" He stopped suddenly, paused for a second then continued. "No way."

By that time everyone but Noel was surrounding him. He looked at Noel and asked her to come over. "Check this out, Noel."

She looked at the section and said, " It's too old for me to read, what's it say anyway?"

Jack looked at her and smiled. "Anyone ever used the term shape shifter around you?" She gave an amused grin and a nod.

"Yeah, but really, I never put much stock in those old tribal stories."

"Really," Jack replied. "This line reads: The spirit touched me and I became as dead. I arose on all fours and I saw my ancestors before me as the animal spirits of the plain.

"Right," Noel chuckled then remarked, "Whoever that was must have been smoking too much peyote."

"Yes," Hollingsworth added, "I read about the tribal passing of the peace pipe parties, I daresay those Indians saw all sorts of things under the influence of that stuff, dear boy."

"Don't laugh at the messenger," Jack said, "I am pretty sure that's what it says."

"We don't doubt that Jack," Jennings replied, "but it does sound a little out there."

Angela decided to give her two cents worth. "It doesn't sound any stranger than some of the things we read in the Bible,… I'm just saying."

Jennings replied, "Yes, well you've got a point there, and I'm not saying it's impossible, just unlikely. Let's keep moving folks, we only have another hour or so to finish up."

After everything was photographed, documented and put on the laptop they walked out and stopped at the entrance of the cave to pray. Jack led the prayer. "Let's hold hands, shall we?"

Noel was a believer but she didn't know whether or not she'd be welcomed to join in so she stood off to the side. Angela reached over to her, smiled and said, "Come and join us, Noel."

Everyone could tell she felt a little awkward when she joined the circle but when Jack said, "Let's bow," she followed and did as the others.

"Father in heaven, we're thankful for You, Your guidance and Your protection. We especially thank You for Noel, her sister Jacqueline and their friend Cal who are fearless warriors in the pursuit of justice. We know you give each of us special gifts to help others and also to search out the truths in Your word and in our world. We ask for Your continued protection and our continued success as we look into the past. In Christ's name, Amen."

When they all looked up they could see a tear running down Noel's cheek. She noticed the stares, smiled slightly and said, "That's the first time anyone other than my parents have prayed for me, or even thanked me for something I've done for that matter." She paused for a second then said, "I really appreciate it," as she wiped the tear way.

"We're all connected in some way, Noel. Even though there are many people who don't believe it, we all share common ancestral parents in Adam and Eve.

Jennings smiled at her, looked at everyone else and said, "We'd better go, the sun's going down."

5

W.C. Coopersmith/ The Nahullo

The trek back was uneventful but each one of them would consider their pre-dusk trips to the stables to be one of the many highlights of the expedition. The Western skies in the evenings were breathtaking. More than one of them commented on how fortunate it was that the mules knew the trails well enough seeing that the rider's eyes were rarely ever on it that time of day.

It was late when they did get back so after they dismounted Jennings said, "I know everyone's super curious as to what's in the journal but we really should eat and turn in early. We can spend all day tomorrow going through it with fresh eyes."

Anyone could tell the others were annoyed at not being able to look at it immediately but agreed it would be better to have fresh rested eyes when going through the book.

After Noel watered the mules she mounted her Harley-Davidson motorcycle and was getting ready to leave when Jennings walked over and asked her if she wanted to join the group in the morning to look at the journal. She said, "I have a karate class first thing tomorrow morning and an appointment in the afternoon but I could do 9 o'clock to 12 o'clock."

"Great," Jennings said, "We'll be in the conference room, see you then."

Angela was with the others getting in the shuttle while Jennings and Noel finished talking. When he joined them Angela said, " Should I be worried?"

He laughed and replied, "Absolutely… not, I just thought she'd be interested in what the Journal had to say especially considering the writer was a native to her part of the world."

Angela looked confused. She said, "A real native, you mean an Indian?"

"Yes, the curator didn't say it as much as he implied it, and I happened to see a picture of what I believed to be his wife and an elderly man who had native American features. And his wife definitely looked Native American also."

"Okay," she remarked, "you have to admit that Noel is a striking young woman, Marvin."

"Yes, Angela, young being the operative word."

The Western sky never disappointed. It was a veritable rainbow of colors blended together against a deep blue and lavender backdrop. Lila took her camera out and snapped a few photos as the shuttle slowly made its way back to the hotel, while the others just enjoyed the serenity of the moment.

When they reached the hotel they unloaded and headed for the restaurant. They had a good time chatting as they ate and none of them could contain their excitement over the day's events. Afterwards they all retired for the evening.

Angela and Lila stayed up a while to talk which inevitably turned to girl talk about guys. Angela asked Lila how long she'd known Marvin.

"Since I was little. He's been active in the community youth programs ever since he graduated from college." "Yes, he's told me that much."

"Well, of course my parents knew of him but have only ever met him once at last year's meet and greet at the college.

Angela said, "I'm curious, Lila, do you know how many lady friends he's had in the past?"

"No, I don't, but there are quite a few of his female students who have a crush on him. Of course, he's popular with his male students too; a real man's man, if you want to use those terms. I see the way he looks at you, Angela. I'd say you've sufficiently caught his eye and his interest. Why else would he have asked you on this trip?"

"It's just that he's never even tried to kiss me. Don't you think that's strange?"

"Not for him, he's a very traditional type. But I'm sure if you let him know you're interested he'll respond."

She smiled and remarked, "I just might do that. Night Lila, and thanks for the talk."

"Sure, anytime, Angela, good night."

Everyone was chatting with nervous anticipation when they entered the conference room the next morning. Noel came in a few minutes after everyone else was seated, smiled and sat at the end of the table opposite Professor Jennings. He bowed his head, said a silent prayer then opened the journal.

"Well," Jack said, "the first page says... What?" Jennings cleared his throat and started to read. (I, W.C. Coopersmith being of sound mind hereby declare that all the accounts written in this book to be true and factual. It was in the fall of the year 1863 when I ventured out again to pan for gold. The long knives once more visited my village and spoke to my people with forked tongues and promised to give our chief much wampum)

"Wait," Lila said, "long knives, forked tongues, wampum, this man was an Indian and he was panning for gold. I wasn't aware they did that."

Jack nodded and remarked, "By then most of the Indians were aware of the value that the English placed on gold and what it could buy. So, it's not as strange as it sounds, Lila."

Jennings agreed with Jack's explanation than started to continue when Lila held her hand up. "Yes, Lila," Jennings said with a slight annoyance in his tone.

"Indians could write in English?"

Noel answered that question. "Yes, Lila, along with the settlers and the soldiers there were also missionaries. They went to the villages who would accept them and taught them English and tried to convert them to Christianity. Without much success I might add. That started in the late 14th century so it's not unusual that he should be able to speak and write English."

"Okay," Lila said with a sheepish look on her face, "no more interruptions, I promise."

"Continuing on," Jennings said. (As I was bending over the water's edge I saw the reflection of a large figure behind me. Fearing for my life I lunged forward as I stood up to run away and felt something grab my shoulder and pick me up. It turned me around to face it. There I dangled in the air face-to-face with a man of very large stature. His features were like that of my brethren and as I was eye to eye with him I looked down and my feet were an arrows length above the earth. I was trembling so much I could barely think or breathe. I spoke to him in my native tongue. He smiled, then he lowered me once more to the earth)

"Wow," Lila said with a slight quiver in her voice, that would be enough to scare the pants off of anyone."

Jennings smiled and continued. (I said, who are you and where have you come from? He signed with his hands as he spoke and told me of his people. We live in the far North country where the wild animals still roam free and are good for food I asked him how is it that you are so large and powerful? He said a spirit warrior passed by many of my tribes tents and I and my brothers are as mountains to them now. At first we were looked upon with fear then some of my brothers became angry and killed many members of the Apache and Cherokee tribes. They were destroyed as a wild animal who kills is destroyed. I and my brothers alone are left. We came here lest we be destroyed as the others)

"Wow," Jack exclaimed, "he was actually conversing with an angelic and human hybrid. The Bible has only ever given sketchy descriptions of these creatures with the exception of Goliath of Gath, his brothers and Og, the King Bashan. What else does he say professor?"

"Well, he goes on to say..." (I asked him where he and his

brothers were living and he said we have only limb covered shelters in the woods a stone's throw from here)

"Uh," Hollingsworth quipped, "whose stone's throw I wonder, ours or his and his brothers'?"

Jennings looked at Hollingsworth, cleared his throat and continued. (Ten minutes had passed when we approached their shelter)

"Obviously his stone's throw," Jack said with a smile.

"Yes," Jennings looked up and replied, "obviously. Now he goes on to say... (His brothers were as large as he and were not pleased when they saw me but motioned for their brother to come over. They talked for some time then turned and beckoned me to approach them)

By this time Lila's eyes were wide open. She said, "There's no way I'd have ever gone with him."

"Yes Lila, he goes on to explain." (Being more afraid to disobey than to obey I went over. They offered me some buffalo meat. I ate with them and now they seemed pleased I was there."

"That was close," Lila remarked, "it's good they had the buffalo meat there to eat."

The rest of the group chuckled at Lila's obvious inference and Jennings said, "Yes, it was good. Now, he continues, (I asked him their names and the one who had brought me there said, (My name is Anoaha and my brothers are Anakha and Anuoha)

Jack commented, "Those names sound almost Egyptian."

"Well," Hollingsworth remarked, "there are some scholars who postulate that the Indians are ancestors of travelers from the lands close to that area where Egypt was eventually located who came over here when the landmasses were connected."

"Yes," Jennings added, "I read something to that effect myself."

"His next entry goes on to say, (I asked them about their mother and he said she died before our war paint years. I noticed a cross and chain around his neck but thinking it was only a trophy I didn't inquire as to where he got it)

"War paint years?" Angela said with a questioning look on her face.

"Yeah," Jack replied, "that was most likely before they were teenagers."

"That's answered right here," Jennings remarked. (When we were old enough the tribal warriors showed us how to hunt, to fight and to kill. Not to ride? I asked Anoaha. No, by then we were too large. We were swift of foot and had no need of horses. I stayed with them for three days more and returned to my dwelling along the river)

Angela said, "I'm surprised he didn't offer to have them stay with him."

Jack chuckled, smiled at Angela and said, "I'd be surprised if the ceilings in his cabin were high enough for them."

Angela looked somewhat embarrassed, nodded and replied, "Yeah, I really didn't think about that." She paused for a moment and said, "Is that all he wrote in his journal, Marvin?"

"No," he replied, "but I think we need to evaluate what I've just read. And so far Coopersmith hasn't asked any questions pertinent to our inquiries."

"How do you mean, Marv?" Hollingsworth asked.

"For instance, do they feel pain like us, do they crave companionship like us, do they dream, are they aware of a creator? And I believe that the Bible says that they're unredeemable."

Jack spoke up. "Wait a minute, what about the chain with across on it? That has to mean something."

"That might just be a trophy of some kind, dear boy." Hollingsworth offered.

"You might be right, I know that in Psalms Chapter 82 verses 6 and 7 God is speaking to the assembly and declares, "You are as gods but you will die like men." "He's speaking to the ones of the heavenly host who transgressed. There are a number of theories as to what became of the offspring who died in the flood it would be interesting to know for certain just how they end up after death. I mean, Mary was overshadowed by the Holy Spirit which resulted in

Jesus's birth, but I guess that was sanctioned by God and the others weren't."

"Yes, that would be the obvious difference," Jennings remarked, "and their offspring were the result of an unholy alliance so it does track that they're not able to be saved."

"We can only speculate as to exactly what happened to them, or any of those who perished in the flood for that matter," Angela added.

Jennings stood up and asked if everyone was ready to have some lunch. Jack said, "Sounds good to me."

They all agreed and as they were leaving the conference room Angela walked over beside Noel and said, "Noel, do you have any thoughts about what was in the Journal?"

"Yes, I guess some of the stories I heard growing up must have had some measure of truth to them, who knew?"

Halfway through their meal the Curator and his wife came over and sat at the table closest to them. The wife introduced herself. "I'm Morning Cloud Bradford. I believe you've already met my husband, Adam." Jennings stood up and shook her hand and gave a nod to her husband.

"Yes, Mrs. Bradford we're extremely grateful to you for allowing us to study your great-great grandfather's journal."

"Yes," she said, "I'm amazed that you were able to solve the riddle. I was wondering if I could sit in and listen while you read it?"

"Of course," Jennings replied, "it's a glimpse into your heritage. By the way, Morning Cloud is a beautiful name."

"Thank you," she replied, "may I look at the Journal while you finish your meal?"

He handed her the Journal and after looking at it she knew it was genuine. She said, "the WC stands for White Cloud, Mr. Jennings. He took the name Coopersmith from a friend of his; Andrew Coopersmith. He was one of the few long knives who actually helped my people. He married my great aunt and was always fond of the Arapahoe people."

Her husband scooted his chair closer to her so they could both read as the others were finishing their meal. When they were done Adam and Morning Cloud joined them in the conference room. Once they were seated Jennings filled them in on what they'd already read and began to read the next entry."

(Only a week had passed and I was busying myself by patching a hole in the roof of my dwelling when the three brothers appeared at the edge of the woods some 30 yards away. I was surprised to see them. When they approached me Anoaha said they had to leave from where they were for fear that they would be discovered. Anakha had seen pony soldiers close by. I asked them to stay with me until they could scout out another location and they agreed)

Jack said. "So, were they able to actually get into his place?" Jennings gave Jack a look and said, "Patience, I'm just about to answer that."

(They had to crawl on their knees to enter my dwelling and on the second day as I was rising I heard a loud banging noise at my back window, then what sounded like a growling noise. It woke up the brothers and Anoaha crawled to the window and opened the shutters. There it stood, a huge brown bear. It must have smelled the meat that still clung to the elk's carcass. I jumped back as the bear tore at the window. Then I saw Anoaha standing outside behind the bear)

Lila piped up and said, "This should be interesting."

Jennings nodded and continued. (He grabbed it around its neck with both hands and jerked it away from the window. I ran to see what was happening. The bear broke loose for only a moment and swiped at Anoaha's chest with its paw. When the bear lunged at him he grabbed the bears upper and lower jaw and tore them apart. Then he picked the bear up and threw it to the ground)

"I bet that was a body slam worth seeing," Jack remarked.

"Yes, no doubt," Jennings replied. (His brothers went out soon after but only looked on without helping. When they saw the bear was dead they skinned it and gutted it and cut it in pieces. The youngest, Anuoha started a fire and cooked the bear meat. I had never seen a bear killed by someone's hands before. As we ate I asked the brothers why they didn't help. Anoaha answered instead and said the bear was mine to kill. His brothers laughed and the youngest said he has killed two bears at once, he needed no help)

"So," Hollingsworth said, "they obviously had a sense of humor, of sorts."

Jennings continued. (There were scars on his chest from the bear claws and even after a short time they didn't look fresh. I asked, how is it that you heal so swiftly? He shrugged and replied. It has always been so. I asked, can you die as other men? He answered, only if our heart or skull is pierced through. In that we are as other men)

Angela interrupted and said, "So, these hybrids had unusual healing abilities? How could that be?"

Jack commented, "If it's true it must have to do with the immortality of the angelic father. Possibly that part of their DNA must have angelic properties, that's the only thing that makes sense. They feel pain, they're not impervious to wounds, so basically; they can be killed, just as the ones that were killed by the Israelites in the Bible."

"Well," Jennings replied, that does answer one question. Let's read on, maybe the others will be answered too."

"Yes," Hollingsworth quipped, "let's."

"Okay," Jennings said, (The next day I was about to drag the carcass off myself but Anoaha looked at me and said No, I will do this. There was an opening at the edge of the trees some distance away from where they came out that went back far into the woods. He picked up the carcass with one hand spun around and threw it beyond the edge. I was frozen for a moment, realizing it must have been over 200 feet that the carcass was thrown."

"No way," Jack said, "that sounds impossible."

Jennings gave Jack a look then continued. (These creatures have unbelievable strength, yet in other ways they behave as regular men. The brothers seem close to each other and seem never to fight among themselves. I questioned them about their mother again. I asked how it came to be that they were not violent as the others)

"This should be good," Jack said.

(Anoaha looked at me and said our mother's mother had been

captured and taken from settlers by the Cherokee tribe when she was very young. She had a silver necklace shaped like... He made a cross with his fingers, and she had a book and would not let go of it. When she grew up she was mated with a great warrior and taught our mother from the book. The tribal elders chanted and smoked a peace pipe when they wanted to see into the spirit world but she taught our mother to pray and our mother told us we would not be as the others, that the Great Spirit her mother had shown her would protect us and we would not die as the others would die)

"That's amazing," Jack said. "Just goes to show you how powerful God's word can be."

Lila said, "Impossible, amazing, me thinks those kind of words are becoming a reoccurring theme with you, Jack."

He grinned at Lila, nodded and replied, "It's just that it sounds like they're saying those three worshipped the same Great Spirit we worship, God, the creator."

"It would seem so, dear boy," Hollingsworth said.

"Yes," Jennings added, "that answers yet another question. Well, maybe two. These brothers were obviously close, so they cared about each other. The relationship aspect and the mother and grandmother's influence may have afforded them some measure of protection, after all, they were half human."

Lila look confused once again. "So, you're saying it's possible they were saved?"

"Maybe," Jack answered, "at the very least it helped to keep him and his brothers from becoming violent like the others."

Adam and Morning Cloud had been silent up to that point, then she said, "It appears that from what you say that these ancestors of mine were believers as were my parents. I am also, but I don't see how these hybrids as you call them could be. Their existence to my knowledge wasn't sanctioned by God."

"Well," Jack remarked, "the Bible does say that with God all things are possible to those who believe. Personally I believe that after the second or third generation there's more human DNA than there is angelic so why couldn't they be saved? Realistically though,

God's the only one who knows for sure. But you're right, Morning Cloud, the initial encounter wasn't sanctioned by God; what do you think, Professor Jennings?"

"I think there are many things we'll never have the answer to until we get to heaven and that we've had a very productive day." He checked his watch and continued. "And we should definitely get something to eat, rest, and check out cave number five tomorrow."

"Quite so," Hollingsworth quipped, "I'm with you, Marv."

After they finished eating everyone except Jack, Jennings, and Hollingsworth turned in for the evening. The three men decided to check out some Bible scriptures Jack had indicated may give them some additional insight into the watchers and their illegitimate offspring.

After reading Jack said that these verses basically chronicle Satan's fall, why he fell and his eventual demise. God cast him from the position that he had but according to the book of Job he still had access to heaven. So he and his cohorts rebellion perpetuated their being cast out but not their ultimate destruction. In the book of Isaiah Chapter 14 verses 12 through 14 Satan says the five I wills. His declaration ends with, (paraphrased) I will be like the Most High God."

Jennings nodded and asked, "How exactly does that help us understand the watchers or their offspring?"

"Well," Jack replied, "it gives us a beginning. The transgressions of the watchers, i.e. bad heavenly host and the rebellion began with Lucifer's pride in his beauty and his self-importance which led to his jealousy of God. That started the snowball effect resulting in the sons of God, (little g) transgressing and producing a hybrid race. All in an attempt to taint the bloodline which would eventually bring forth our savior, Jesus."

Hollingsworth cleared his throat and said, "So what you're saying is that we're just pawns in a spiritual interdimensional war waged between God and his ill-conceived creation, i.e. Lucifer on the one hand, and after an undetermined span of time he decided he wanted to circumvent God's plan and replace it with his own?"

Jennings was smiling by that time and said, "It does seem that that's what happened, but you're assuming God made a mistake. If you believe God is infallible then you also have to believe none of what happened took Him by surprise and that He has everything under control even though it may not look like it to us."

"That's right," Jack commented, in Luke Chapter 10 verses 19 through 28 Jesus makes a statement which basically prophesies Satan's end and in first Kings Chapter 22 verses 19 through 28 there is a conversation between God and a member of the heavenly host. The Lord says, (paraphrased) Who will persuade Ahab to go to battle and be slain? And a spirit suggested, (paraphrased) I will become a lying spirit in the mouth of Ahab's prophets and persuade him to go into battle. Then the Lord said, (paraphrased) You shall persuade him, and also prevail. Go out and do so. So God permitted the evil spirit to do as he suggested."

Hollingsworth looked confused. He said, "What does that prove and how does that help us better understand the watchers or their offspring?"

"Well," Jack replied, "it tells us that the destruction of these bad angels as well as Satan hasn't been fully realized. Their ultimate destruction will be in the lake of fire and that won't happen for a very long time. Meanwhile, they have God's permissive will to operate in the heavenlies and on Earth to the degree that God allows them to."

"Not good news," Jennings remarked.

"Quite," Hollingsworth added. "Even still," he continued, "why were these creatures, I mean, bad actors allowed to continue their carnal like behavior even as late as the 19th century?"

"For all we know," Jack replied, "they're still doing it, they're just clever enough now knowing how much more sophisticated mankind is to hide it."

"Yes," Hollingsworth added, "A large part of the world is civilized to the point where we wouldn't be bowing down to them and worshiping them as they did back in the day. Still, there have been stories even recently where there have been sightings of beings of unusual size and strength in some remote back villages. And, if these bad actors are clever enough at concealing their identity they could already be infiltrating the halls of power on every continent."

"Okay," Jennings's remarked, "we're not going to solve the mysteries of the universe tonight. The discussion has been intriguing; however, we should be getting some rest."

The next day as they were mounting their mules Jennings asked Noel if there were anything special about cave number five. She quipped, "You tell me Professor, I've learned more about these caves from you and your group than I knew going in and out of them since I started working for my sister."

Jennings smiled and said, "Let me rephrase the question. What have you seen or heard from the locals, any rumors, legends, anything out of the ordinary?"

"Yes, there have been sightings, unexplained moaning, you know, the usual supernatural ramblings of people still stuck in the 18th and 19th century mindset."

"So you're saying you've never witnessed anything unusual at all?"

"Well, there was this one time after I instructed the tour group I was leading to exit the cave. I turned around to make sure no one in the group had left anything behind and I saw a bluish whitish figure in front of the furthest cave wall. It was just for a second and then it vanished back into the wall."

"Other than the color was there anything unusual about it?"

"Yeah, I'd say it looked almost as tall as that section of the wall. Eight feet or so, it was just a trick of the eye, nothing more. I shrugged it off immediately."

Jennings looked somewhat skeptical but replied, "It's good that you could do that, Noel."

Jack had come close enough to hear the last few sentences. He remarked, "Did this image look like an Indian or just some guy?"

"An Indian, come to think of it. No matter though, it's just a result of too many stories from my childhood. There was nothing there, really."

Jack rolled his eyes at Noel and said, "If that's what you have to tell yourself. Say, by the way, which cave was it?"

"The one we're going in today. Why, are you going to dig into the wall to see if you can find him?" Jack and Jennings both laughed. Jack said, "No, but I brought the book with me and I just might try something."

He slowed down and rejoined Lila who was a little annoyed at him leaving her. She gave him a look and said, "Smitten much?"

"What, do you mean... with Noel? Not at all. I was just listening to one of the experiences she'd had in cave five."

Within a few minutes they were at the cave's entrance. Once they were inside Noel motioned for Jack and Jennings to follow her. Lila saw the interaction and decided to tag along.

Angela looked around and said, " "Lila, a little help please."

She gave Angela a semi disgusted look and replied, "Oh, alright, I'm coming."

Within a few minutes they were at the back of the cave. Noel pointed to the wall. "There, that's where I saw the figure. See, not there, it was only a trick of the eyes, coupled with my own imagination."

They turned to go back to the others when there was a slight popping sound. They turned around and saw the same image Noel had described. It was pointing up to the cave's ceiling, then just as quickly it disappeared.

Noel turned to the two men with a surprised look on her face and said, "Did you, I mean, did you see..?"

They both gave a slow nod and Jennings replied, "Yes, we saw it too.

Was that..?" "Yes, it was exactly what I saw. Did you see? It was pointing to a spot where the wall and ceiling meet. I wonder what it was trying to say?"

Jack said, " I'll go back to the entrance and get the small step ladder. There may be something up there it wants us to see."

Noel shook her head and remarked, "Did you just hear yourself? You said it wants us to see something."

"Well," Jack replied, "why else would it reveal itself for a second time when you're here? Did you look long enough the last time to see if it pointed?"

"No, are you kidding; I diverted my eyes as soon as it appeared."

"It may have pointed that time too," Jack said. "It may be that you have a connection with it. You are, what part Indian?"

"One quarter, or there abouts; what's that got to do with anything?"

"I'm just saying it wasn't looking at me or the professor, it was looking directly at you, Noel."

"Gee, thanks for pointing that out, Jack."

Jack went to get the ladder and when he got back he handed it to Professor Jennings. Jennings gave him a look as if to say, what, me?

Jack looked at him and said, "Well, you're a good 4 inches taller than me, Professor. I just thought…"

"Oh, you two, really!" Noel quipped. "Here, give me the ladder, I'll do it."

Jack got a smirk on his face and said, "That'll do, I just thought you might be scared, is all."

"Right," Noel replied, "flesh and blood, never, this was a whole other animal."

As she stepped on the top rung of the ladder, she said, "There seems to be a crevice." She put her gloves on not knowing exactly what might be in the crevice. Her arm went in up to her elbow then she got a semi-shocked look on her face.

She pulled out a sack containing a journal size book. It was covered with a quarter of an inch of damp moldy dust. When she stepped down from the ladder she brushed off the film and opened it to the first page. There was a look of surprise on her face, then she said, " It looks like… Yes it is, the same writing as in the other journal. And there at the top right-hand corner of the first page are the initials W.C.."

"So," Jennings said, "the apparition we saw must've been the spirit of one of the hybrids White Cloud spoke of in his journal."

"Yes, Professor," Jack commented, "what relation would be to

Noel and how would he know it was there unless White Cloud told him or showed him?"

"Well Jack, unless White Cloud had a ladder he couldn't have put it there. Maybe he gave it to one of the three brothers to hide it."

"But why, why would he be hiding it in a…"

"Jennings laughed, held his hand up and said, "Were you going to say a cave, Jack?"

"Okay, Professor, I regretted that as it was coming out of my mouth; of course he'd hide it in a similar location."

"I wonder if there's more than two," Noel queried?

"Let's take one journal at a time, shall we," Jennings said. "You're right, we need to complete the first one then this one. You know, it could be that the apparition sensed the Indian in Noel, that's why it looked at her."

"Sensed, really," Noel said with a smirk. You mean like a dog senses something?"

"No," Jack replied, "your long raven black hair, your dark brown eyes and your Amazonian like stature."

"So, you think that thing can actually see?" Noel quipped. "Well, yeah," Jack replied, "you don't think it just pops out sporadically to see if anyone happens to be standing there do you?"

Jennings chuckled. "You mean like a Jack-in-the-Box."

Noel looked a little miffed and said, "Very funny. Professor, I guess that was a silly question. Let's go and show the others what we've found."

The three of them got a dirty look from the rest when they returned. Angela said, "You couldn't stay and help us set things up?"

"Quite," Hollingsworth added, "very slack-ish of you three. I should think you'd want to expedite the info gathering."

Jack looked at them and said, "We were a little busy entertaining an apparition and finding a second journal." He held the book up and continued. "This one is also by White Cloud Coopersmith."

Their jaws dropped then Angela said, "A what, you were entertaining a what?"

"Yes," Jennings answered, "That was my reaction too. All three of us saw it, so it was real, whatever real is, that is."

Lila went over to look at the journal and took it from Jack. She said, "How did you find it?"

Noel replied, "I know this is going to sound out there but the apparition showed us."

"Yes, out there indeed, dear lady," Hollingsworth said. "Exactly where was it located, Jack?"

"High up on the wall in a crevice. Noel used the ladder to get to it."

Angela chuckled slightly and commented, " So, you men had to have a woman take the risk, huh?"

Jennings looked a little sheepish then replied, "To be fair she is taller than me and I must admit probably somewhat braver." He paused for a second then said, "She did volunteer."

"Oh, okay I guess I'll give you that, Marvin. My other question is, why would this apparition appear to you three?"

Jack replied, "I have a theory about that."

Noel interrupted and said, "He thinks the apparition knows that I have Indian ancestors and that's why it looked at me when it appeared."

Jennings knew it was a possibility this conversation could go on all day. He said, "Okay people, we have four hours to document this cave; we better get started. That is if the rest of you aren't afraid to go where we saw the figure."

"No," Angela replied. "Not me," Lila remarked.

Hollingsworth put his hand on his chin as if he was thinking. He said, "Exactly how big was this thing? It's just that I had a really traumatic experience with an apparition of sorts when I was young, and I'm not looking forward to experiencing that again."

"Really," Jennings said with a slight smile." "Oh, I'd say eight feet or so, but other than it's imposing size, blueish white transparency and it's stoic demeanor it was seemingly harmless."

"Oh, right, Marv," Hollingsworth said, "reassuring much?"

After they finished taking pictures and documenting the images

Jennings said, "Okay, let's pack it up and head back. We can check out this new journal tomorrow."

Noel gave Jennings a look. She said, "No way, I'm not waiting until tomorrow, I'm going to read it tonight. I did climb the ladder and put my hand in a hole to retrieve it after all."

Jennings laughed and replied, "That's fine, Noel, maybe you could give us a synopsis tomorrow."

She nodded and said, "That all depends on whether I fall asleep while I'm reading it or not."

They were tired when they returned so everyone ate a light supper and turned in early except for Jack and Lila. Jack had asked Noel if he could go over the book with her. After she agreed, Lila insisted on coming with Jack. They met Noel at her apartment around 7 o'clock. After she'd offered them some tea they sat down at the kitchen table with Jack on one side of her and Lila on the other. The first page had a few red drops on the edges that looked like blood.

Noel said, "That doesn't look good."

Jack commented, "There could be any number of reasons for that, go ahead, let's look at the first page."

"Very well. Let's see it starts out with (This is the second of three journals)

"Wait," Jack said, "there's another journal, I wonder where that one's hidden? We'll have to let the others know."

"Yeah," Lila remarked, "a riddle to find the first one, an apparition to find the second. I wonder what we'll have to encounter to find the third journal, if there is one?"

"I'm sure we'll find out," Noel quipped. "Now, let me continue." (I have witnessed many things in the wilderness, things which cannot be explained. Anoaha and his brothers exist in this world in many ways as others do. They speak of finding a place to live where they can stay without hindrance or fear of being found out. But they also speak of having a family. It's strange, other than their size and obvious strength they seem almost normal)

"Right, normal," Jack said sarcastically.

Noel gave him a look then continued. (I laughed at them when they told this to me. I said, Anoaha, who could endure such a union. He held up his hand and moved it side to side and said he had already found such a one. She was cast out of her tribe to survive on her own. I asked, where is she now? He said she is with child and waits for our return. He goes on to say an old Apache medicine man who lives by himself on the river's edge, north of where we are now has let her stay with him while we seek another place to stay)

"Well," Lila said with an indignant look on her face. "He just left her there pregnant and with some old nasty smelly medicine man?"

Noel and Jack couldn't help but laugh. Jack said, "That's okay Lila, this happened a long time ago. Go ahead, Noel."

(I asked him what tribe she was from. He said the Arapahoe tribe and that she was cast out because of her unusual size. They saw her as a bad omen. I asked him if she were normal in other ways? He answered and said she is very good to look upon and possesses great strength. He held his hand to his chest to sign how tall she was, which would be almost a head taller than an average size man."

"Wait a minute," Lila said as she stood up. "How did he find her? Oh wait, if she's a hybrid too they could be related."

Jack held his hand out and said, "Calm down, Lila. I'm sure they are operating under an entirely different genome scenario than us. Besides, what are the chances? She could've just been abnormally large, no aberration involved."

"Chances indeed," Noel added, "I'm with Jack. It's probably not the same issue as humans would have."

"I have another question," Lila stated. "Does the journal give any names? We need names."

Noel was looking a little irritated. She said, "If you'll let me continue there may be some names further on, Lila."

"Okay, I'll stop talking."

"He continues with, (It was five months later when the brothers came again and with them was Anoaha's squaw and papoose. I was made small by his mate and his male child was quite large too. I asked the name that was given to his child. He said his name will be Running Bear."

Noel stopped reading and got a questioning look on her face. They waited a few minutes then Jack said, "Something wrong, Noel?"

She looked up and replied, "I know that Running Bear was a fairly common name among Indian tribes back in the day but my grandmother said her grandfather's name was Running Bear and that he was a mighty warrior who was feared by all."

That got Jack's attention. "Was there anything unusual about his size?"

"Only that he was larger than most men."

"What about your grandmother?"

"She is tall for a woman. Taller than me come to think of it. I never questioned why, everyone in my family is taller than average; Jacqueline is the shortest and she's 6 feet tall."

"Keep reading," Lila said, "maybe some other names will come up. By the way, how old is your grandmother?"

"Old, she has to be at least ninety. And she's in really good shape for a ninety-year-old too."

Jack checked his watch and said, "We can finish this later. Oh, wait, when should we meet, Noel?" She hesitated then replied, "Let's meet in the lobby at 7a.m.,I'll text the others."

"7a.m. it is," Jack replied, "looking forward to it."

Other than the barely believable apparition, cave number five proved to be less than informative. Most of what they'd found related to the tribes in the area and their hunting parties and two of their intertribal wars. The only thing they did find of any significance were cave paintings of winged Indians presumably referring to the Spirit Warriors which most of the tribes attributed to the spirits of their ancestors.

They all met in the lobby of the hotel and took a bus to Noel's grandmother's residence. The bus was relatively new but anyone could tell that some of the occupants were more accustomed to riding the puddle jumpers used to access back roads and remote locations in the area. There were several people on board carrying chickens and one had a potbelly pig that oinked during the entire ride. If the smell hadn't been so bad it would have almost been comical.

When they entered Noel's grandmother's house Noel filled a large vase of water and put a beautiful bouquet of flowers that she'd brought for her grandmother, then she introduced everyone.

"Oh Noel, they're beautiful, thank you so much." She looked up at Noel and continued, "Now, you said your friends had some questions they wanted to ask about my grandfather?"

"Yes, Gramma Rose, your grandfather's name was Running Bear, right?"

"Well, yes it was. My mother was Arapahoe and her name was Chenoa which means Dove. She was very young and my grandfather mated with her after his first mate died. He was much older than her, 20 years or so I believe. He was born in the late 19th century, around 1880."

Noel was smiling at her grandma the whole time she was speaking and waited for her to finish. "We were wondering… Gramma Rose, if you knew anything about your great-grandparents?"

"Oh yes, of course, I never knew if they were true or just exaggerations and folklore. You know there are a great many stories pertaining to our people, Noel."

"Were any of them surrounding your great-grandparents, Gramma Rose?"

She gave Noel a look, smiled and replied, "Yes, but I hesitate to say only because they sound so bizarre. You see, I never really told anyone just for that reason."

"We'd like to hear, if you don't mind that is."

She gave a sideways glance and replied, "Oh, all right. Well, as I said my great-grandfather by all accounts was feared by everyone. I guess though, you could replace fear with respect. It was said he had the strength of ten warriors and could squat under a horse and raise it up on his shoulders and back. No man could stand against him and my great-grandmother was a powerful woman as well."

"Do you remember their names, Gramma?" "Remember, no,

but I wrote them down in my diary just before my mother passed away many years ago. Let me see, oh, yes, I keep it in the desk drawer next to me."

She leafed through the pages and a few minutes later she said, "Yes, here are the names of your great-great-grandparents. His name was Anoaha and hers was Aiyana, which means Eternal Bloom. They had Running Bear and he mated with my grandmother Chenoa and they named their son Chisum. He mated White Flower, they had me and named me, Lamaze, which means pretty flower. They never called me Lamaze, just Rose."

As Rose was saying the names everyone standing there was having the same jaw-dropping reaction. The entire expedition/trip was to find more information about the past that would give them a better understanding about the earthborn and here they were listening to a direct descendent of the very ones they were seeking to gain knowledge of.

"What about my grandfather, Gramma, you never spoke of him?"

She lowered her head. "Oh child, he died in the second world war. He was a powerful man, yes, but just a man. His medals are in the desk somewhere. They sent them to me, you see."

She rummaged through the second drawer and said, Oh, here they are. I keep them in this case." She handed them to Noel.

She glanced at them and handed them to Professor Jennings. He smiled, looked at Noel's gramma and said, "Your husband must've been a remarkable individual."

"He was to me long before he went to war." Jennings took out the medals one by one. The first one was the Congressional medal of honor then there were two bronze stars followed by 5 purple hearts.

"There is a letter with them, Gramma Rose, do you mind if I read it out loud?"

"No, not at all, go ahead."

"This letter is from Eagle Feathers commanding officer, Colonel John T. Jackson. "These medals hardly represent the true accomplishments and bravery of the one we affectionately referred to as, the Eagle. To all of us who served with him he was a force to be reckoned with. There never was a soldier before him nor will there ever be one after him that could equal his accomplishments. My sincerest regrets for your loss and for our country's loss as well. Colonel John T. Jackson."

"How is it I never knew this, Gramma Rose?"

She smiled and replied, "This is only the second time that I've opened the box since I received it."

Professor Jennings was looking very puzzled. The fact that they now knew that not only Noel's great great-grandfather was descendent from a hybrid but that her grandfather must have been too even though he never owned up to it.

He looked at Gramma Rose and asked, "Would you say that your husband was superhuman?"

She laughed and replied, "Some might say so, but no, he was tall and he was strong as I said, but it was his faith in God and duty to his country that made him a mighty warrior, Professor. There was nothing superhuman about him that I could point to. Well, except possibly his heart. He truly lived up to the name Eagle Feather. He was powerful like the eagle but when it came to his family, friends and people in general he was as soft and unabrasive as a feather."

"Well," Jack decided to say, "now it makes perfect sense."

"Gramma Rose looked at him and said, "How do you mean young man?"

Jack looked at Noel then back at Gramma Rose and said, "Your two granddaughters. They are definitely cut from the same cloth as their grandfather."

Noel smiled at Jack and Lila gave him a, well, not a smile. Gramma Rose stood up and even Professor Jennings did a double take. Noel saw the reaction and said, "I told you she was taller than me." Even at ninety she was an imposing figure.

She said, "I must confess something." She bowed her head slightly as she looked at Noel. "Even though my granddaughters reflect our native heritage and are brave beyond measure, they do not come from our loins."

No one moved. After she said that the silence was deafening.

So much so that you could've heard a pin drop. They all knew the implications of what she had just said but no one spoke.

Finally, Noel said, "I don't understand, Gramma Rose, what do you mean?"

"I never wanted to be the one to tell you this. Your mother and father adopted both of you girls when you were very young. Your sister was three and you were just a baby."

"How, I mean how is it that we are so tall and strong?"

Her grandma smiled and replied, "It wasn't planned, they were just fortunate that your biological parents were very tall and athletic. They had left you and your sister with some friends while they were out shopping and they were killed in a terrible car crash with an eighteen-wheeler."

There was some awkwardness for a moment then Jennings stood up followed by everyone else. Before they left she said, "Why are you all so interested in our ancestry?"

Noel replied, "Oh, we found a journal that had the name Running Bear in it and just wondered if there were any connection to your grandfather, Gramma."

"And so, was there," she asked? "Yes, but it's not important Gramma, thanks so much for your help, and your revelation."

"My pleasure, dear. And please, don't think less of your parents, to them you are theirs."

Noel gave her a kiss on her cheek, smiled and said, "I know Gramma Rose." As they walked out her gramma said, "You all have a blessed day."

When they all sat together on the bus most everyone could tell Noel's grandmother's revelation had had a measurable impact on her but it was Professor Jennings who spoke up and asked her about it. "So Noel, are you alright?"

She shook her head slightly and replied, "Yes, I only wish my parents had told me and Jacqueline. It's totally surreal if I'm being honest."

She froze for a moment then said, "I know my sister will want to find out something about our biological parents eventually. Me too, I guess."

The professor said. "I know I would if it were me. But, I guess I have to agree with Jack. You and your sister are unusually tough ladies, no matter who your real parents were."

Jack leaned in close to Noel and said, "Are you bummed out that you and your sister don't have any superpowers, I mean anything unusual that you can do or that you know of?" She gave him a side glance then remarked,

"We do have one, we're really good at ignoring obvious questions, Jack." He got an excuse me look on his face and said, "Sorry."

When they got back to the hotel Noel got off the bus and left the others immediately. Jack started off after her but between Professor Jennings and Lila they were able to convince him that she needed some space.

Angela and Lila both felt a little sorry for Noel even though she and her sister did have an Amazonian stature and exotic good looks. They expressed those feelings that evening after they finished eating. The reaction from the three males on the trip were basically the same.

Professor Jennings looked at Angela, smiled and said, "Yeah, I think I just might have to rethink our relationship. Noel would be quite the catch." His grin turned into an all-out chuckle. She was setting close enough to him to give him a good nudge in his ribs.

Lila gave Jack a look and quipped, "Don't tell me that you're not attracted to her."

"Attracted, yes, but I'm more intimidated than anything. It would be somewhat emasculating to be in a relationship with someone who not only overshadowed me physically but could manhandle me with little or no effort."

Hollingsworth was thoroughly amused by the conversation but kept silent. "So," Jennings said, "what's your take on all this, Byron?"

Hollingsworth leaned back and clasped his hands behind his head, smiled and replied, "Whoever's fortunate enough to land

Noel and her sister will most likely have more testosterone flowing through their veins than you two or myself."

Jennings and Jack nodded in agreement then Jennings commented, "We only have a short time before we're finished documenting and investigating the caves, so I suggest we get some rest. That is if we can, at any rate. What we found out today from Noel's grandmother is as unsettling as it is interesting."

While they were eating and discussing the day's events Noel was calling her sister Jacqueline to set up a meet. When Jacqueline arrived at Noel's apartment she could see her sister was upset.

She said, "What's up little sister?"

Noel motioned for her to have a seat. She just sat there for a few moments, not sure how to begin, and just as she was getting ready to say something Jacqueline's impatience got the better of her.

"It's late, if you're not going to say anything."

Noel stood up and blurted out, "You and I were adopted."

"Wait, you and I were what? Have you been drinking or something?"

"No," Noel replied sharply, "you know I don't drink, sit down and I'll explain."

Jacqueline reluctantly sat down and said, "Okay, explain yourself, I mean, explain what you just said."

Noel went over in detail the visit with their Gramma Rose and their conversation and how she had told her that their biological parents were killed in a car crash and they were adopted by their mother and father.

"So," Jacqueline said, "you're telling me mom and dad are not our real parents?"

"Yes, apparently our biological parents were tall and athletic and must have had at least some Native American in them for us to look the way we do. It's just a coincidence that we matched up so perfectly with the ones who adopted us."

"Any other bombshells?" Jacqueline asked.

"Now that you mention it, that's not the only news I have. Gramma Rose's ancestor appeared to me while I was in cave five some time ago. I just passed it off as a trick of the eyes. But the other day it appeared to me again. And everyone who was with me saw it too. It looked right at me and pointed to a journal which had information about our adoptive parent's ancestors."

"Okay Noel, stop, this is way more than I want to hear right now."

"You and me both, Jacqueline. It's hard enough to deal with one life altering revelation, much less two."

They just sat there hugging each other for a while then Jacqueline stood up and said, "I guess at some point we'll have to let mom and dad know that we know. I just hope we'll be able to sleep; good night, Noel."

6

The narrow escape/ Dynamic duo

E veryone was surprised when Jacqueline showed up with Noel the next morning. They'd only ever seen the two sisters together one-time before and even though Jacqueline was 5 inches shorter than Noel anyone could tell they were sisters. Both of them could have been models but their selfless upbringing would never have gelled with the modeling world.

Jennings stood up and looked at everyone, then remarked, "Shall we continue our research people?" Then he looked at Noel. " Do you want to continue being our guide?"

"Yes, of course, Professor. I'll meet all of you at the stables shortly." Jacqueline looked at everyone and added, "I believe I'll come with you today, Noel; my next tour doesn't start until tomorrow."

Once they'd made it to the stables and were mounting their mules Noel looked at her sister and said, "Any particular reason you decided to come along?"

"Yes, after we get the tour settled and in place I want you and I to look in cave 5. The apparition you saw may come out again if we're together. Maybe this time it'll actually say something."

"You mean you actually believe me?"

"Let's just say I'm not as skeptical about these things as I once was, little sister."

The trail was a little more treacherous that day. Evidently there'd been small rockslides all along the trail the night before and the canyon maintenance crew hadn't finished cleaning everything out of the path.

Jennings looked at the sisters and said, "I guess we should've waited a while."

Jacqueline nodded, "You're right, Professor, they usually set up signs when this happens. I'll have a word with the head maintenance man when we get back. They should have had the trails cleared out by now, just be careful and keep it slow." She repeated what she said loud enough for everyone else to hear.

Once Noel and Jacqueline helped them set up their equipment in the cave they mounted their mules and headed to cave five. They stood at the entrance for only a few minutes then Noel motioned for her sister to go in. She said, "Come on Jacqueline, no need to be afraid."

Jacqueline gave her sister a look and said, "You know not much frightens me in the natural…, but what you said you saw was anything but that."

"Yes, but he had kind eyes."

Jacqueline squinted her eyes at Noel and said, "Yes, kind eyes, 8 feet tall with a transparent body; from what you told me. The fact that he had kind eyes isn't all that comforting."

Jacqueline shrugged, put her hands on her hips and said, "Okay, I'm ready."

When they got to the end of the cave they just stared at the wall for what seemed like 10 minutes. Jacqueline touched the wall, turned around and said, "Let's go, he must be haunting another cave."

Just as the two turned around to leave they heard a noise behind them. They turned around slowly and there, half in and half out of the wall stood the eight-foot apparition. He held his hand up as a sign of peace. They looked at each other then back at the apparition. He slowly put his hand to his heart extended his arms outward with his palms up.

"No way," Jacqueline said in a whisper, "he just made the sign for love and bountiful."

Noel responded, "You think he knows us?"

"Yeah, I think he does. Wait, his countenance just changed and he's signing something else."

Jacqueline was looking intensely at his movements and trying to interpret as he was signing. "Let's see, that sign is for you, then, depart, next, danger; now he's signing, run!" They started toward the entrance of the cave and when they were halfway out the ground began to shake and parts of the cave walls started to crack.

They made it outside and mounted their mules and carefully made their way back to where they'd left the others, all the while dodging small rocks that were raining down onto the trail. The others were already out when they reached them and immediately small pieces of the trail were breaking off and dropping hundreds of feet below. Just as Lila was trying to mount her mule a section of the ground beneath her gave way and she went over the edge trying with all her might to hold on to something.

As the others looked on in horror Jack jumped off his mule but by the time he reached the edge she was too far out of reach and barely visible because of the falling debris. Lila was screaming as she plummeted toward the canyon floor. Everyone was so focused on the tragedy that was playing out before them they didn't see that Jacqueline had tied off the rope she had around the saddle horn, wrapped the other end of the rope around her waist and quickly scaled down the side of the mountain unseen by everyone there. That all happened in a matter of seconds with Noel not far behind her.

Then, suddenly, there Jaqueline was under Lila catching her in one arm and grabbing the edge of a rock that was jutting out from the side of the canyon wall with the other. Lila's dissent stopped immediately. By then the debris had stopped falling and the look on everyone's face went from despair to relief, then to amazement.

Before they could process what was happening Noel had already reached Lila and her sister to help them back up. When she reached them she told Lila to climb onto her back.

"I can't," she said, "I'm too scared."

Jacqueline helped her up far enough so she could put her arms around Noel's neck and shoulders. It took them ten minutes but they managed to get back up to where she fell from. The quaking had finally stopped. However, everyone but Noel and Jacqueline had sustained bruises from the rocks falling. Fortunately, no one was hit in the head or seriously injured. When the three women stood up everyone was looking at the sisters as if they just witnessed a miracle, which of course they had.

Professor Jennings eyes were still popping when he asked, "How did you do that? One minute you were on your mule and the next you were under Lila stopping her from falling?"

Jacqueline shook her head. "I don't know how I did it. I wanted to stop her from falling to her death and I just reacted."

Angela said, "But we didn't see you go down there, there was nothing but rocks and the canyon floor below her, then you were there; it's simply incredible."

Jack exclaimed, "The debris from the falling rocks must have temporarily kept you from our view."

Jack was hugging Lila from the time the three stood up and then he went over and hugged Jacqueline and Noel. He looked up at Noel and said, "Lila's not heavy by any means but you climbed up carrying her on your back with no effort. You two are like, like superheroes. I wish you could come back with us to Massachusetts."

"Calm down, dear boy," Hollingsworth quipped, "You'll have a coronary." He gave a slight bow to Noel and Jacqueline and said, "I won't be as unabashed as my young colleague but I will say what I just witnessed was not only brave, but it was also beyond selfless. Why, I don't think I've processed it still. Well done ladies, well done indeed."

When they returned to the stables Jacqueline contacted the canyon maintenance coordinator and informed him of the damage. She said, "Listen, Warren, you either need to be more hands on regarding the people you hire or hire more responsible people. There should have been signs put up on the trails entrance this morning. There were rocks and debris everywhere on all the main trail arteries and not a sign of any of your people."

She listened to his response, nodded and replied, "Good, see to it." When she finished she turned around and everyone was staring at her.

She looked at the group and said, "Okay, stop; I'm no hero, so please, look at me like you would any normal person, and please, do the same for my sister."

Professor Jennings smiled, looked at her, then Noel and said, "I think I speak for everyone else when I say we appreciate what you and Noel did to save Lila. And we apologize if our admiration for you two is making you uncomfortable. We're just glad you were there to do what we couldn't."

Lila spoke up and said, "If I had to fall I'm just glad you were there to do whatever it was you did." She looked at Noel and added, "I apologize for being so jealous of you, Noel, you risked your life to save me and I'll never forget it."

Noel smiled and acknowledged Lila's words, then said, "Gramma Rose's advice about rock-climbing really paid off. I'm glad I could do what I did, even though I'm not quite sure how we did it either. So what now Professor Jennings?"

"We keep doing what we came here to do."

Jack agreed and remarked, "You two super gals will be interested in what I found in the cave today given the fact that I'm positive it relates directly to you, even though you don't have any recessive angelic DNA, that we know of at any rate."

Noel was the more curious of the sisters. She said, "Why, what did you find?"

Jack looked at Hollingsworth as if wanting him to say something but Hollingsworth pointed back at Jack and said, "You're the one who figured it out, dear boy, be my guest."

He gave the sisters a glance, nodded and said, "Okay, there was a section close to the entrance of the cave which depicted a large rectangular shape and a symbol representing a spirit resting in a tree."

"What," Angela remarked, "You mean resting on a tree."

"No, the spirit entered the tree. Next to it was a depiction of three trees, tall and sturdy and even more majestic than the tree the spirit entered. Representing Anoaha and his brothers. There was a

119

succession of trees after that; but only one had a flower growing from it indicating what I believe is your Gramma Rose; then a symbol in the shape of a ship representing your father who was a hero in the Navy and two flowers growing from it. I believe those two flowers represent you and Jacqueline and that entire section of the wall represents you and your sister's adopted family tree."

"How," Noel exclaimed, " Gramma Rose just finished telling me that we're not actually their descendants and these images have been here long before we were ever born."

Jack replied, "You have to remember that some of these symbols are prophetic and consider this; there's nothing to say that your biological parents weren't special too. And if you and Jacqueline are not true descendants of Anoaha then the line stopped with your adopted parents. Did you ever notice anything special about either one of them?"

Noel nudged her sister. " Something just came to mind, Sis."

"What?"

"Remember how we used to go to the garage when dad was lifting weights? We'd play video games out there while he was lifting."

"Yeah, that's right."

"Well, once when you weren't there I asked him how much weight he had on the bar and he replied by saying; more than enough. It never registered at the time but if I'm not mistaken he had five separate weights on each side of the bench press."

What's your point, little sister?"

"I happened to go in the garage the other day to get something for mom and glanced at the weights. Each of them are a hundred pounds apiece. Dad was benching 1000 pounds and he did it a lot more than one time too."

Professor Jennings commented, "And you never realized that until just now?"

"It's been so long since we were in there when he lifted, and we we're young at the time. I guess we never noticed how much each weight weighed."

Jack said, "Okay, yeah, I don't know anyone who can bench press a half ton. And you two never lifted weights?"

"No, I haven't," Noel replied.

He looked at Jacqueline and she said, "Me either, never needed to; I guess were just naturally fit."

Hollingsworth smiled and commented, "Naturally fit would be one way to describe you two. Now, I don't know about anyone else but I'm starved. So, if we're finished contemplating their ancestral line; I say we go get something to eat."

That garnered a chuckle from everyone in the group. Then Professor Jennings said, "Yes, I agree, I believe we have one more cave to go and a third journal to find; but for now let's get on the shuttle and head to the hotel's restaurant." Noel and Jacqueline left the group to go talk with their grandmother and the rest headed for the shuttle.

After they got to the restaurant and were all seated at the table enjoying their meal, Jack said, "If the symbols we saw really were related to Noel and Jacqueline's ancestry, there may be something in the last cave that's similarly predictive. As a matter of fact, I'm beginning to see some of what we've recorded in a whole new light. I guess that'll have to wait until we get back home though."

He scanned the table and continued, "I really do wish one or both of the sisters could come back with us. Their unusual adoptive ancestry would be invaluable to our research and our understanding of the earthborn and their abilities."

Professor Jennings nodded in agreement and remarked, "I'm still a little perplexed though."

"About what, dear boy?" Hollingsworth replied.

"Well, the ones that we know to be descendants of Anoaha, Gramma Rose and Noel's and Jacqueline's adopted father show no signs of evil."

"Well Professor," Jack said, "the further away from the fallen Angels the more human the descendants. And the last time I checked if you're human, your savable."

"Savable," Hollingsworth quipped, "is that even a word?"

"Maybe, maybe not," Jack replied, "but my meaning is valid. The Nephilim were an abomination to God only because it was the result of the angel's transgression. Those that they transgressed were not evil, they were victims. Consequently, with each passing generation the original transgression may not have been imputed to the resulting offspring. Noel's and Jacqueline's adopted father is a perfect example. He has a residual power, i.e. his obvious strength, but not the evil bent. His would have been the fourth or possibly the fifth generation from the original transgression."

"I agree, Jennings said, "everything we've seen fairly points to that."

Jack was still reeling. "I know I said it before, I just wish they could come back with us. Their input would really help bring a conclusion to this expedition."

"I agree," Angela replied. She paused for a moment then continued. "We can't force them to come back with us. They have a business, family, friends and standing in the community. Not to mention a massive amount of ancestral roots; even if they're not angelic that we know of."

Jennings was nodding the entire time. "Of course that hasn't been proven, Angela. Their real parents were obviously of Indian descent, just not from the line we originally thought. They could still have residual angelic DNA. What they did on the trail was nothing short of miraculous. So, we'll just have to glean what we can from the caves, the journals and what we've discover through Jacqueline and Noel's life and what their grandmother told us."

Hollingsworth chimed in. "I do believe we've done enough to put together a rather comprehensive paper on the earthborn. I am disappointed we've yet to locate any large skeletons. An old college chum of mine texted me when he found out we were coming here. He found some giant bones while exploring the caves near Yellowstone's Hot Springs. He used the Indian name Nahullo or (giant ones). He was told that there were similar ones in the caves of the Grand Canyon."

"Really," Jack said with a slight air of wonderment. "It's strange we haven't come across any. Maybe we should go back to the cave where we saw Anoaha and ask him."

Angela and Lila gave him a look, then laughed out loud. Lila said, "Do you speak Arapahoe, or any other Native American language for that matter?"

"No, maybe he'll use sign language like he did before, or we could take a translator."

Angela smirked and said, "And what would you tell this translator? Oh, I know, there's a spirit of a giant Indian in cave number five who may or may not have the location of a cash of large Indian bones and could you please translate for us?"

"You know that just may work," Jennings quipped. "Most of the Native American descendants I've come across still have a belief in the supernatural. It actually might be worth it to try."

Hollingsworth chimed in again. "Where would we find such a translator, pray tell?"

Jack said, "Noel's and Jacqueline's gramma should know of one, let's ask her."

Jennings looked at Jack and said, "We should touch base with one of the sisters, we don't want to offend or upset them in any way."

Jack stood up and pulled his cell phone from his pocket. "No sooner said than done." Jack hit Noel's number on his speed dial and two rings later she answered.

"Yes, Jack."

"We were wondering if your Gramma Rose knows of any Indian translators?" "She does, but I know of one too, why?"

"We need one to go with us into cave five to see if Anoaha will appear again. Professor Hollingsworth believes there may be some giant bones hidden in or around one of the caves and we thought Anoaha may direct us to them if we ask."

She was silent for a moment then she replied, "My great uncle, White Feather would probably be willing to help, he's a firm believer in the spiritual realm. He seemed quite interested when I told him of Anoaha's apparition."

"Great, would you contact him and ask him if he'd be willing to help?"

"Sure, he's an early riser; would first thing tomorrow be good, we can meet at the stables around 6 o'clock?"

"That'd be great," Jack replied. "Could you let us know either way?"

"Sure, I'll call back as soon as I talk to him." "Thanks Noel, you're the best."

Everyone could tell just by listening to the conversation that it was a go. Angela and Lila both gave Jack a disgruntled look.

Angela said, "We'll have to get up no later than 5 o'clock to get dressed, have something to eat and make it to the stables by 6 o'clock."

"Yeah," Jennings remarked, "sounds about right." Just then Jack's cell phone vibrated and dinged. "Hey Noel, so what's the verdict?"

"He jumped at the chance to actually see the spirit of one of his ancestors. And he speaks four Native American languages so I'm sure he'll be able to translate if we're lucky enough to see Anoaha again; I can hardly wait to see if he shows."

"You and me both," Jack replied.

"Good, then be at the stables by six. That should give us enough time to get our gear loaded, mount up and get to the cave by 7 o'clock."

"See you there, Noel. Oh, wait, will Jacqueline be coming?"
"Yes, she'll be there."

"There was a great amount of anticipation on each one's part that evening. So much so that there was little sleep to be found. Still, everyone was up by 5 o'clock the next morning. They were excited to see if there would be an appearance by Anoaha and whether Noel's great uncle, White Feather would be successful in communicating with him if he did grace them with his presence.

After they'd dressed and eaten they headed to the stables in the shuttle. They mounted their mules and started the trek down the canyon path to the cave. White Feather never rode a mule, he said mules are for squaws. He rode a beautiful black stallion that was a good eight hands higher than any of the mules.

As he looked down on everyone else he directed his gaze at Noel. " So, you have seen the spirit of Anoaha, and you say his spirit has great height."

"Yes Uncle, it was as high as the ceiling in a house, and he wore the garb and feathers of the Arapahoe."

"Good, I will speak to him if he appears. What would you have me ask him, niece?"

"See if he knows of the resting place of the Nahullo bones."

"You and your friends seek the bones of the giant ones? There are myths of those of great height, both of the Indians and the long knives. Which do you seek?"

"Whichever we can find."

"Very well, I will question him in that way."

When they reached the cave they dismounted and tied off their mules to the hitching post that ran alongside each one of the cave entrances. Fortunately for them the sun had come up early that morning which had displaced some of the dampness of the cave's interior.

They all looked at each other as if to say; are we ready for this? After that slight pause White Feather led the way. Because of his size and the length of his stride he stayed a good 4 yards ahead of the rest. When they reached the end he turned, looked at Noel and said, "This is where Anoaha appeared?"

"Yes," she replied, "he simply emerged from the wall."

He looked at the wall then back at them and said, "You may not need to speak with him to find the answers you seek. Only a few minutes passed and the apparition appeared. He looked directly at White Feather, put his right hand to his chest then raised his hand to give the sign of peace. He put his hands to his ear, turned his back to the group and disappeared back into the wall."

Jack blurted out, "He didn't say anything."

White Feather put his finger to his mouth and said, "He did speak, he said to follow him."

"Where," Jennings remarked, "into the wall?"

"Yes, there is where he wants us to go, into the wall."

"There must be an entrance of some kind," Hollingsworth said.

White Feather walked up close to the wall and noticed a smooth area just below a rock jutting out in the shape of a hand. He pressed his hand against the imprint on the wall. Suddenly, there was a rumbling noise and a section of the rock moved back leaving enough space for them to go through one at a time.

One by one they made their way through the narrow passage. White Feather was the only one who had to bend slightly to get through.

Once they were all in Noel said, "I don't see any skeletons." No sooner had she said that than the air became chilly and they could feel a draft coming from somewhere.

Jack walked 20 feet further into the cave, stopped, then pointed. "Look, there's another tunnel. Lila, bring me the flashlight."

They followed Jack down the narrow passage and after having gone about 100 feet they came to an opening. As the flashlight illuminated the cavern that lay before them they could see hundreds and hundreds of skeletons scattered everywhere, virtually covering the entire floor as far as they could see.

"Well," Hollingsworth remarked, "I daresay we found the motherload of giant skeletons."

"I'll take as many photos as I can," Angela said. And look at the size of some of those skulls. It's hard to believe no one has stepped foot in here for centuries." "

"So it would seem," Jennings remarked. He shone his flashlight around 360° and said, "Anyone notice how clean and web free this cave is?"

"Quite," Hollingsworth quipped. And does anyone else feel that warm flow of air? There must be another entrance to this supposedly secret section of the cave."

"I feel it now," Jack replied. "I think it's coming from over there."

He walked another 30 feet to discover the same smooth handlike shape that allowed them to enter the skeletal graveyard. He pressed his hand against it and the wall moved back just as the other section had earlier.

He motioned for the rest to follow him. When they had all exited the opening they could see a road between two tall rock formations which seemingly went on forever. The road was wide enough for any size vehicle to pass through and given the fresh tire tracks it was obvious there had been one there recently.

"Well," Jennings said, "we should have known these bones didn't magically appear in the cave overnight. Someone must've been here recently."

They all stood there with a questioning look on their face. Jack put his hands palms up. "So, are the rest of you thinking what I'm thinking?"

Lila spoke up first. "Yeah, who, why and how."

"Exactly," Jack quipped, "who brought these bones here, why did they bring them and how did they happen to come to have them? Most of the large skeletal remains that have been made public are explained away by oh, let's see, anomalies of nature, carnival sideshow gimmicks, photoshop trickery or that they were simply manufactured. Hey, these bones show signs of injuries; injuries one might sustain in a battle or possibly an execution."

"Absolutely," Jennings said. "Most assuredly," Hollingsworth added."

Noel and Jacqueline sat down on several flat rocks at the base of the precipice. Noel raised her hands as if asking permission to say something.

Jennings smiled, "Yes Noel, what have you?" She looked at Jacqueline, they both nodded, then said simultaneously,

"We've been here before, several times."

They all got a semi shocked look on their faces and Angela said, "And you never knew there was a secret cave?"

"No," Noel replied, "we tried climbing here years ago but we were never successful. There aren't enough places to put your hands and feet and the face of the rock is too soft to hold the metal clips."

"That's right," Jacqueline added, "who knew there was a secret door to a secret cave." Jennings looked at Noel and asked, " So where does the road go to?"

Noel raised her eyebrows slightly then replied, "Well, the two of us were considerably younger when we came here and we had to climb over several piles of large boulders that had fallen across the road. But as to where it leads to; it eventually comes out between cave number two and number three. The first part is kind of tricky though, you'd need a four-wheel-drive to start out with then once you get over that section you go down a steep hill that ends up about 300 yards from where the road turns, just up ahead. It would have been impossible to get through with a vehicle then; it's obviously passable now, given these fresh tracks."

Hollingsworth looked at her intently and said, "Just how long ago was it, my dear?"

"Eight years or so, wouldn't you say, Jacqueline?"

"Yes, at least eight years."

Jennings stood there with his hands on his hips looking around. "I doubt seriously that all those bones got there in eight years, so the rocks that were blocking the road must have fallen after most of these bones were already placed here. I'd say over a period of a least a thousand years or so."

"I concur," Hollingsworth quipped.

"Well," Jennings said, looking at the sisters, "Shall we go back the way we came or go that way?" He pointed towards the opening to where the road vanished."

"The way we came, definitely," Noel replied. "Whoever was here may still be on the road going out and they may not be friendly either. However, I might be able to find out who used the road recently. One of the canyon maintenance workers may have seen them; I'll ask when we return. We should probably go; I think we've found out more than enough for today; I just hope we don't encounter any more rockslides on our way back."

"Right," Jennings quipped, "I'm sure that we all agree on that."

They retraced their steps and traversed the cave safely making sure the hidden doors were closed behind them, all the while keeping an eye out for any unknown figures alive or otherwise.

Once they were out they started along the trail and were careful to stay as close to the face of the canyon wall as possible and were staying on the alert for any more falling debris.

Everyone could tell Noel; her sister and their uncle were excited to have seen Anoaha but one of the members of the group wasn't letting things stand as they were.

Jack gave his mule a slight nudge so he could catch up to the sisters. When he rode up between the two of them he looked at one then the other and said, "I think the others believed the story your Gramma Rose told you but I'm not buying it. No normal person, or should I say average person could do what you did to save Lila, your real parents may not be descendenst of Anoaha but I'll bet there was definitely something special about them."

Jacqueline replied, "How would we ever know?"

"I know," Noel said, "we'll ask our father and mother. I'm sure once they know that we know they'll tell us."

Jack remarked, "Even if they don't you can still find out. You're both over twenty-one so by law you can ask for the adoption records to be unsealed."

Noel moved her horse closer to her sister, leaned over and hugged her and said, "That'll be plan B, we should definitely talk to our parents as soon as we get back."

By that time Lila had caught up to them. She said, "I just had an idea, you girls should totally talk to your parents and ask them who your real parents were."

Jack smiled and the two sisters nodded. "We were just talking about that, Lila." Jacqueline said, "but hey, great minds and all that."

She noticed the blood on Lila's arm and asked, "Are you okay, your arms bleeding?"

"Yeah, it hurts but I'll live, thanks to you two. I don't mind telling you I was scared to death when I started to fall."

"We all were," Jack replied. He pointed up ahead. "Look, there's some of the maintenance crew."

"It's about time," Jacqueline commented. "The trails actually somewhat passable now."

It was another hour before they got back to the stables which were still being worked on. Fortunately, it was confined to the newer section. Once they dismounted Jennings said, "Okay people, this has been an eventful day to say the least. And I don't know about anyone else but I'm beat and ready to eat, and not long afterwards I'll be ready for sleep."

"Really," Hollingsworth quipped, "I don't know what we'd do without your poetically generated insight, dear boy. The eating part of that little run does sound good to me though."

As they were walking to the shuttle Jack and Lila walked up behind the sisters and tapped them on the shoulder to get their attention. When they turned around Jack hugged one while Lila hugged the other. Then Jack said, "We just had to put some skin to our thanks. Seriously, you two are awesome."

Jacqueline responded with, "Well, we want to thank you for getting us to consider asking our parents about our actual heritage. I only hope our adoptive parents know something and are willing to tell us if they do."

"I'm sure they will," Jack remarked, "if you're any indication of what they're like they've got to be super nice people."

Noel leaned over and hugged Jack, then looked at Lila. "Most men are too intimidated by my height to even speak to me so it's nice to be complemented by one." Then she said, "Lila, that was just a sisterly hug, nothing more."

"I know, Noel, no worries."

While the original members of the expedition headed back to the hotel, Noel and Jacqueline jumped on their four wheelers they kept parked near the stables and headed to their parents' home. On the way Jacqueline texted the head of the parks maintenance crew and conveyed to him her displeasure at how things had been handled that day.

She got back a frowning emoji and a text that said, (We had two people call in sick today so I was shorthanded but you're absolutely right, I need to have some backup plan in the event that something like this happens again, I'm on it)

Both Jacqueline and Noel were anxious to see the look on their adoptive parents faces and were really excited that they might find out something about their biological ones.

They could never have been prepared for what they were about to find out. They hadn't called ahead so their parents were surprised to see them. As soon as the girls entered the house they could tell something was up. Their father said, "Have a seat girls."

Once they were seated their mother went over and sat between them on the couch. She smiled and began. "We got a call from your Gramma Rose."

She cleared her throat then continued. "You are our daughters and we couldn't have loved you more than if you'd come from our own bodies. You know that don't you?"

They embraced her and Noel responded with tears. "We do, we do know that Mother. But we have to know who our birth parents were. If we weren't from your loins how are we so tall and strong like you and father?"

She looked at their father and nodded as if giving him permission to speak. He sat up straight in his chair and said, "Your real mother's name was Elana and your father's name was Franco. They were dear friends of ours and early on we were around you girls so much you might well have thought we could be your parents. Elana and Franco were renowned circus performers."

"Were they of Native American dissent? Jacqueline asked.

"Yes, she was one third Arapahoe and he was one half Cherokee. They were incredibly gifted physically and something to watch when they were performing. Circus Olay had expressed interest in them joining their troop but your parents wanted to stay close to home and close to their roots, so to speak."

Noel looked at her father and said, "How did we never know you were superhuman, and Mother, are you as well?"

"Your father could never have married a weak woman, but, no, I'm totally human, just taller and stronger than most." A tear rolled down her cheek as she continued. "I hope you don't think less of us or love us less now that you know."

You could see tears filling both Noel's and Jacqueline's eyes. But Jacqueline is the one who spoke. "That would never be possible, we were just disappointed when we found out. You could have told us before; we would have understood."

Their father went over sat down and embraced their mother, looked at the girls and said, "To answer your question about me. Well I'd heard the stories about my ancestors of course but it wasn't until I was ten that I realized I was different."

"Really," Noel said rather abruptly, "Nothing before then?"

"That's right, I guess the need never showed itself before then. Anyway, I was with a friend of mine and his parents. We were picnicking near the lake; you know, the one by Pioneer Ridge. While we were eating in the picnic area some of the neighborhood troublemakers thought it would be funny to push my friend's parents car into the lake."

"What, no way," Jaqueline blurted out."

"Exactly, so when it started rolling down the hill Henry's father ran along side of it and jumped in to stop it but in doing so he hit his head hard and slumped down into the seat with the door still opened. By then the car was almost at a 45° angle plummeting towards the lake. Henry and I had already reacted and were running toward the back of the car. I ran ahead and when I caught up to the car I grabbed the back bumper."

"Let me guess." Noel said, "you and Henry had just recently watched a superhero show?"

"Probably, I don't recall. Anyway, as soon as I grabbed it I dug my heels into the ground and the car stopped immediately."

"Had Henry's mother already called for help?"

"She must have because the rescue squad and the police showed up after everything was over with. The newspaper chucked it up to adrenaline on my part but when I grabbed the bumper I could feel the power surging through my body and at that moment everything changed. I had to hide my unusual strength all through school and whenever it was necessary to do so."

The girls were silent momentarily then Noel said, "Do you have any pictures of them?"

"Yes," their mother replied, "I've kept them just in case this day ever came; I'll go get them."

She came back holding a shoebox and handed it to Jacqueline. Noel scooted closer so they could look at them together. She took the top of the box off slowly as if she were opening a much-anticipated Christmas present.

Once the top was off the first photo they saw was a miniature billboard type picture of their parents in their costumes. She looked up at her mother and asked, "Were they aerialist?"

"Yes, acrobatic aerialist to be precise. Their act drew crowds from all over the country. Their long muscular bodies made what they did even more impressive. They would've been so proud of you girls, as proud as we are."

Noel looked down and back up at him and said, "So, there wasn't any..., anything super about them?"

The father raised his eyebrows and glanced at their mother and said, "They never said of course but I had my suspicions about your father. You see, people who are like me in some way whether it be strength, speed, hearing, sight or whatever, tend to want to keep it a secret for obvious reasons. Franco, your father was spotting for me one day when I was attempting to bench-press 1,500 pounds."

"So he knew about your unusual strength?" Jacqueline asked.

"Yes, we were best friends, so yes, you can imagine how devastated we were when they died. Anyway, I was struggling a bit under the weight. It was pressing on my chest so I said, "A little help please."

"A little help," Noel said with a chuckle.

"Yes, well it was 100 pounds more than I had successfully bench pressed before. At any rate afterwards your father insisted I did most of the pushing to get the weight back on the bench rest. So, if he wasn't like me exactly, he wasn't far from it. He would lift your mother Elana up like most men would pick up a feather."

"I wish we could've seen them perform," Jacqueline said.

"Yes," their mother replied, "I've often wished we would've had enough foresight to film them. One time we were watching them perform and he must have forgotten to hold back. We've seen it often enough to know that the routine called for a single back somersault. Well, she went so high in the air that she did three. I knew what'd happened and your mother realized it too while she was in midair and adjusted accordingly. The entire arena stood up and applauded. Nothing was ever said, but I know his strength was far beyond what's considered normal."

They continued going through the photos and Jacqueline turned to Noel and said, "You look just like her you know."

"Yes," their mother added, "I've always thought so. She wasn't as tall, only 6'2" but Franco was 6'6" and they were an extraordinarily handsome couple."

"Can we keep these, Mother?" Noel asked.

"Of course, I only wish I'd have had the courage to show them to you girls before this." A single tear rolled down her cheek, then she looked up and asked, "Are we diminished in your eyes?"

"No," Noel replied, "we couldn't have asked for more loving and supportive parents. We're blessed to have been raised by you and father. You showed us how to live by reading us the Bible every day and living its message out in front of us. We are who we are because of you and your guidance. I do have some questions for a new friend of ours, however. He's somewhat of a Bible expert I'm told."

"Will you two stay for dinner?"

"Absolutely, Mother," Noel quipped, "we always had good eats growing up too, right Sis?"

"Right, what can I help you with, Mother?"

7

The trip is extended/ More journals.

While they were having a good time of fellowship with their adoptive parents the group was back at the hotel's conference room going over what they'd found recently and were also discussing the subject of the third Journal.

Angela said," We really should try to find it, so we can have some closure and to see if there's anything we've missed."

"I concur," Hollingsworth remarked. "Whoever is responsible for collecting and hiding those giant bones has to be descendants of those that first made it their mission to conceal what the Bible clearly conveys."

"Jack was keeping quiet up until that point but decided to interject his thoughts regarding what Hollingsworth had just said.

"You're right Professor, I'm sure you all have either watched or heard about the movie, 'The DaVinci Code.' It puts forth a conspiracy theory about a secret society charged with keeping the true identity and nature of Jesus a secret down through the ages."

Hollingsworth looked more than a little flustered at that statement and said, "I believe that movie was concocted by some liberal Satanic theorist group, no doubt. The very idea fabricating a story that Jesus and Mary Magdalene were married and that she was pregnant when He was crucified. Propaganda of the highest order."

"Well," Jack replied, "I'm sure that hiding those giant bones from the world at large is more than a theory. There are those who'd do anything to prevent the public from knowing anything about those bones. Which by the way would prove conclusively that the Bible and specifically the Old Testament account of Genesis is true. I think we should extend our time here if possible to try and expose their duplicity if nothing else."

"Here, here," Hollingsworth quipped, "I for one am not ready to leave; what say the rest of you?"

"I'm in agreement with that," Jennings replied, "but there's a matter of the financing for an extension. If everyone else is an agreement I'll make the call."

Angela and Lila raised their hands then Angela said, "How much more are we talking about, Marvin?"

"If we extended it by one week I'd say between five and six thousand dollars, that's if we want to continue to stay at this hotel and to continue using Noel and Jacqueline's services."

"I have some money saved, Marvin, if that's what it takes."

"I don't think that'll be necessary, Angela." He looked at his watch and said, "I'll call this evening, for now I think we should finish logging in what we photographed today and elicit Jacqueline and Noel's help tomorrow in an attempt to find out who those tracks belonged to then look for the third Journal."

"Capital idea," Hollingsworth quipped, "the game is afoot as Sherlock Holmes would say."

They spent the next few hours documenting and downloading photos into the computer. Jack and Lila were at the far end of the conference room table looking over some of the cave paintings when Jack stopped suddenly and got a questioning look on his face.

Lila noticed the look and said, "I know that look, Jack, what is it?"

"I didn't pay any attention to this before with all the craziness going on, you going over the cliff and the rockslide, but." He stopped and started to speak in a whisper. "Do you remember the flowers I thought represented Jacqueline and Noel?"

"Yes, I do, what of it ?" "These paintings here, do you see them?"

"I see, what do you see, that's the question?"

"The two flowers I attributed to Noel and Jacqueline are depicted again. One is being taken by a bird that's flying away and the other is stationary."

"Let me take a closer look. You're right, Jack, the flowers are identical to the ones coming out of the ship. I never got the whole ship thing. I mean if their father isn't actually their biological father then why are they shown together?"

"It's fairly simple, Lila, the images don't distinguish between adopted versus biological it merely connects what will eventually be."

"I wonder if they were successful in finding out about their real parents?"

"I guess we'll know soon enough, Lila, I'm sure they've already confronted them. You know, those two are fearless."

"Yeah, my still being alive testifies to that. Are you going to tell the others what you found?"

"No, let's see how it plays out. The birds are definitely identical but it's impossible to tell which flower is taken by the bird."

By then the day was fairly spent and the group decided to get something to eat. They scooted two tables together as they had since they arrived, ordered their meal and while they waited they discussed ideas as to how they might find the elusive third Journal.

"Well," Jennings said, "we found one journal down and one up, maybe the third is somewhere in the middle."

"Make sense, dear boy, but the middle of what?" Hollingsworth quipped.

"It may be simpler than we think, Professor Jennings," Jack offered. "It's been about the caves before; it could be about them again. We had clues for the first one and the second one Anoaha showed us the way. There are six caves so maybe just maybe the third Journal is in the middle cave."

"There isn't any middle cave as such, dear boy," Hollingsworth remarked. "The middle of seven would be the fourth cave with three before it and three after it."

"Technically that's true Professor, but if we lived in the nineteenth century the middle of six could mean there's possibly a crevice or pocket somewhere between cave three and cave four."

"So using that logic," Angela commented, "the middle of cave three should be hiding the third Journal, but what more information could there possibly be?"

"It could reference us, Angela, our very presence here," Jack said.

"I think that's highly unlikely, young man." Hollingsworth said with a degree of superiority.

Jennings gave Byron a questioning look and replied, "I wouldn't be too sure about that Byron, we may not be blood descendants or grafted in like Jacqueline and Noel but not everything on these walls are about them, so it is possible."

"Agree to disagree Marvelous Marv; but I suppose time will prove one of us right."

"Yes it will, Byron. Well, it's for sure we won't settle this today, let's come at it fresh in the morning. We can talk to the sisters tomorrow and get their input. They may have some insight. Meanwhile I'm going to call the head of the Archaeology Society and give him just enough of what we've found to whet his appetite. Maybe we'll get lucky and they'll see their way clear to free up some more funds. For now though, let's all get some rest; it's been an extremely long day."

Jack and Lila had decided to lounge around in the hotel lobby for a while so Jennings went to his and Jack's room to have some privacy. The time difference was only an hour or so to where he was calling. His contact in the Archaeological Society was Professor John Cameron. They had been friends since their university days. The call was only a few rings in when he answered.

"Yes, Marvin, how goes the expedition?"

"Better than expected John, which is why I'm calling. We found some physical proof of the Nahullo. That's what the Native Americans called the giant ones. We also found a treasure trove of cave paintings and ancient Indian hieroglyphics proving that when the landmasses were connected there must've been numerous travelers from the European continent."

"Well, sounds like you and your group are having quite the adventure."

"Yes John, so much so that we're discovering that two weeks just isn't enough to detail, document and collect everything, would it be possible to extend our expeditions finances for another week?"

The line was silent for only a moment then John said, "Let me contact the other members to see what they think. I'll get back to you soon. However, if you could send photos of only some of what you've discovered that may go a long ways toward convincing them, Marvin."

"That sounds promising John, I'll send them to you immediately and thank you."

"Thank me when you've gotten a positive response, Marvin, we'll talk later."

While Professor Jennings was waiting for his return call he went to Byron's room and knocked on the door. Hollingsworth popped his head out and said, "Yes, dear boy, you've gotten word so soon?"

"No Byron, but I am optimistic that Professor Cameron will be successful in convincing the other four members."

"I see, of course that does make sense that he'd need everyone's approval. I'm sure they'll agree, aren't you?"

"Fairly certain, yes." Jennings paused briefly then said, "Not to drastically change the subject but what's your thoughts on the hybrids descendants, Byron, are they more human than not?"

Byron gave a questioning nod and replied, "Logically, it's just as young Jack said. The only real transgression that the initial hieroglyphics we found referred to would have belonged to the fallen Angels and the first offspring. The remaining interaction over the generations so to speak were more or less between humans so the original sin wouldn't be passed on, at least no more so than us, seeing we're all born into sin. The bad blood would have eventually been thinned out. That's my take anyway."

"I see, Byron, so you're saying whatever residual abilities these individuals have are just that. We see no signs of evil, just the opposite in fact. The girl's father is five generations separated from the initial incident from what we know, possibly even more."

"The proof is in the pudding Marvin my friend, that's what I always say. Human is as human does and all that rot, a what?"

Jennings smiled at Byron's British-like platitudes and replied, "I agree."

He'd no sooner finished replying than his phone vibrated and beeped. Hollingsworth couldn't hear the voice on the other end of the call but he could tell by Jennings remarks that the other members of the society must have given the okay.

"So, Marvin, good news I take it?"

"Yes, they were apparently impressed with the photos I sent and are going to release another six thousand to the expeditions account."

"Capital, simply capital. I knew you'd be successful, Marv. Now, I should think you'd want to give the others the good news."

"It'll keep until tomorrow, I'm sure Jack's already in the room wondering where I am, see you in the morning old friend."

"Yes, till then, Marv."

They were all up early the next morning and met in the dining area. By the time everyone had ordered Jacqueline and Noel showed up. They pulled another table next to the other two and Jennings offered to buy them breakfast."

Thanks," Noel replied, "we talked to our parents and look, here's a small photo taken from a billboard." Noel handed it to Jack and said, "The photo is of our biological parents; they were acrobatic aerialist, isn't that unbelievable?"

Jack nodded and replied, "No, that actually explains a lot. Did you ask your adoptive parents if there was anything unusual about their abilities?"

"Yes," Noel replied, "our dad suspected our biological father had some but our mother was totally human except she was tall and very athletic."

"I'll say," Lila blurted out after looking at the old photograph. "They look incredible, why couldn't my parents have looked like that?"

Angela put her hand on Jacqueline's arm and said, "We're all very happy for you two, what now?"

"Well, it's like Jack said, it explains at least to a degree why we are how we are from a strictly physical standpoint. Our adoptive parents taught us right from wrong and raised us to be responsible and to not only look out for ourselves but to use whatever abilities we have to help others."

"Who could ask for more?" Jennings said. He stood up and continued, "So, I have good news, we have the funding we need to stay another week, is everyone on board with that?"

He looked at Noel and Jacqueline then said, "Will you continue to be our guides?"

"Of course," Noel replied.

Jacqueline hesitated then said, "I'll help out if needed but I do have other parties lined up. But hey, I'm sure my little sis is more than capable of taking care of you guys just as she has before."

"Great," Jack exclaimed. "Now that the food is here, let's bless it, eat it and continue the adventure."

After they finished eating Jacqueline said she needed to go meet the next group but that she wanted to be kept in the loop concerning any new developments.

"I'll fill you in," Noel remarked, "I'll be staying with this group until they leave."

"I figured as much little Sis, take care."

Everyone got their gear together and hopped on the shuttle, Noel sat next to Jack and Lila. She looked directly at Jack and said, "At some point I'd like to talk to you to see if there's anything the Bible says about, you know, whether we are savable or not."

Hollingsworth was sitting behind them and cleared his throat.

Jack turned and said, "Yes, I know we're not sure that's a word, Professor. Then he looked back at Noel. "Sure, sometime this week. I'll do some research in the meantime."

She smiled at Jack and Lila then said, "Thanks."

Just before they mounted the mules Hollingsworth said, "So, are we going to search for the Journal, perchance?"

"I think we should," Jennings replied. He looked at Noel and said, "We believe there's a third journal and it may be somewhere between cave three and four. Would you mind if we spent some time carefully searching the area between those two caves today?"

"No, not at all, I would say I've never noticed anything unusual between the two, but hey, you guys found the skull, two journals as well as other things that I obviously overlooked so I'm in no position to be skeptical."

Fortunately for them that day the sun was out but the heat was not. At least not nearly to the degree that it had been. As soon as they passed the entrance of cave three they did a grid search in ten-foot increments never going up further than 8 feet.

There was approximately one quarter of a mile between cave three and four so if in fact the Journal was located somewhere in the middle it would be at about the six-hundred-and-sixty-foot mark. But with all the cracks in the face of the canyon walls and the rocks jutting out, finding a crevice, hole, indention or whatever would be anything but easy.

They reached cave four without finding anything noteworthy. "Perhaps the sun wasn't at the right angle in the direction we came from," Hollingsworth remarked.

Jack had developed a down cast look having not found anything but perked up at Hollingsworth's suggestion.

"That could be it. That could be why we didn't see anything. Did you bring that handheld floodlight Professor Jennings?"

"Yes, Jack, I have it in my backpack."

"Okay, it'll take some time but I believe if we use the floodlight and shine it up and down going backwards from cave four to cave three we just might get lucky."

"I'm game," Lila said. "Me too," added Angela.

Noel gave Jack a doubtful look and said, "I hope you're right, we'd better be going though, there's another group heading this way and the trails not all that wide."

They studied the exterior practically inch by inch and it took what seemed like forever to make it to the halfway point. At almost exactly the 660-foot mark Jack noticed a crack that wasn't like the rest. It actually formed an almost perfect rectangle. It was about 6 feet up. He pulled a tiny crowbar from his backpack along with a small hammer and begin to enlarge the crack one side at a time.

"I think this may be it, if I can just open the crack enough."

Suddenly the section of the rock popped out. He turned around and looked at the rest and said, "Anyone care to stick their hand in the hole?"

They all looked around at each other and Noel said, "Really, no one." She put her hand in first then her arm up to her elbow. "Wait," she said, "I definitely feel something. I've got the edge. I've almost got it."

She pulled out a small dusty sack similar to the one that'd contained the other journals and said, "Eureka." She shook the dust from the sack and handed it to Jack. "It's all yours, I hope it's what you're looking for."

"I guess we'll find out soon enough," Jack replied.

Just then Noel got a text from Jacqueline. (We're coming up on your location in a few minutes. Are you close enough to a cave to step in as we pass by)

Noel called her back. "Hey Jacqueline, we are, we'll slip into cave four; see you in a bit."

When she got off her phone she said, "Okay, everyone we need to walk quickly and carefully back to cave four, go into the entrance far enough for Jacqueline and her group to go by."

Everyone gathered up their equipment and put it into their backpacks. They were about to mount up when Noel said, "We're close enough to cave four to walk the mules down the path. Let's go, I can hear Jacqueline's group coming."

Once they'd made it to the cave and entered they heard an explosion somewhere off in the distance. Noel handed the reigns of her mule to Jack and ran back up the trail in the direction of Jacqueline's group and caught up to them in a matter of minutes.

She looked at her sister first then the group, then back at her sister. She said, "Did you hear that explosion?"

"Yes, I can't be sure where it came from but it sounded like it could be in the vicinity of the cave we found the bones in."

"Yes, I agree but we can't investigate now, we need to get these people to safety, the explosion could trigger more rockslides."

"Right, I'll get the others and be right behind you."

When she made it back to the cave Jack was poking his head out of the entrance. He said, "What's up, Noel?"

She stood in the entrance and said rather hurriedly, "We need to get back. The explosion may have been loud enough to trigger more rockslides. Jacqueline and her group are already heading back. For now I think it's safe to mount up but if we encounter any falling debris everyone needs to get off their mules and walk as close to the canyon walls as you can get. The mules can take the falling debris better than we can. I'll take the lead, let's go."

They moved slowly up the trail passing cave three then cave two. And when they'd had gone only 100 feet past cave two, small rocks and rock dust began to fall enough so that they all dismounted and put themselves between their mules and the canyon wall just as Noel had said.

"We'll have to walk them the rest of the way, folks."

They finally made it to the stables thirty minutes later where Jacqueline was waiting. "Where's your group, Sis?"

"They left in the shuttle about 10 minutes ago. I was just getting ready to come back and look for you."

"Thanks Sis, but we managed. Did you see anything of the trucks and men?"

"Yes, they were heading for the hotel just as we got off the trail."

"I guess there's no chance they're staying around here?"

"Probably not, Noel. I wish we'd have been able to stop them somehow. I'm sure they were the ones responsible for the explosion."

"That's okay," Jennings remarked, "we have pictures and now that we have our extension we'll go back there and retrieve as many bones as we can so we have physical proof of their existence."

"That may take some doing, Marv," Hollingsworth said. "I for one am against digging or moving rocks by hand."

"We can at least check it out," Jennings quipped, "we do have six more days now."

"Very well, Marv, if we must. But I do think it would behoove us to involve Park security and the local authorities. What if those ruffians decide to come back?"

"That's a good point old friend, we definitely aren't equipped to deal with them." He looked at Noel and Jacqueline and said, "Well, most of us aren't equipped any way."

That elicited a smile from the sisters. Jacqueline looked around at everyone there and said, "I know the chief of police, he's worked hand-in-hand with the Park security people before. I'll contact him and tell him what we heard and saw and suggest that he contact Jake Sutter the head of Park security. I'm sure those people Jacqueline saw are either working with the ones we dealt with before, or they could be a separate group altogether, either way whoever goes after them better move fast."

Jacqueline pulled her cell phone from her backpack pocket, scrolled down and hit the speed dial number for the chief. "Hey Chief, this Jacqueline."

"I know your voice Jacqueline, I've asked you out often enough, what's up?"

"There was an explosion in the canyon about forty-five minutes ago and I saw a truck I didn't recognize pull out from between cave two and three. It must've belonged to whoever set the explosion."

"Did you get the plate number?"

"Only a partial, I saw the numbers 4419 and the only letter I saw was P."

The chief didn't say anything for a moment, then he said, "Is everyone all right, you obviously had a group with you?"

"Yes, everyone's fine. Noel had a group with her too, she's here with me and her group."

"Good, I'll get in touch with Jake Sutter and we'll coordinate our efforts and let you know what we find out."

"Great Sam, be safe."

"You too Jacqueline, see you soon."

When she finished Jennings said, "Well, that sounded promising, from what we heard you say at least."

"It did, yes, and as much as I'd like to assist the Chief and the others I do have a business to run. So, were you successful in your searching for the third journal?"

Noel nodded in the affirmative and showed her the sack containing the Journal.

"Looks like you people have some light reading to do and I have to go reschedule the tour that was cut short; that is if they still want to try again, catch up with you later, Sis."

Noel turned and looked at the others and said, "Well, should we get cleaned up and eat?" She checked her watch. "It is after twelve."

"Yes, by all means," Hollingsworth replied, "eating sounds good to me, dear girl."

The rest agreed. Jennings added, "We can read the journal after lunch in the conference room if it's not occupied."

They all met in the dining room when they finished showering and changing. After they ordered Noel came and sat down next to Angela. She said, "Mind if I join you folks for lunch and for the reading of the third journal?"

"Of course not," Jennings replied, "it's possible you and your sister are mentioned again. I assume it's the last and most recent documentation of W.C. Coopersmith."

She smiled, "Yes, exactly, according to my adoptive father our real father must've had some unusual ability. But the first journal said that the last one in my father's line to have been erratic was at least five generations ago and all those who conceived after that were natural Native Americans."

"Yes," Jennings remarked, "but according to something else that was said in the Journal the original transgressor transgressed multiple times before he was taken out. So, Franco could have been a fourth, fifth or even six generation descendent from them."

"I guess we'll never know," Noel said rather somberly.

After their orders had come they discussed whether or not they should try to excavate the cave entrance enough to retrieve some of the skeletal remains of the Giants.

Jack looked at Noel and said, "If you'll take me, I for one am willing to at least try."

"Sure Jack," she replied, "I will." She looked at the rest as if looking for their reaction.

"I'm game," Jennings said. "But I doubt Angela and Lila are on board." He looked at one then the other and continued, "Am I wrong?"

They both hesitated and Angela replied, "Well, I can be there for moral support."

"Me too," Lila added.

Hollingsworth was silent then decided to say, "Oh, alright, I suppose I could buy a pair of gloves and help, reluctantly, mind you." That elicited a chuckle from the ladies.

"So, it's settled then, we'll check out the Journal this afternoon and set out first thing in the morning for the bone cave."

Noel nodded in agreement and said, "I'll have to get my sister's okay, I do still work for her but I'm sure she'll be fine with it."

As they entered the conference room there was anticipation on some of the faces and trepidation on others. The former were the adventurous types and the latter were those who had more skin in the outcome of the journals content.

Jennings held the Journal up for everyone to see then said, "Anyone here have a burning desire to be the one to read this or shall I?"

No one raised their hands so Jennings nodded and said, "I'll do the honors then." He cleared his throat and began. (I have watched as Anoaha's son grew to a large size and increased in strength. His manner was that of his mother. He possessed a quiet spirit and was very mindful of his parents' wishes. I spoke to them of all the white man taught me of the true Great Spirit, the maker of all we see. It was then that Anoaha showed me the cross he was given by his mother. He told of the stories she read them from the book the white missionary had given her. He was the one who had taught her the language of the long knives)

Noel interrupted and said, "Didn't he talk about the cross in one of the other journals?"

"Yes," Jack replied, "I believe a cross was mentioned."

He continued. (I could see the words I spoke and those already spoken had fallen on eager ears and we spoke of the book and it's great wisdom many times)

Before he could continue Noel said, "Sorry Professor." She looked at Jack and said, "This brings up something I wanted to ask you about. Since Jacqueline and I must have some of the latent angelic DNA in us is it possible we can't be saved?"

Jack smiled and replied, "The passages Professor Jennings just read answers the question, Noel. The Bible says whosoever will, it also says if you confess the Lord Jesus with your mouth and believe in your heart that God raised him from the dead you will be saved. You and your sister are both a whosoever and correct me if I'm wrong but haven't both of you made that profession of faith ?"

"Yes, we have from our early teens."

"Well," Jack said, "then you have your answer by answering my question. There's another verse I'm sure you're familiar with. With man it is impossible but with God all things are possible. We can't be 100% sure that Anoaha and his brothers were the first generation or what the Bible calls the Nephilim, they could have been second or even third generation which means you and Jacqueline may even be the seventh or eighth generations away from the original transgression. So, as our esteemed Professor Byron Hollingsworth said, "The proof is in the pudding, human is as human does and I believe he also said, "We are all born into sin and need to be saved."

He turned to the rest of the group and asked, "Am I right?"

Jennings nodded in agreement and Hollingsworth said, "Here, here, my young savant."

Angela and Lila got up from their seats and walked over and hugged Noel. It's unanimous, Noel, you're as saved as any of us. Professor Jennings would you continue reading?"

"Yes, he goes on to say (Running Bear grew to be a mighty warrior. He helped all those in need and brought meat to families who'd lost husbands in battle. He truly possessed the heart of a servant)

He paused momentarily to let Noel speak. "You have a question?"

"So, even as far back is our great- great grandfather there was a tradition of selflessness."

Jack spoke up. "Absolutely, a legacy he apparently started that's been passed on to future generations. We only know bits and pieces of your ancestry, Noel. Your adopted father and biological father could very well have been related in some way. There've been instances where couples have married who were raised in different states and through genealogy research they found out they were related, howbeit many times removed. So, Professor, any prophetic words from White Cloud?"

"I'll read on." Jennings scanned through a number of pages sometimes reading in a whisper, then he said, "The last ten pages were just about his crops, the weather and hunting parties. Now he starts talking about his departure...(My end-of-life comes swiftly but I have seen many things, I have lived many years and will never forget my encounter with the three brothers, and their kindness to me for my kindness to them. Anoaha's papoose has grown in size and strength. I have seen him pray often and his mother and father also. He told me one day we will die and go to the Great Spirit and to the Son He sent as will all those who come from his loins, we have prayed that this will be so and trust the Great Spirit to do as we have asked)

"Stop!!" Jack exclaimed. "That sounded like a prayer prayed in faith and from what we know it's certainly been answered, Noel and her sister are proof of that."

"I agree," Jennings said, "a prayer that obviously came down through the generations. By my estimation Anoaha would have prayed that well over 200 years ago and it has certainly come to fruition."

"Is there anything else in there that could be considered prophetic?" Professor Hollingsworth asked.

"Other than what I read? Let me skim through some more pages. He goes back to nonspecific everyday life for about ten pages then…, wait, there's some references to the caves, he says Anoaha spoke of a cave within a cave within a cave."

"Where?" Jack practically blurted out again. "Does it say where?"

Jennings couldn't help but grin. Then he held his hand up and said, "Slow down, Jack, I think he's coming to that. Let's see, yes, here it is. Oh great…, another riddle. (Between the first, between the last, a hidden cave to see the past. It's canyon home is there it's true, reveals the past and future too)

"Great is right, Marv." He looked at Jack and asked, "Any ideas dear boy?"

"Yes, forget most of what it says, I believe the cave full of bones is the initial cave he speaking of. I say we go and dig our way back into the bone cave and find the hidden one W.C. Coopersmith is referring to."

"I agree," Jennings replied, "there must be an additional cave with writings and paintings of the past, present and future."

"Was that the entirety of the journal, Marv?"

"I'm afraid so, Byron, but it may just be all we need. That is if Jack's right." He looked at Noel but before he could ask she said, "I know what you're going to say. And of course I want to come and help, let me call Jacqueline and let her know."

After she finished the call she looked at the others and said, "She won't be able to make it."

They all ate a light dinner and turned in early even though the night's sleep escaped most of them. When they got up the next morning Jack, Jennings and Noel were all about getting an early start but the others, not so much. After they ate and gathered what was needed to do some excavating they took the shuttle to the stables, mounted the mules and headed out.

It took them an hour and a half to get to cave five where they'd found the entrance to the bone cave. Jennings pressed his hand where

White Feather had and the wall started to move. It opened a crack just enough for them to see that it was blocked by rocks.

"Just as I expected," Jack said. "I guess we'll have to try the other entrance. That means backtracking to the road between caves two and three."

"You're right Jack," Jennings said with a touch of exasperation in his voice. "Too bad we couldn't have gone there first."

"Hindsight and all that," Hollingsworth remarked.

It took them over three hours to backtrack and reach the outside of the bone cave entrance. When they finally got there Jack looked at Jennings and said, "There has to be a palm like imprint here too, doesn't there?"

Jennings didn't reply he just kept looking all around. He knelt down and said, "I believe this is it." He pressed his hand against it and a section of the wall opened wide enough to get through but the opening itself was completely blocked by rocks.

"Well, I guess we'll have to dig our way in, Professor Jennings."

"Yes, it could take a while and those stones aren't light."

He'd no sooner finished saying that then Noel walked by them with her leather gloves on and started chucking the stones out one by one. Jack tried to toss one of them further away to make room for the rest and had considerably more trouble picking them up than did Noel.

He whispered to Jennings, "I guess some of her father's strength must have been passed on to her."

Jennings smiled, nodded and said, "No doubt." Then he looked at the others and back at Noel and said, "Let us know if you get tired young lady."

Twenty-five minutes later Noel had cleared out enough of the rocks for the rest of them to get through. She took her gloves off and stood there momentarily, turned around and saw the rest staring at her and said, "What?"

Lila said, "I guess we shouldn't be surprised but seeing you throw those rocks around like they were small cantaloupes was kind of awesome."

"Oh yeah, the adrenaline has always brought out my strong side, I hope it didn't scare you guys."

"No," Hollingsworth commented, "but had we known you were a one women excavation crew I could've left my gloves in my room."

They laughed and Jennings said, "Well, Noel's made a nice path, shall we go in?"

There were still a few rocks to traverse but once they were all in they could see the other door completely blocked. Angela said, "I wonder how these men whoever they are planned on getting in with more bones?"

"I don't know," Jack replied, "possibly since the cave was compromised they didn't intend on bringing anymore here." He scratched his head then continued. "The other cave referenced in the Journal must be around here somewhere."

"Precisely, that's the only thing that makes sense," Hollingsworth said. Then added," Do we need to reference the riddle?"

Jack shook his head indicating the negative. "We need to find a palm print similar to the ones we used before."

They walked back beyond where the bones ended and scoured the area for any sign of palm print like smoothness. Forty-five minutes passed and Hollingsworth gave a slight yell, "Over here, people."

Jack got there first and knelt down beside Hollingsworth. "I think You've found it, Professor." He placed his palm on the smooth section of the wall and it opened just enough for them to get through. It was pitch black so they all hit the button on their battery-powered lanterns.

The light illuminated the entire cave and Angela immediately started snapping photos of the walls that were covered with wording of some kind, and paintings.

Jennings said, "These are similar to the ones my colleague sent me."

"Exactly," Jack replied, "these paintings and wordings reference the exploits good and bad, mostly bad of the Nahullo, until we get to here."

He pointed to the painting of three large treelike images. It's obviously referencing the three brothers and it looks to continue on to Gramma Rose, her first son and the two red flowers."

Jack stopped suddenly. "It can't be," Jack said under his breath.

"What," Jennings asked.

"This whole section is about Noel and Jacqueline."

That got Noel's attention. She walked over to them and tried to see what Jack was talking about. "What do you see, Jack?"

"I see us and you and Jacqueline. Each of these depictions tell a story that was yet in the future when they were done."

"Extraordinary," Hollingsworth quipped.

Jack went over each one from the brothers meeting with White Cloud, Anoaha's taking of a bride, the birth of Running Bear, Gramma Rose's birth and her son, and here are Noel and Jacqueline, the two flowers."

He pointed to another drawing and said, "You're not going to believe this." By then they were all standing behind him listening.

"Just as the previous images and writings spoke of Noel and Jacqueline's ancestral line and their father's exploits these speak of Noel and Jacqueline."

"Okay, wait," Noel interjected, "we're not related through our adoptive parents line."

Jack nodded. "That's right but just as I told Professor Jennings, these pictographs and writings don't follow the future according to who is related to who only what will be."

"So what is it we won't believe, dear boy," Hollingsworth said rather impatiently.

He pointed to the area he was referencing and said, "What do you see?"

"No way," Angela said with a surprised look on her face." "What, what is it?" Lila asked just as impatiently as Hollingsworth had.

"It's Noel and Jacqueline saving you, two red flowers raising up a yellow flower; and there's a depiction of a precipice surrounding the three of you. And what's this just prior to that?"

Jack shook his head at Angela's question and said, "Noel will have to explain that one, I haven't a clue."

Everyone looked at Noel. She looked at the image intently for a moment and said, "Oh yeah…, oh, this is really bizarre. It must be referring to what happened seven years ago. Jacqueline and I were climbing the twin faces of Comanche Ridge. We were having a contest to see who could get to the top first. I was climbing and had reached about 80 feet and lost my footing. I was trying to grab rocks as I was sliding down with no luck and before I could even scream Jacqueline was there grabbing my arm. I would've died just as Lila would have but Jacqueline was just there. Later when I asked her how, she shrugged and said, "I saw you falling and knew I had to save you. I don't know how; I was on the ridge opposite you then a split second later I was on the other side next to you grabbing your arm."

"Astounding," Hollingsworth said with an air of amazement. "she obviously has the ability to travel through dimensions at will. Has anything like that happened since that you're aware of?"

"Yes, I suppose it happened to her again when Lila was falling. I don't think she knows how to control it; it must just happen whenever she feels another's life is in danger."

"I guess abilities vary but if you're going to have an ability that's a good one to possess," Jack said.

"Any further revelations dear boy?"

"Nothing new that I can see, Professor."

He pointed a little further down the wall and said, "There's a bird flying away with a red rose in its beak, that's the same as the one we saw before." He looked at Noel and smiled." That's either you or your sister. I believe one of you will be coming back with us when we leave, or possibly shortly thereafter. The rose is identical to the one representing you and your sister saving Lila."

She looked down slightly and then back up with her eyes only and replied, "I haven't said anything to Jacqueline but I was considering going back with your group…, only temporarily mind you."

"Really!" Jack remarked. "Well that would be really…"

He looked at Lila then back at Noel and continued. "Really okay, yeah, okay."

Lila punched Jack in the shoulder and said, "You don't have to minimize your obvious gleefulness at the prospect on my account, Jack, I'm sure Noel has something more in mind for coming with us other than you."

She looked directly at Noel and said, "Am I right?"

"Yes Lila, I've been wanting a change of scenery for a while now. For some reason I feel if I go with your group I just might find what I've been missing here, I can't explain it, I just feel it."

"Your Mr. Right could be waiting for you there," Jack quipped, "you never know."

"That could be it, Jack; all I know is my gut feelings are usually there for a reason."

Wanting to get back on track Jennings said, "Okay Jack, this cave has given us a little more insight than what we had before but I can't help but think there's a better reason for its existence than what we've seen so far..., Any thoughts?"

"There's something fairly obvious that we've overlooked or just taken for granted."

"Which is?" Jennings asked with a perplexed look on his face."

"The sliding rock walls. They very likely weigh more than a ton, easy. We see the door slide open and slide close and we just take it for granted." "Precisely, dear boy," Hollingsworth quipped. "That takes some sophisticated engineering."

Jack touched his nose with his index finger and pointed to the professor. "As you said, precisely."

He paused then continued. "This tells me they had some serious engineering skills back in the day or they had help from an outside source, either way those sliding rock walls are pretty impressive."

"Okay," Jennings said, "most of what we're seeing here is a repetition. I think we've gleaned as much as we can so I think we should be getting back."

They all agreed and started to make their way through the opening Noel had made. Within twenty minutes they were back on the road that came out between cave one and two. They were getting plenty of exercise that day and by the time they made it to the end of the road it was dusk.

Noel said, "It'll be dark by the time we get close to the stables so when it does use the battery-powered lanterns to light the path."

Lila gazed up at the sky and said, "Wow, the sky looks like it's on fire. The orangey reds and blue streaks resembles a blaze, I've never seen anything like it."

They all stopped for a moment to admire the site then Jennings said, "God really is the master artist."

Noel nodded in agreement then said rather matter-of-factly, "We still have a long ways to go people, let's keep moving."

Jacqueline was waiting for them at the stables and after they dismounted she said, "You guys really enjoy worrying me, don't you?"

Noel explained how they had to backtrack, what they'd found and how they were late getting started in coming back."

"So, she said rather abruptly, "I hope it was worth it."

Noel held up one of the skulls they'd found in the cave and said, "We've been here our entire lives and we've never seen anything like this, not to mention the skull we found early on, the three journals and a revelation in them or the bone cave full of giant remains. So, yes Sis, I'd say over all this group has made everything that's happened during their stay here worth it."

Jacqueline smiled at her sister and replied, "I totally agree, I was just really concerned for yours and the others' safety."

"Well," Jennings said, "by the time we document and catalog all that we found our extension will have expired."

He looked at Noel and said, "I hope you'll be able to make up your mind by then young lady."

She nodded and knew what Jennings had said would elicit a questioning look from her sister. She turned around and sure enough there was the look, with just a touch of concern.

"So little sister, you're thinking about flying the coop?"

"Yes, for a while now, Jacqueline, we should talk, but not now, later."

"Okay, we certainly will. Now that I know you all are safe I'm going back to the lodge to check on my group, see you good people tomorrow."

Everyone could tell there was a certain amount of tension between the sisters but they were silent on the shuttle ride to the hotel. Once they were back Jennings said, "Okay people, we have two and a half days to document and catalog the rest of our findings. It's been a long day so I suggest we eat a light dinner and retire to our rooms."

As everyone was heading to the dining room Angela touched Marvin's arm and said, This has been the most interesting and exciting time of my life, Marvin. It's made my feelings for you all the more real. I couldn't have imagined when you asked me to come how much I'd enjoy it and how amazed I am at what we've discovered."

She hugged him and said, "I'll be indebted to you forever for asking me to come with you."

Jennings was a bit surprised at how generous she was with her thanks."

"You know I'd never would've been the one to initiate this as you have, Angela. Some would say I'm a boring professor, but I couldn't agree more. This experience has been all the more enjoyable for you being with us. Even though it has had its share of…shall we say, scary moments."

She smiled and said, "Thanks for that. You know my heart was pounding before I said anything and all the while I was saying it not knowing how you felt."

"This is how I feel, Angela." He gave her a long, respectful kiss then stood back and looked for her response.

"Well, for a boring professor you certainly are a good kisser."

He smiled and replied, "I'm glad you think so." He winked and said, "Not a word of this to Lila's mother, now."

"I promise, not one word."

After everyone had eaten, Jennings walked Angela to her room, returned her hug and said, "See you in the morning, have a good night's sleep."

8

The revelation/ The journey home.

The next morning while they were all eating breakfast Jack got a text from one of his friends. It read (Hope your expedition is going well; I'm finishing up two summer classes and the basketball training camp is going great. Be a good bud and send me pics of some scenery so I can see what I'm missing)

Just as he finished reading the text Jacqueline came in and sat down next to her sister. "I've got some news."

"Good, bad or indifferent," Hollingsworth quipped. "Good I'm glad to report. The park security working with the local police department was able to find the perpetrators that tried to destroy one cave and closed the entrances to the last one we found."

"That is good news," Jack said with a flare. "How many men were there and what did they find, anything interesting?"

"Two men and one woman and an assortment of pipe bombs and bomb making materials, plus half a wall of surveillance photos featuring us. I guess if it came to it we would be targets also."

Lila looked at her intently and said, "You mean?"

"If, you mean, eliminate us, I guess we'll never know for sure. Sufficed to say whatever they had planned for us is now null and void."

"I think that may be our que to skedaddle," Hollingsworth quipped.

"Skedaddle, Byron, really?"

"I thought it was appropriate wording given our location, Marvelous Marv, in the West and all that."

"We have one more day here group. Let's take one more trip to the Canyon and just enjoy the scenery."

"I agree Professor Jennings," Jack replied. "I'll take some pictures to send to my friend Carson."

They gathered their gear for the last time and headed for the stables. Jacqueline and Noel jumped on their four wheelers and by the time the others arrived the sisters had all the mules saddled and ready to go.

After they were mounted Jacqueline looked at Professor Jennings and asked, "Well, was it worth the trip, Professor?"

He smiled and replied, "It was more than worth it. We have an abundance of photos as well as physical artifacts, not to mention the skulls and bones of the Nahullo. And we mustn't forget Anoaha's visitation."

"Don't forget the journals," Jack added.

"Yes, of course, we do have copies of them at least; we couldn't very well deprive W.C. Coopersmith's descendants from cherishing the originals."

Hollingsworth cleared his throat to get everyone's attention." We mustn't forget these two lovely young Amazonian guides whose services I was responsible for procuring."

"That goes without saying," Jennings replied. "Shall we begin?"

"Yes, lead on dear ladies," Hollingsworth said in his best British accent.

The weather was unusually mild that day and the Arizona sky was breathtaking. They stopped at the entrance of each cave and said a prayer thanking God for His protection while exploring them.

Jack brought a box of chalk so he could identify each cave that they stood in front of. When they got to cave five Jack asked, "Shall we see if Anoaha is out and about?"

"Once was quite enough for me dear boy, let's not disturb the old fellow; I think that's best don't you?" As he looked at Jennings.

"I agree, that is unless Jacqueline and Noel want to."

They all looked at the sisters to see their reaction.

"No," Noel replied, "he's not going anywhere, let's move on."

Pictures were being taken at every angle of the Canyon wall and the sky, then Jack said, "Wait."

Everyone disengaged from what they were doing and looked at him.

"I want to take a group picture of us all standing together with the Canyon in the background to send to my friend Carson Lennox."

They lined up in two rows with the tall ones in the back. They stood as close as they dared to the edge for the full Canyon affect. Jack set up the tripod and set the timer for ten seconds, giving him enough time to get into the picture.

Once in position he said, "Everyone say cheese." Then he rushed back to get into position.

Jack sent the photo to Carson and texted (You missed a once in a lifetime adventure my friend, too bad it coincided with two classes and basketball training camp) "I never heard you talk about this Carson Lennox, Jack,"

"Well." Lila interrupted after the first word." "It's because even though Jack and Carson are good friends they've had a rivalry ever since kindergarten. Carson has almost always bested him. Carson was the star athlete, star pupil, most popular; you name it he bested Jack in almost everything."

"But you're still friends?" Jennings said with a questioning look.

"Yes, I'm not so petty as to let his popularity interfere with our own friendship."

"Most mature of you, dear boy, most mature indeed," Hollingsworth said with an earnest tone.

"Yeah, well, I'm engaged and he still doesn't have a clue who his life mate will be, so there's that."

He'd no sooner finished the sentence than he got a text from Carson. It read (Thanks for the pic, beautiful view of the canyon and who's that tall Amazonian type on the back row, she's gorgeous?"

He texted back (One of our guides, who just may be coming

back with us in two days) (Great, Jack, that way I'll get to see her in person)

Jack sent him back two thumbs up emojis, looked at Noel and said, "It seems you've made quite an impression on my friend even from 2000 miles away."

"Really, and just how tall is your friend?"

"Tall enough, I believe he's 6'8" tall."

"Is he handsome or not so much?"

Jack didn't answer he looked down at his phone and pulled up a picture of Carson. "This was taken last year."

She looked at it intently then said, "So, he's very handsome."

"Yeah, he thinks so too, one of his few flaws."

"Would you introduce us when we get back?"

"So, you've decided for sure that you're coming with us?"

"Yes, I believe I have, now."

"That elicited a slight chuckle from everyone there. It was obvious that Noel found Jack's friend appealing and that fact had eliminated any doubts she may have had about leaving.

They continued down the trail for a short time and Jacqueline said, "Around this corner coming up is one of the most beautiful views of the canyon walls. It's a real rainbow of colors when the sunlight hits it. We should get there just in time. Careful though, the trail does narrow a bit."

It took them about fifteen minutes to round the bend to get to the spot Jacqueline referred to but it was more than worth a few extra waggles of the mule's backside. The sun came out from behind the clouds and the canyon walls were ablaze with brilliant colors of reds and purples at the top and at the bottom shades of greens and blues and also white quartz like colors which blinded the eyes if one were to look at it intently for any period of time.

Noel said, "If you wait a few minutes the sun's position will mute the color somewhat which will be more conducive to taking photos. All you'll get now is a lot of bright spots that will obscure the image in the photo."

They sat there on their mules as if frozen in time and sure

enough just as Noel had said the sparkle faded just enough to get a clear spotless photo of the canyon walls. Everyone used their phones and several of them used not only their phones but also their more expensive cameras they'd brought along.

"Wow," Jack commented, God really outdid Himself here, didn't He?"

"Yes," Jennings replied. "Some would say it took millions of years for this canyon to be formed but to me this was all God in conjunction with the flood."

"Quite right, Marv, creation scientists have proven in simulations that a good bit of what we see here could have happened rather rapidly. And, while we're on the subject of the flood, did anyone read about a test done in nineteen seventy-six with a scaled down version of Noah's Ark. They put the scaled-down version of the ark in a simulation tank and threw every conceivable hurricane condition at it and it wouldn't capsize. That's especially interesting if you consider up until that time sea vessels and their construction had never even been heard of."

"Yes," Jennings replied, "and that wasn't the only test done, and they all came to the same conclusion. The ark could have withstood a 200 mile an hour hurricane and never capsized and even if turned over on its side it would immediately right itself. Who could design such a thing but God?"

"Obviously, not anyone," Lila remarked, "but we're all choir members here, no doubters. Right now I choose to just enjoy God's handiwork, not analyze it."

Jacqueline nodded in agreement then said, "As much as we'd all love to stay here longer we really should be heading back people, it'll be dark in two hours."

Anyone looking at the group as they mounted their mules for the last time could have detected a certain resistance. They pushed the short haired steeds less than before wanting the ride to last a little bit longer. And even though they'd never forget the harrowing experiences of the expedition the rewards of the adventure overshadowed them by a mile.

It was almost dusk by the time they made it to the stables. Once again the sunset was breathtaking. It seemed every color of the rainbow was displayed and positioned to complement each other. It was as if a master artist had taken it upon himself to create this gigantic masterpiece.

They'd never seen skies this beautiful back home, or maybe it was just the rush of everyday life that never allowed them to look up and enjoy them. Jacqueline dismounted first and looked at her sister while she took the saddle and blanket off her mule. Noel knew she was upset that she'd be leaving the next morning, or would she?"

"Hey, Sis, are you taking another flight tomorrow?"

"No, I'll be going with them."

"How?"

"Simple, I took a page out of your be prepared playbook, Sis."

"Really, how so?"

"I booked a flight for last week and paid for the right to cancel and reschedule. As soon as I found out what flight they'd be taking I switched, easy peasy."

"Oh, so you're really leaving me?"

"Not forever, Sis, I need a change."

"And if this Carson Lennox turns out to be Mr. Right, what then, Noel?"

"I'll come back here to be married. And if he does turn out to be Mr. Right, we'll decide then what to do."

She walked over and hugged Jacqueline. Everyone took the opportunity to snap a picture of the Amazonians hugging and Jennings said, "One thing's for sure, Jacqueline, we'll never forget you and I can't speak for the others but I'll definitely be returning here at some point in the future."

They all shook their heads in agreement then Hollingsworth said, "Wild horses couldn't keep me away my dear."

"That's sweet, Professor, I do so hope you all will come back to visit, your expedition has answered a lot of questions for Noel and I and brought up almost as many more. Things won't be nearly as exciting now that you guys are leaving."

"That might be a good thing," Jack quipped. Then he said, "Well, I guess we should head back to the hotel, people, we have an oh dark thirty flight (meaning very early) to catch in the morning."

"Right you are, dear boy, right you are."

The shuttle dropped the group off at the hotel while Jacqueline and Noel jumped on their 4-wheelers and went to talk to their adoptive parents. Jacqueline was the first one in the door and when her mother saw her she could tell that her daughter was upset.

She said, "Where's Noel?"

"Right behind me and she has some news for you and Dad."

Just then she came through the door with a semi-woeful look on her face. When their father came from the kitchen he could tell something was wrong too.

"Okay girls, what's up now?"

Noel said, "Let's sit down."

Once they were seated Noel went through the entire sequence of events for the last three weeks hitting only the highlights. "It's been a real wild three weeks Mom and Dad. I've found out more about myself in that short amount of time than in my entire life. I want to experience new things, be with new people. I'll be back, I'm not going to be gone forever."

Her mother and father scooted over closer to her and her mother said, "We always knew that one or both of you would be going somewhere at some point in your life sooner or later; it's going to be hard but we want both of you to be happy, I just wish it would be later rather than sooner."

"I know, I'll miss you and dad terribly but I do need to go pack, Mom."

"Sure, I'll help."

"Not me," Jacqueline blurted out, "I'll see you before you leave tomorrow. And Noel, I'll be smiling on the outside but frowning on the inside."

"Okay, but our flights at six thirty so you have to be there before then to say goodbye."

"I will be, I'll be there at six, hopefully just before you board the plane."

"I'm holding you to that Sis; till then."

The willingness to rise early wasn't there as it had been in the beginning. The thought of leaving the adventure they'd experienced almost from day one and going back to a certain level of tedium wasn't something any of them were looking forward to even given their discoveries.

The expense increased of course what with all the artifacts and bones they were bringing back. Fortunately, Jennings contacts with the Minister of the Interior and the Archaeological Society he was affiliated with ran interference and were responsible for facilitating their even being able to remove the artifacts in the first place.

They'd be placed in a museum soon after their finds were authenticated and documented by the proper people, but it was sufficient for Jennings and the others that his name and the names of those with him would be engraved on a plaque next to the items.

Jacqueline showed up just as she'd promised. She gave her little sister a hug and a kiss on the cheek. Then said, "Keep in touch."

"You know I will, Jacqueline, I love you."

Tears filled Jacqueline's eyes and she replied, " I love you too, little Sister."

She gave a hug to all the rest and received an especially long-lasting hug from Jack and Lila. "I'm so glad you were there that day, Jacqueline. I couldn't imagine living without Lila."

"Yeah," Lila added, "I couldn't imagine living without me either."

Even though everyone was obviously sad to be leaving, Lila's quip started them all laughing. The usual smiles, waves and goodbyes lasted a good five minutes until all of them had disappeared into the chute connecting the terminal and the plane.

After everyone boarded and were seated the captain gave his usual speech. Then the flight attendant gave her safety tips as the plane was taking off. It went smoothly for the most part. There was five minutes of turbulence as the plane ascended then stopped just as suddenly as it started after the plane leveled off at 30,000 feet.

Prior to loading Jennings asked the luggage handler to make sure all the bags containing the artifacts were secured emphasizing how fragile some of them were. He assured Jennings they would be secure then said, "I'll see to it personally."

Noel was seated directly behind Jennings and next to Jack and Lila. A half hour into the flight she happened to look back behind her and slightly to the right and thought she recognized the man sitting there. Not wanting to draw attention to herself she waited ten minutes before leaning forward and whispering in Jennings' ear.

"The man two rows back on the opposite side of the aisle looks familiar. I think we should keep an eye on him."

"Okay, I'll check him out when I get up to go to the bathroom. Noel leaned back but kept her eyes on Jennings to see when he'd get up. Fifteen minutes later he unfastened his seat belt and stood up. He didn't walk toward the back but rather walked toward the front of the plane and engaged one of the flight attendants.

She gave him a stern look at first but then smiled when he smiled at her. "This bathroom is occupied but there is one in the rear of the plane, Sir."

"Oh no, I have a question."

"Yes?"

"I assume there is an air marshal on this flight?"

"Why do you ask?"

He gave her the position of the man Noel told him about and said, "I believe that man is here to do harm, is there any way I can talk with the air marshal?"

"No, but I can certainly slip a note and ask him to keep an eye on the man, just in case."

"Great, that's great, thank you so much."

The flight attendant gave him a look and said, "Just so I have an idea of who you are, I need to see your ID, I'll return it to you when you get off the plane."

He reached in his wallet and gave her his license and his card with all of his information on it. After glancing at it she said, "Okay, Professor Jennings you can return to your seat now."

He smiled and said," I really do have to use the restroom." She nodded and said, "It looks like this one up here is clear now, use it and please return to your seat as quickly as possible."

As soon as he returned Noel leaned forward again and said, "Well?"

"She said she'd slip the marshal a note."

"I think she must have done it while you were in the restroom. She walked to the rear of the plane and walked back by us to the front within 3 to 4 minutes. The air marshal has to be close to the rear of the plane."

"Yes," Jennings said," that does make sense, that way he or she can keep an eye on everyone. Let's hope you're wrong and he just looks like one of the men involved in the explosions."

"Yeah, hope is right. I'll stop talking now."

Noel stood up slowly and practically every male on the plane did a double take. She had to bend over slightly to walk down the aisle, which was fairly unusual, especially for a woman.

Noel sized up all the ones likely to hold the position of air marshal as she walked down the aisle and pegged the rather stern looking broad-shouldered man with a bulky jacket as being him. The bulky jacket he was wearing could easily have been concealing a weapon.

She smiled at him and as she walked by he returned the smile for reasons that would be obvious to most men. He was in the very back row and tall enough to see pretty much any one on the plane.

When she sat back down she didn't lean forward as before but whispered loud enough for Jennings to hear. "I think it's the tall man with the chiseled jaw, black hair and bulky jacket, Professor."

"Good to know, we may need his help if that person is who you think he is. He may very well be here to steal our finds; we'll just have to wait and see."

Lila and Jack had been listening to them the entire time and Lila whispered, "I thought they caught all of those men?"

"Maybe, maybe not." Noel replied. "All I know is I'm going to shadow the baggage man after we land."

"Yeah," Jennings said, "I think it would be good for Jack and I to go also. We went through way too much acquiring those artifacts to let someone steal them now."

"I agree," Jack added, "We'll just have to hurry to go down the escalator to the tarmac level and be there as he unloads them off the plane; it won't be easy."

"Whatever it takes," Noel said." I just had a thought, what if he's not the only one, there could be two or three to deal with?"

"I couldn't comment on that," Jennings said. "But if he does have help we'll definitely have to be on our guard." He gave Angela a questioning look.

"Yes, Professor?"

"I think you and Lila should be the last ones to get off the plane. We should know by then what we're dealing with."

Jack tapped Jennings on his shoulder and said, "Who's going to let the air marshal know what we're up to?"

"I'll go back and slip him a note letting him know we think the guy's going to make a move."

Jack said, "Wait, Noel, how are you going to know for sure that it's him?"

"I'll reach for that bulge in his jacket, and if it is him he'll react like a professional, grab my arm and pulled out his weapon."

"Yikes," Jack said, "that sounds kind of dangerous."

"I agree," Lila remarked.

"Well, I'm betting my reflexes are faster than his."

"Then what?" Angela turned and said in more than a whisper.

"Then I'll give him the note and hope he doesn't try to handcuff me, it'll be fine, I'm not afraid."

"Okay," Lila said with a touch of exasperation in her voice, "I hope you're right, Amazonian 007." That elicited a muffled chuckle all around. Noel smiled and pulled the slip of paper from her jacket pocket, spent two minutes writing on the paper, got up and walked toward the back of the plane.

Everyone that looked at her before looked again as she walked down the aisle."

"Gee," she said under her breath, "you'd think they'd never seen a tall women before."

Two steps before she got to the supposed air marshal she looked directly at him, smiled, then winked. On her way there she thought better of reaching for the bulge in his coat and decided just to hand him the note. When she did of course he assumed she was engaging him on a purely romantic level but when he opened it up and read it his countenance changed.

He reached in his pocket and showed her his badge and nodded as she walked back by him. She nodded in recognition.

"Well," Jack said when she sat back down, "is he the air marshal?"

"Yes, he flashed his badge as I walked back by and nodded, so I think he's on board."

Lila nudged her and said, "What exactly did the note say?"

"It said, my group and I are just on our way back from an expedition and have numerous artifacts in the luggage area and we're relatively sure there's a man on board who intends on taking them; could you help?"

I took his showing me his badge and nodding as a confirmation that he would."

Jack looked puzzled and said, "They're really not supposed to reveal themselves under any circumstances, that is unless there's a viable threat."

Lila gave him a look and said, "Duh, that's why we agreed that Noel should take him the message."

"Right, it's a good thing you came with us, Noel, I don't think any of us here are disarming enough to have pulled that off."

Lila cut her eyes at Jack and gave him a slight jab in the ribs. "Hey, what was that for?"

Angela said, "I know precisely what that was for, Jack; what about us, are we chopped liver?"

Jack blushed slightly and replied, "You two are obviously

attractive but you're not as imposing as our 6-foot five-inch friend here is. There's a difference, come on, you know there is."

Everyone close to them heard his response; some snickered and some just gave them a weird glance while Lila and Angela both chuckled. Angela remarked, "Yeah, we get it, tall girl more engaging; you could've whispered though I believe the pilot and copilot heard you."

They could tell Noel was only a little offended, she said, "I'll except imposing. I'm only hoping my trip down the aisle was worth it."

"I guess we'll find out," Jennings said. He looked at his watch and continued. "We should be hearing from the captain soon, according to my calculations we're coming up on fifteen minutes before we're supposed to land."

He looked at Jack and Noel and said, "We'll need to be ready to move. Angela, you and Lila will be responsible for getting the overhead bags down."

Hollingsworth had been sleeping for practically the entire trip. Jennings reached over across the aisle and tapped his shoulder and whispered, "Byron, wake up old friend."

"What, what, are we there?"

"Close, will you help Angela and Lila get the overhead bags?"

"Right, of course, just so. What about you, Marv?"

"Jack, Noel and I are getting off quickly to be sure our extra luggage is secure, know what I mean?"

"Yes, very good, I shall endeavor to do as you asked; you can count on me."

The plane started its descent and the captain came on the intercom. He said, "Everyone please keep your seats and seatbelts on, we should be landing and ready to get off in approximately fifteen minutes. The temperature is a balmy 76°. We hope you enjoyed your flight and will fly with us again."

The flight attendant walked the isle with a trash container in her hand to retrieve the last of the used cups and trash then walked back to the front checking as she went to see if everyone's seatbelts were still fastened. As soon as she passed by, Jennings, Jack and Noel put their hands on the seat belt release so they'd be ready to move as soon as the doors opened to let the passengers off.

Fortunately for them they were only four rows from the front so they'd be better than able to be the first ones out. They knew they had ten minutes at the most to traverse the shoot, get to the escalator, and exit the building before the luggage handler started to unload the baggage compartment of the plane.

The plane landed and taxied into position and two minutes later they were given the okay to start unloading. The three of them were up and out like a light, running swiftly through the shoot then on to the nearest escalator, skipped down so fast they caught the attention of two airport security men then headed toward the ground exit sign.

They bolted out the door with the two security guards not far behind. As soon as they turned the corner they saw a man wearing a dark hoodie with a gun in his hand demanding that the baggage handler hand him the ones labeled artifacts.

"There's no way that's the same man that was on the plane," Jennings said under his breath. "You're right," Jack replied. "He couldn't have gotten down here before us."

The man pointed the gun at them as he walked toward him. He said, "That's far enough, I was sent here to retrieve the contents of these bags and that's what I intend on doing."

By then the security guards arrived on scene, the tall one pulled out his cell phone to call for help. He looked at the hooded man and said, "There'll be back up here within minutes so I suggest you put your gun down. Soon you'll be outnumbered 5 to 1, so put the weapon down now."

Three more-armed security guards came to the scene and this time the man dropped his gun and put his hands into the air. After he was handcuffed Jennings walked over to him and asked, "Who hired you to do this?"

"I don't know, I don't know who hired me. Two thousand was transferred to my account with the promise of two thousand more when they took possession of the bags. It was all done anonymously over the phone. Why, what difference could that possibly make?"

"Oh, let me see, so we'll know who to go after and prosecute."

By that time the security guards had handcuffed him and were ready to take him away when the police showed up. After they spoke to the guards they took off their handcuffs and put theirs on.

"Let's go," the officer said."

"What am I being charged with exactly?"

"You'll find out soon enough, come on."

Jennings, Jack and Noel followed the police as far as the terminal they'd exited and sitting there on one of the benches with semi-worried looks were Angela, Lila and Hollingsworth. Hollingsworth was the first to speak. "So, I take it that we're still in possession of the goods, Marv?"

Jennings smiled and replied, "Right you are, dear boy, right you are."

They all laughed a bit and Hollingsworth said, "Adequate, an adequate impersonation of me, I'll give you that dear boy, now what?"

"We go to the baggage claim area and get our stuff, hail a couple of taxis down and head for the college. Waiting there will be members of the Archaeological Society who will relieve us of our treasured finds and do their thing before displaying them in the Western History Museum."

"Surely the skulls won't be exhibited there," Jack said.

"Well," Jennings replied, "the skulls ordinarily would be exhibited in the Natural History Museum but there's a new museum that's just recently opened with a section for biblical artifacts and finds; that's where the skulls and bones will be displayed."

"That's better," Jack said. "That's definitely more appropriate than a secular museum, Professor. I only hope there's not someone on the inside to sabotage the exhibit or try to steal the artifacts again."

"I've been assured by the museum's curator that they'll have more than enough security."

"Famous last words, I only hope he's right, Professor."

Lila's mother and Jack's father were there to pick them up and just as they suspected her mother's first words weren't did you have a nice flight and a good time it was directed at Professor Jennings and Angela. "Well, you two are acting awfully chummy, I hope you kept your promises."

Jennings smiled and replied, "Yes, Mrs. Harper, we were only away from the group once but even then we were in plain sight of others."

"Ditto for Lila and I," Jack offered.

"Good, glad to hear it, are you ready to go, Lila?"

Lila gave a reluctant yes then she gave Jack a hug and said," See you at the opening."

"What opening is that?" Her mother asked."

"Once everything we brought back is authenticated and placed in the museums there's going to be an opening to the public and to make everyone aware of our contributions to the exhibit, Mother. Two openings in fact, one at the Western History Museum here in Montclair and the other at the recently opened Creation Museum."

"Well, I'll be sure that your father and I come too." She said goodbye to Professor Jennings and thanked him for watching out for Lila. After they got into the car and drove off Jennings looked at Jack and said, "So, she didn't tell her mother that she almost died?"

"Are you serious, she'd never even let her out of her site if she knew about that, past legal drinking age or not. Her mother is fanatical about her safety. It's a miracle she let her go with us, and rest assured had she known about the near tragedy she would have flown to Arizona and took her back immediately."

Angela raised her eyebrows and said, "If she were in her early to mid-teens I could almost see the extreme but at her age my mother had already been married four years."

Jack nodded in agreement and added, "Her mother isn't going to be too happy either when she finds out I'm picking her up almost as soon as they get back home and driving us to meet up with Noel and Carson to eat out."

Hollingsworth was still waiting for his cab and said, "Really,

I can't see what all the fuss is about; he shook Marvin's hands and said, "Best expedition ever, totally, to put it in the young people's vernacular these days. Keep in touch my friend, and definitely let me know if you'll ever be returning to Arizona at any time. Tata everyone."

Before he left he eyed Noel and said, "Be careful my dear, don't let just anyone in on how special you are; Godspeed everyone, see you at the openings."

They all said their goodbyes and Noel gave Hollingsworth a hug as his cab was pulling up. He waved out the back window as the cab drove away.

Noel said, "Well, I guess I need to find an apartment and a job ASAP."

"How are your finances?" Jack asked.

"Good, I have a twenty-thousand-dollar CD and forty-five thousand dollars combined in my checking and savings account. Not much to spend my money on living rent-free at home and I've been working for Jacqueline for six years."

Jennings and Jack both looked impressed. Jennings said, "Wow, how very frugal of you, even so, if you need any help with anything let me know."

"Yeah, me too," Jack added."

"That's sweet but I should be okay for a while."

"Wait," Jack said with a touch of excitement. "Do you play basketball?"

"Yes, I've been known to make a few baskets in my day, why?"

"Carson is good friends with the coach of a women's semi-Pro basketball team here and if he's not looking for help or a player he may know someone who is."

"Great, Jack, give me a text or call if your friend knows anyone."

"I'll do better than that, he said he wanted to meet you as soon as possible, how about I set something up and give you a call?"

"Sounds good, well, here's my ride, I'll be checking out some of the apartment buildings close by. She hugged Jack, Jennings and

Angela as the cab was pulling up. She smiled and said bye as she was getting into the cab.

Jack's father had been taking in all the conversations. He finally said, "Well, with all the hugging going it seems everyone must've gotten along well."

"Yeah, Dad, it was an experience like no other, I'll fill you in sometime." He shook hands with Jennings and Angela and said goodbye as he was getting into the car with his father.

"Jennings looked at Angela and said, "That just leaves you and me, Angela, my car's in the parking lot, can I give you a ride?"

"Yes, I'd like that, maybe we could have dinner tonight."

"No maybe to it, how about I pick you up at 6 o'clock; I know a great Italian restaurant downtown."

"It wouldn't happen to be Luigi's Italian Restaurant, would it?"

"Yeah, are you familiar with the place?"

"Yes, very, I guess I'll see you at six then, bye for now."

Noel checked her phone for apartments available in the area and found one close to the university Professor Jennings was always referring to. When she got there she asked the cabdriver to wait just in case the apartment buildings website hadn't been updated.

When she walked in the inordinately short desk receptionist took a long look up and said, I think I'm in love, oh, I mean excuse me." He cringed a little to think that he had just said that out loud. "I mean, how may I help you?"

"The names Noel, do you still have an apartment available?"

He checked the room registry and said, "Yes, I have two available, one's on the first floor and the others on the third floor; which would you prefer?"

"The third floor, does the apartment have windows?"

"Yes, I believe there is one in the bedroom and one in the living room."

"Great, I'll take it."

"Okay, if you will just give me your information and sign the registry I'll get you the key cards." He looked at her information and said, "Oh, I see you're from Arizona, they must grow women tall there, huh?"

Noel didn't give him a reply. The man cleared his throat and said, "The elevator's just down the hall and to the left."

"I prefer the stairs."

"Really, okay, they're right next to the elevator, have a pleasant stay."

She paid two months in advance and walked out to pay the cab driver and told him she'd be staying there. Soon after she went into her apartment to unpack, she got a call.

"Hey, Jack, I didn't expect to hear from you until tomorrow."

"Yeah, that was the plan but my friend Carson is so anxious to meet you he wanted me to call and set something up. He was wondering if we that is Lila and I and you two could go and have dinner tonight."

She checked her watch and said, "I suppose, I'm at the Seven Days Inn apartment complex near the college."

"Good, I know it, how about Lila and I pick you up at five thirty and then we can meet up with Carson at the restaurant."

"Sounds good to me, I'll be outside waiting, see you then."

After she got off the phone with Jack she called her sister. Jacqueline answered after two rings. "Hey, little Sister, how goes it?"

"everything's good so far or are you still upset?"

"A little, I just finished interviewing someone to take your position."

"I hope you can find someone, Jacqueline, for yours and my sake."

"Why yours."

"Then I'll feel less guilty about leaving you, of course."

"Don't, Noel, you need to live your own life and if that means trying something new or moving away, so be it. Call and let me know what this Carson guy is like. Maybe I can live vicariously through you."

"Seriously Jacqueline, you need to find someone."

"Yeah, maybe someday, don't forget to call mom and dad."

"I'll do it now, we'll talk later, bye."

She was already feeling a little homesick even though she hadn't even been gone twenty-four hours. Hearing her mother's voice would probably only increase the feeling but she knew Jacqueline was right and went ahead and made the call."

"Hey Mom."

"Hey honey, have you found a place to stay yet?"

"I'm in an apartment and the rates are reasonable, it's only eight hundred dollars a month plus utilities. It's small but it's clean and I have a good view of a nearby lake."

"Okay, honey, don't forget to call us once a week." She paused momentarily and said, "Is that too much?"

"Not at all Mom, I won't forget, love you, bye."

9

Carson and Noel/ Museum openings

While Professor Jennings and Angela were enjoying their meal Jack and Lila were on their way to pick up Noel to meet and have dinner with her and Carson at The Corner Bistro. Noel had a little trouble getting in Jack's car; it was one of the smaller compacts so she stayed slightly hunched over the entire ride.

Lila turned around and said, "You can sit up front on the way back, Noel. I should've known there wouldn't be enough headspace back there for you."

"No trouble, maybe Carson will give me a lift back to my apartment."

"How is the apartment anyway? That is if you don't mind my asking."

"It's adequate, I'm not a prima donna you know, I'm not used to anything fancy."

"Oh yes, we know that." Jack said with conviction. "Here we are. Oh, and there's Carson walking in now."

Once they were in and seated Carson looked across the table at Noel and said," Well, you're even more impressive in person."

Noel blushed slightly and replied, "Yeah, right back at ya. Jack tells me you're a real jock, when's your next basketball game?"

"Tomorrow night, would you like to come?"

"I would..

"Good, give me your address and I'll pick you up on the way."

Jack nudged Carson slightly and said, "Maybe you could take her to her place tonight, that way you'd already know where to pick her up."

"I'd love to." He looked at Noel for approval.

"Sure, I'd like that too."

After they'd eaten and sat around and talked for a while Carson said, "I usually try to get to bed early when I have a game the next day, care if we leave now?"

"No, not at all, I'm really beat, ours was an unusual flight to say the least, sometime I'll have to fill you in on our adventure coming home."

"Okay then." He stood up and waited for Noel to stand. When she did he said, "This was great, Jack, I finally have a woman I can truly be eye to eye with. Thank you both for the intro again; I owe you two big time, shall we go?" "Yes, I'm ready."

It was about a twenty-five-minute trip from The Corner Bistro to Noel's new digs. So, after they were only five minutes into the journey, Noel said, "There's something you should know about me Carson, and it could affect how you see me and if you want to see me in the future."

He glanced at her and replied, "I really can't think of anything that could make me not want to see you again." He got a really questioning look on his face and continued. "From where I'm sitting you look pretty perfect to me."

"I'm glad you think so, but I have an ability, one that could be passed on, if you get my meaning."

"What ability might that be?"

"Well, there's only one that I'm aware of now, there could be more."

"Is this something you care to share?"

"I'll show you when we get to my apartment building." There were a few weird glances back and forth between the two of them during the remaining ten minutes of the drive. When they arrived

Carson pulled into one of the empty parking spaces, looked at her and said, "Okay, I'm ready."

She smiled and replied, "You can stay in the car and afterwards you can either wave me back in or wave me goodbye."

"Okay, are you sure you don't want to wait until we at least get to know each other better?"

"By then, it could be harder for you to walk away, best to rip the bandage off sooner rather than later." Noel got out of the car walked to the front and leaned down and gripped her hands firmly under the front bumper.

Carson put his head out the window, grinned and said, "Really, you think you're going to..."

Before he could finish the sentence Noel raised up to a standing position complete with car. Then she let it back down slowly and gave Carson a questioning look. "Well?"

He sat there for a moment fairly stunned then he slowly put his fingers together palm facing him and waved her back in. She got back in the car and said, "Well?"

He still had an inquisitive look on his face and after a few minutes had passed, he said, "How exactly are you able to do that?"

"Would you believe me if I told you it was genetics?"

"That's what you're going with, genetics?"

"Well, my adoptive father could bench-press 1000 pounds. My biological father was strong too evidently or something like it so there's a possibility I might pass it on to any children I might have." She paused, then continued. " So, are you upset, confused or turned off? You should tell me now."

"Seriously, I think it's awesome, who wouldn't want to date someone who's not only beautiful but powerful too? I'm in it for as long as you are."

"Okay then, let's see where this goes, how about a cautionary kiss just to see if there's a connection there."

Carson smiled and replied, "Okay, but a first kiss, nothing overboard."

"I can do that." They both leaned in close and kissed only for a moment then sat back up.

"That was good," Noel said, "just enough to tell me you liked it and that you are cautiously optimistic and willing to wait for something more passionate."

"Exactly, Noel, except for the waiting part. No, seriously I'm totally cool with waiting. You are an amazing woman and I'm so glad you decided to come back with them. I'll pick you up at five tomorrow, how's that?"

"Great, I look forward to it, good night."

"Goodnight, Noel."

Carson was so enthralled with her that he almost forgot about her unusual ability. No worries he thought, if we ever get mugged I'll just let her take care of the mugger. He chuckled to himself, then after he was home he texted Jack.

(Did you know about the super side of Noel, Jack?)

A few minutes later he called Carson. "Yeah, I kinda did. I thought it was her secret to reveal, not mine, sorry."

"That's okay, just checking, I don't know whether to be happy or elated, I guess I'm both, she is truly amazing."

"You should see her sister in action, but that's a story for another time my friend, get some sleep."

Meanwhile Professor Jennings and Angela were having a discussion of their own. Apparently he was positive in his mind that Angela was the one but she came from a family where the engagements were long and drawn out. He said as they were walking up to her door, "I really feel a connection with you, Angela, would it be too soon to ask if you and I could be exclusive?"

"No, not too soon for me, I thought though that we should give it a few more weeks, maybe three. If the both of us still feel the same then, we'll see."

"That's fair enough, it would be nice to know now but that's fine, I'll call you tomorrow."

"Great, I'll be waiting."

Hollingsworth was finding out already how much he missed the companionship as well as the intellectual stimulation. He called Jack and asked, "Mind if I give you a hand setting up for the openings?"

"No, I'd welcome your help Professor."

"Splendid, splendid, give me a ring when you need my help."

"Will do, Professor, good night."

The next morning everyone that'd been on the expedition was experiencing some level of boredom. Jennings called them all and asked if they would want to participate in setting up their part of the exhibit. Naturally they all agreed with the exception of Noel.

The group met outside the Western History Museum to help unload the trucks. They carried the crates inside and carefully took out each one of the artifacts and placed them on a staging area.

Noel was busy trying to find a job but it seemed everywhere she went her height worked against her. After the last rejection she decided to give it a rest and try again the next day. She'd no sooner thought that when Jack called.

"The coach I told you about wants to see you so he can evaluate your abilities, do you think you can control your you know what?"

"Yeah, pretty much, it's not like I forget I have the ability and even though I could pretty much score at will, I'd never actually do it, so thanks for setting that up."

"It's this evening that he wants to see you."

"Okay, where and when?"

"I'll email you the address, good luck."

"Thanks, Jack." She knew she'd have to call Carson because of the change of plans. They had exchanged digits just after they left for him to take her to her apartment. She didn't want to disappoint but she did need a job. Carson answered right away."

"Hey, Noel, what's up?"

"I have a job interview tonight so I won't be able to make it to the game, sorry."

"I am disappointed but there'll be other games, I'll see you tomorrow." She checked out a few more ads just in case, went to buy some clothes and new shoes and by that time it was time to check out Jack's coach friend. The gym door was open so she walked in and to her surprise there were nineteen other girls or young women standing around.

Just as she'd walked up to one of them, the coach came out with Jack not far behind.

"Okay ladies gather round and listen up. I need to see each one of you dribble, pass, shoot and rebound. The best way to do that is for you to split up into four teams and play ball. So pick your teams and let's get started."

Everyone was sizing each other up but eventually four teams emerged. Johnson said, "Half-court games, ladies. You can dunk if you're able; just try to keep the contact to a minimum, let's go."

The coach and Jack watched from the sidelines and it wasn't long before Noel was standing out in every discipline the coach had named. Forty minutes later he blew his whistle and said, "Okay ladies, line up, I've made my decision, only five of you have made it and I don't want to hear any moans, groans or nasty comments from those of you that didn't make it. Line up."

Once they'd lined up the coach said, "Noel, Camilla, Tamara, Holly and Christine, you've made it; the rest I'm sorry to say you didn't, maybe next year."

There were some inaudible grumblings as the fifteen not selected gathered their clothes, put them into their backpack's and walked out. He looked at the five he selected and said, "You ladies are good enough to play first string and you may have the opportunity to actually do that at some point. For now you'll be second string on the Rockets Semi–Pro Women's basketball team. You'll be paid three hundred dollars a game, two games a week, with a third game occasionally and then weekend games if we make it to the playoffs, any questions?"

They all shook their heads indicating the negative. "That's all for tonight then, give me your email addresses before you leave and I'll send you the game schedule, have a good evening. Oh, wait a minute, I need you to give me your uniform sizes before you leave also."

Jack walked over to Noel and said, "I knew you were holding back, was it hard?"

"Yes, well, this is not like an actual game though, more like a practice. The real test will come when I play with the team against another opponent." She hugged Jack and said, "I can't tell you how much this means to me."

"Hey, you saved Lila's life, there's nothing I could ever do to repay that. I just hope it turns out well for you, Noel." He turned to go then turned back around. "Oh, do you need a ride home?"

"Sure, I'd appreciate that."

"Okay, I need to talk to the coach for a moment first, I'll be right back."

The coach was collecting the balls when Jack walked over. "Hey coach, were there any standouts of the five?"

He gave Jack a look, grinned and replied, If I didn't know better I'd say she was a ringer of sorts. I caught her getting one rebound where she barely flexed her calves and went above the rim."

"Yeah, she can jump for sure. Will you send me a schedule coach, Lila and I would like to see all the games this season if possible?"

"Sure, I'll send it to your email address, and Jack?" "Yes."

She's going to be amazing. Her abilities will put us into the playoffs for sure."

Jack nodded and walked back to Noel and said, "Ready?" "Sure."

Once they were back in the car Noel looked at him and said, "So what did the coach say?"

He grinned and replied, "He said you'll do."

"Is that it?"

He laughed and said, "The coach thinks you're amazing, or rather he said that you could be. Just remember,

if you show them too much of who you really are it could end your career before it even gets started."

"How so?"

"These games are covered by several local newspapers. And there are always those scouts from professional teams looking to find new talent."

"Yeah, I see what you mean. I'll just have to keep my ability in check. Will you and Lila be coming to the games?" "Me definitely,

Lila may, it all depends on whether or not they fall on her girls night out."

He dropped her off and when he got home Lila said, "How'd it go?"

"She's a shoe in of course, the coach was over the moon and picked her first out of nineteen other women."

"I should have known that; anyone could see how awesome she is. I'm just glad she intimidates you."

"Right, she would intimidate pretty much any man. Well, Carson may be the exception, he's pretty intimidating himself."

"Yeah, he is, Jack, jealous much?"

"Me, no, they do make a striking couple though, I hope things work out for them."

"Me too, Jack."

The week went by quickly and the time came for the first opening at the Creation Museum. The entire expedition's crew helped with the setting up process especially the showcase containing the plaque with their names engraved on it.

The group gathered around that part of the exhibit which displayed their archaeological finds and looked at each other with no small amount of pride. Their names were on the plaques which they admired of course but it was the adventure involved in the acquisition that they would remember the most.

The venue was opened and within a matter of minutes the building was packed with people ranging from toddlers to the elderly, all with the look of anticipation on their faces.

A reporter from the local Gazette was there, and not for the right reason either. He said, "How long did it take you people to fabricate these, they look so realistic?"

"These look realistic because they are, every piece here has been authenticated and registered by a nationally recognized archaeological society." Professor Jennings said matter-of-factly.

"What, a Christian archaeological society? Come on now, those skulls are almost twice the size of an average man. And those three journal copies, they look fake. How long did it take for you, or some other creationist to do them?"

Noel walked in and heard just enough of the slanderous remarks to be upset. She bent over and looked the reporter in the eyes and said, "Is it my imagination, Sir, or is my skull bigger than yours? I suggest you leave if you're only here to disrupt this event."

The reporter backed up a few steps and Noel continued. "Oh, and I happened to be the guide for the expedition with no skin in the game and I can say for certain that all of these are genuine with the exception of the journals which had to be copied so the originals could stay with the descendant of the one who wrote them."

His face turned red and his jaw tightened so much you could hear his teeth grinding. Then he said, "I print what I choose to print."

"Yeah, like so many others today in the news, you report it with a bias slant that suits your narrative, regardless of what's actually true."

He folded up his notepad and walked out. Angela started clapping and said, "Way to stand your ground, Noel."

"Right, standing her ground with a scary face," Jack said. "I was scared and she wasn't even looking at me."

Noel smiled, walked over to their part of the display and said, "Just think of all the years I was so close to them and never knew they even existed."

"We couldn't have done it without someone like you, Noel," Jennings said.

"Here, here," Hollingsworth added. "And I might add, without her and her sister one of us wouldn't have made it back."

"Right, that would be me," Lila chimed in.

"Okay," Jennings said, "lets mingle, there're some people here who are anxious to talk to us."

After the reporter left things calmed down considerably and everyone there enjoyed the rest of the evening. Jennings, Jack, and Noel were especially busy talking to the group, mainly about the contents of the caves and how well everything was displayed and documented.

There would be two additional days for the opening and on

the second day Professor Jennings was slated to give a talk to those present with a brief question and answer period afterward. He was apprehensive about being too specific concerning their encounters and wanted to get everyone else's take as to what or what not to share. He contacted each one and they all agreed to meet with him at the venue that afternoon but he wasn't able to get in touch with Noel right away.

When he finally reached her, she asked if Carson could come. Jennings said, "That depends on whether or not you've revealed anything to him about your ability." She hesitated then replied, "Yes, I thought that it was best to let him know up front to avoid having a problem down the road."

"How very forthcoming of you and what was his reaction?" "Surprisingly calm, if I'm being honest. I really wasn't expecting that."

"You didn't happen to mention anything to him about your ancestor, did you?"

"Oh no, I thought that would be a bit much for him to take in. That would be a story for a later time, maybe."

"Can you meet with me and the others this afternoon at the venue?"

"Sure, Carson's got the afternoon off; we'll be there with bells on."

Jennings chuckled a bit and replied, "Bells are optional, Noel, see you then."

Jack and Lila were a little late getting there and the others were chatting when they came in. They were as surprised as the others to see Carson there. As soon as they were all seated Jennings stood up and said, "Noel asked if Carson could come join us and I agreed, is there anyone here that doesn't?"

There were looks back and forth between the others then Jack said with an affirming tone, "No, none, please proceed Professor."

"Okay, I wanted to get everyone's opinion as to what to not share as I said before, seeing that some of our experiences were a little out there; any questions?"

Jack raised his hand. He said, "And no I don't need to use the bathroom." Jennings remembered the back and forth from the trip, chuckled a bit and said, "Go ahead, Jack."

"I assume that since Carson's here he knows about Noel's abilities and looking at him he doesn't seem to be too upset. However, I've known Carson for years and I believe we could tell him practically anything that we experienced and he would take it in stride. Having said that, unlike most people he's a pretty unique individual. So, if it were me I'd leave out our encounters with Noel's ancestor and how Lila was miraculously saved by Jacqueline and Noel. Everything else should be palatable."

Carson looked questioningly at Noel. She understood the look and whispered, "I'll fill you in later." He nodded, put his arm around her shoulders as only someone his height could, then directed his attention back to the professor.

Hollingsworth cleared his throat as he often did and said, "I totally agree with master Jack, most people will enjoy hearing about how we found the skulls and bones and documenting each one. And they would no doubt be thrilled at how the saboteurs were thwarted and the discovery of the journals by solving riddles and such but the supernatural aspect they may not be quite ready to swallow, my dear friend."

"Is everyone agreed then, keep it in the realm of the normal?" Lila raised her hand briefly." Yes, Lila?" She looked at Noel and said, "I'd love to tell them how you and your sister risked your lives to save me but how without revealing how special you are?"

Noel gave her a genuinely affirming smile and said, "There's no need, I didn't do it to be praised and it wasn't the risk for Jacqueline and I that it would've been for someone else."

They discussed among themselves momentarily then they all agreed something should be said about Lila's near-death experience but it would have to be presented as something believable and then only if her mother wasn't present.

"I know," Angela said, "we'll just tell them about your biological parents and how athletic and amazing they were and how they were these death-defying aerial acrobats."

That garnered another questioning look from Carson to Noel. She whispered again," That's true they were professional acrobatic aerialist, there's more, I'll tell you later."

Carson whispered back at her, "You've become more intriguing by the minute, it's making me feel really ordinary."

"You're not ordinary, so hush."

"It's settled then, I'll stick to the believable, it's pretty exciting all by itself anyway," Jennings said.

"Precisely," Hollingsworth added, "no need to let the masses know everything; shall we adjourn?"

Everyone agreed and as they were standing Jack looked at Carson and said, "This wasn't too much for you, was it old friend?"

He looked at Noel then to Jack and replied, "No, not at all." He looked back at Noel adoringly and said, "She's just the tall mysterious woman I've been looking for, so, not too much by any means."

On the way back Noel said, "The one thing that I didn't tell you that Jennings was referring to was seeing my ancestor."

"Your ancestor as someone who's been dead a long time?"

"Right, we all saw him, I'm not sure why but we did. Now you know pretty much everything."

"What about the unusual save they were gushing about?"

She looked down and back up at him and said," Well, at one point when we were on the trail heading back to the hotel from the canyon there was an earthquake and the rocks gave out from underneath Lila. She was falling fast and all of a sudden Jacqueline was under her grabbing her arm. I climbed down as fast as I could and carried her up on my back. Jacqueline is the one who really saved her, all I did was carry her back up the cliff."

"Oh, is that all. And just how far down was it where she was falling?"

"Three possibly four hundred feet. But she didn't get that far she only went down maybe 20 feet before Jacqueline was beside her and grabbed her arm."

Carson gave her a somewhat stern look and said, "Okay, I don't care how strong you and your sister are, you wouldn't have survived that fall so I'd say that was pretty brave, and yes you two were risking your lives. Although I suppose it's safe to say, with your abilities it wasn't as much of a risk as it would've been for someone else."

The next day went by rather quickly and the time came for the second opening. There was a whole line of people waiting outside to get in as the members of the expedition showed up. There were smiles, greetings and quite a few photos taken as they made their way to the door. And when Jennings opened the doors they were virtually hurried in by the rush of the crowd.

Once everyone was seated Professor Jennings got up and stood behind the small podium, cleared his throat, took a sip from his glass of water and said, "The purpose of our expedition initially was to prove or disprove the existence of the Nahullo, or latter-day Giants referred to in the Bible as the Nephilim. The earliest recording of these entities were in Genesis Chapter 6 but as it says they existed after that also. Meaning after the flood of course."

One of the men in the group raised his hand and said, "There's been quite a debate even among Bible scholars that these individuals were not all that large and that they were only somewhat bigger than the average person of the day, can you speak to that, Professor?"

"Yes, I can. Using the measurements of their day, meaning cubits and span we calculate even going by the smaller lengths that these individuals would've been well over eight, possibly 9 to 10 feet tall. We know that Goliath and his four brothers as well as Og the king of Bashan and most if not all of the inhabitants of Canaan at the time Joshua and the Lord's army took the city were the result of the cohabitation it spoke of in Genesis Chapter 6. Using information and photos given by a colleague of mine as well as some local folklore from the area and an excerpt of one of Buffalo Bill Cody's journals I was successful in obtaining funding from the Archaeological Society I'm affiliated with."

The man raised his hand again. "I'm a little confused Professor. Doesn't the Bible say that the ones who transgressed were chained up into everlasting darkness until the day of their judgment?"

"I'm glad you brought that up. As one of the members of our

expedition so astutely pointed out that even though those who initially transgressed were chained up, it didn't stop it from happening over and over again. Now I'm sure as each incident took place God expeditiously carried out the same sentence on them but the Bible also talks about the principalities and powers and wickedness in the heavenly's. That indicates to me that a lot of the mischief that went on back then could even still be happening today. No doubt this is likely where the antichrist will come from. So does that answer your question?"

The man indicated by his gesture that it had. So the professor continued. "Now, the expeditions group consisted of me as well as each one here in the front row. I'll call their names out and asked them to stand as I do so. Professor Byron Hollingsworth, Professor Angela Drake, Jack McKinney, Lila Harper and Noel Danvers. They each stood, turned and faced the group of people, gave a slight bow and sat back down.

One of the men that came in late raised his hand and asked, "Who's the Amazon?"

"Yes," Jennings said looking at Noel. "Her name is Noel Danvers, she and her sister Jacqueline were not only our guides but life savers more than once.

That comment got their attention which led to more than a few whispers back and forth between some of those present. He showed slides of all the cave paintings and the photographs they'd taken then he had Jack walk over and uncover several of the skulls and bones. He held one of the skulls next to his and said, "As you can see it's quite a bit larger than mine and I'm told I have an unusually big head."

He put the skull down, raised his hands to his side palms up and said with a questioning look on his face, "What's that all about?" There was faint laughter from those members of the expedition and from more than a few in the audience. Then Jennings continued.

"The metaphysical world is referred to quite often in the Bible. And because of all of the fairytales we hear growing up and stories about ghosts we want to lump what's talked about in the Bible in with them. For those of us who know the Bible to be the inerrant word of God, the metaphysical world is all too real. The writer of Hebrews says it all too well, and this is paraphrased. The things that we see in this physical world were created and exist only because of the world we can't see. I'll sum everything up this evening by saying that our past, present and future has been, is, and will be, only because of our Creator. Now, I'll allow a few more questions and then we'll be closing for this evening."

A woman in the front row raised her hand and stood up. "Did you or anyone in your expedition see any tangible evidence of the world you are speaking of while you were at the Grand Canyon?"

Professor Jennings looked up for a second trying to decide what he would answer. "My group and I discussed that very thing when we were trying to decide exactly what all we would disclose. And while neither I nor anyone in my group believe in ghosts there is a section in the Bible when King Saul is conferring with a sorceress of which there were more than a few back in the day."

One of the reporters raised his hand and said, "Wasn't that actually supposed to be a witch, Professor?"

"Yes, she was. Saul had a question for his deceased mentor, the prophet, Samuel. The text infers that the one he was speaking with was no more than a charlatan but because God wanted him to have an answer for this question he allowed Samuel to speak to him from his place in paradise."

The same reporter raised his hand again. "If I'm not mistaken it indicated in that same passage that the witch was actually scared when Samuel appeared."

"It's good to see that some of you reporters actually know your Bible. Anyway, to get back to what we were discussing the fact that we saw what we saw tells me that God does make exceptions. I said all that to say this, we did encounter a spirit of sorts during our expedition for reasons I can only imagine, the result of which was our discovery of the second Journal left by W.C. Coopersmith. This was not a mass hallucination nor was it a result of anything we tried to conjure up. It just happened, any other questions?"

No one else seemed to have any questions so the professor thanked everyone for coming and told them the following night would be the last night of the opening.

Practically everyone there wanted to shake hands with the members of the expedition and they were especially enthralled with Noel and her boyfriend Carson. She politely spoke with everyone, shook their hands and apologized for coming on a little strong the night before while engaging with the reporter.

The ones who were there the night before just smiled and gave an understanding nod. One man, however, said, "Yeah, I was here, he totally had it coming. He just came to make trouble anyway, I'm sure."

By then those of the expedition had reassembled and began to straighten things back up that were slightly disheveled from the group that night and said their goodbyes for the evening.

Professor Jennings, Angela and Noel and Carson were the last ones to leave. On the way out the door Noel told the professor how well she thought he had handled everything. He smiled, nodded and said, "Well, thanks for the encouragement and I apologize for not being able to refrain from saying what we said I shouldn't, but unfortunately someone had to ask the question, so I felt obligated to tell them."

"No worries Professor, I'm sure more than a few that were here tonight would have their own story to tell about that subject, goodnight." He and Angela shook hands with Carson and gave Noel a tip toe hug and said good night.

After Carson dropped Noel off she called her sister. "Hey, Sis, how's the new help doing?"

"She's not you but she's eager to learn and Cal's helping out. He's between deployments and he's a great draw for the female tourists."

"I'll bet, Mr. Handsome and Mr. Muscles rolled all into one."

"How's everything going in the east, Noel, is Carson going to be a keeper?"

"I believe so, he's a tall handsome athletic drink of water and he's okay with who I am."

"Really, you told him already, how'd that go?"

"I showed him and it went fine, he was surprised but I guess that's to be expected."

"Every man should be so lucky as to have someone like you, little sister. How long will you stay?"

"That would depend on Carson I suppose. I can't very well ask him to leave, if and when we get serious. We'll just have to play it by ear I guess."

"Yeah, that's best Noel, you're not anything if not sensible, I hope it works out."

"What about you, Jacqueline?" "If you're referring to the male companion department I've almost given up. I thought I might try a dating site. Let's see, I'd say, tall early to mid-20s businesswoman with abilities far beyond those of mortal women who likes the outdoors and sporadic moments of danger seeking a man with similar likes and abilities. Must be at least 6 feet tall. How's that?"

"It's a start at least, however you may want to leave out the superhuman reference, Sister." Noel checked her watch and said, "I've got to go there's a two-hour time difference here you know."

"Sure, I get it, love you, Noel." "Love you too, Jacqueline, I'll call you soon."

"Yeah, you'd better."

Noel drifted off to sleep that night thinking about how wonderful it would be if she and Carson could make a go of it.

The next morning everyone on the expedition found themselves somewhat exhausted. They reckoned the first day back they were all running on pure adrenaline but just like the sugar high leads to a sugar low the adrenaline had run its course and now they were going through the motions on fumes.

Jennings called everyone and asked if they were experiencing a letdown and invariably the answer to that question was a yes. He texted the group using his avatar and a racehorse emoji. Then he texted everyone to meet at the Montclair high school athletic track. It read (I believe we need to do some good old-fashioned exercising to get out of this physical funk we're in.)

He got a thumbs up and a smiling emoji from everyone except

Jack who was the only one that asked (What time should we be there?) He texted back (Let's meet at twelve then we'll decide how far to run) His phone pinged four times with a checkmark emoji in each text and a 12 noon it is.

Everyone had already started running by the time Noel got there but it didn't take her long to catch up. As she was passing Jennings he said, "Your long legs serve you well."

She turned to look back at him with a smile and replied, "Yeah, that and two years on the track team in high school."

Once they finished the run they sat down on the nearby bleachers huffing and puffing. Angela sat next to Marvin, turned to him and said, "All set for tonight, fearless leader?" The rest turned to see what his response would be.

"Yes, I guess so, I just hope no one asked any questions that I don't want to answer. I am considering leaving out any specifics on the heroics by Noel and Jacqueline; too many queries could be generated by that story, not to mention Lila's mother would be terribly upset and mad that she was left in the dark about it. And I really couldn't blame her. The truth is that if Jacqueline and Noel hadn't been there to save her, Lila would most likely have died."

Everyone agreed it would be best to leave that part of the trip out. They finished wiping the sweat and drinking the water and were standing up to leave when Jennings said, "I haven't said it before, but you people not only helped make this expedition successful but you made it enjoyable too. As far as I'm concerned I couldn't have asked for a better group, see you this evening."

They all gave him a hug except Hollingsworth. He smiled, shook Jennings hand and said, "If this was indeed my last expedition, and I hope that it's not, I couldn't have asked for a more exciting one, Marvin, so for that I thank you. Yes, and I especially thank you for letting this old sod be a part of it."

"Well, it wouldn't have been the same without you, old friend, see you later tonight."

The doors were open a half hour before Jennings was to give his talk and all the seats filled up rather fast. Those who were part of the expedition were seated up front facing the crowd this time in case any one of those present wished to ask any of the members a question directly.

He was showing slides of the cave drawings and stills of the artifacts and he explained what they were and what they meant from the notes he and the others had taken. Halfway through a reporter that was attending said, "Excuse me, excuse me, I noticed some of the rudimentary stick figures are larger than the others; what's the significance, do you know?"

"Yes, at one time there were tribes of unusually tall and large natives who dominated some parts of Arizona as well as other states. There is also a section in one of Buffalo Bill Cody's journals attesting to that fact."

"Yes Professor, I've heard that story. Is there any indication as to what happened to that tribe or others like it?"

"Yes, they were taken out by a coalition of four or more tribes in the area mainly because the Nahullo or exceptionally large Indians were pretty much wreaking havoc on every other tribe taking them out one by one."

"So, the enemy of my enemy brought the tribes together to eliminate a common threat?"

"That's correct, and as you can see by a number of our finds those stories and others like them are born out."

Jennings hoped that would satisfy the curiosity of the reporter but it didn't. He looked directly at Noel and said, "Would it be okay if I asked the young lady at the end to stand up?"

Jennings looked at Noel. She stood up rather slowly. Then the man said, "I can't help but notice that this woman is not just beautiful but very tall and extremely fit looking."

Jennings gave him a look then replied, "Is there a question in there somewhere, Sir?"

Noel said, "I'll answer that Professor. My parents were very tall and they were also quite famous in their day. They were acrobatic aerialist."

"You say they were?" "Yes, they were killed in a car crash when my sister and I were very young. We were raised by good friends of theirs."

"Were they special too?"

"Yes, they were much like our parents."

"And what do your people think about your ancestors and all the scalps they took and the settlers they killed?"

Jennings decided to bring the question back to the expedition. He said, "I can answer that question and then I insist we get back to the purpose of the night. Noel Danvers and I had that conversation while we were checking out some of the caves. She realizes that there was plenty of blame to go around on both sides and I can tell you beyond a shadow of a doubt Ms. Danvers is one of the finest and bravest women I've ever known. Her and her sister risked their lives as I said in one of the other sessions on a number of occasions while we were in the canyons to ensure our safety. You had your time, Sir, are there others?"

The questioning went on for half an hour or so and everyone was mostly interested in the large bones and Jack's translations of the writings and images. The last question asked was by another reporter. "Who, Professor Jennings do you think was the most valuable member of the expedition besides Ms. Danvers and her sister of course?"

Everyone focused on Jack immediately.

"I'd have to say Jack Harper without a doubt; he has one of the most brilliant minds I've come across when it comes to translations and just plain insight into the meaning of symbols, and he even solved the riddle which was instrumental in us finding the journals which by the way we have quite a few copies of if anyone's interested."

Another member of the audience raised their hand.

"Yes, go ahead." "Could you sum up the trip and tell us whether or not you accomplished what you set out to do, Professor Jennings?"

He paused then replied. "I believe our efforts were very productive. The bones we were given permission to bring back with us prove the existence of the Nahullo and in addition to that the three journals we found prove the relationship between White

Cloud Coopersmith and the three brothers who were by all accounts at the very least second-generation Nahullo."

"Excuse me, Professor, I just want to clarify, I must have come in after you explained; the Nahullo is the name the Indians gave the very large tribe members, is that right?"

"Precisely."

"So, how do you square these with the fact that none of these giants exist today?"

"One, there are only a few primitive peoples around today who would deify these creatures the way they were in the past and if there are others in this day and time they'd probably be a bit too clever to show themselves. Besides, there are an abundance of very large men now just as there have been in the past."

He showed them the same photos that he'd shown his classes over the years then continued. "These are only a few of the many photos depicting oversized men in various parts of the world. And there are many basketball players who are over 7 feet tall and of course Yao Ming is 7'6" tall. Also there was a man born in1918 named Robert Waldo that grew to be 8'11"tall. Additionally, there are actors and wrestlers and all manner of individuals who are extremely tall and large who could have latent recessive Nahullo or Nephilim genes. There's a man currently living in Europe who's 8'3" born to relatively normal size parents and his height is not related to gigantism as was Mr. Waldo's.

"So you don't think it's only just a matter of breeding, Professor, as is the prevailing theory?"

"Of course that may explain some of it but certainly not all. Now, are there any more questions pertaining specifically to the expedition? I'll take two more questions, and I might add even though this is the final night of the opening I hope all of you will come back to just look around at some point."

There was a hand raised in the back of the room. "Yes, the gentleman in the back."

"Yes, Professor, you never elaborated on just how Noel Danvers and her sister were involved in saving those of your expedition."

"That's correct, I didn't. Sufficed to say had they not acted when and how they did one member of our group would most certainly have died. I won't give the name of the one or the details of the save, you'll just have to take my word for it. Noel and her sister are remarkable women and that's all I'm prepared to say. Anyone else?"

"Yes, the gentleman in the front, go ahead."

"Could all of the bones you found to be a hoax of some kind, Professor?"

Jennings smiled and replied, "There are photos in one of our expedition albums on the table just in front of me that you're welcome to look at, Sir. In it are extensive photos of the skeletal boneyard containing thousands of giant skeletons put there by persons unknown most likely over the course of thousands of years in an effort to disqualify any notion of these giants existence."

"So why would anyone go to such lengths, Professor Jennings?"

"Why indeed. My theory is that if you wish to discredit the Bible you hide or destroy anything that would prove it to be valid." Jennings checked his watch and said, "Again, I want to thank you all for coming. There are cards on the table as you exit that you can have, I hope you all have a blessed evening, good night."

Once again the group stayed to collect anything that wasn't taking up permanent residence in the museum. While they were working Jack commended Marvin on how well he handled the morbidly curious and the naysayers.

Jennings said, "Thank you for that, Jack."

Jennings took his jacket off the chair as he was putting it on he looked at everyone and said, "Who knew four short months ago that we, meaning all of us would have shared in such an amazing adventure?"

"I know, right," Jack replied.

By then they were all huddled around the professor. Hollingsworth said, "Well dear boy, you're the one who initiated our little jaunt, maybe you can explain just how it is we survived and, when can we do it again?"

Everyone started laughing because they were sure Professor

Hollingsworth was going to say something negative. Jennings patted his old friend on the shoulder and replied, "I'm ready anytime you are."

He looked at the rest of the group who were weren't looking quite as ready and said," Well?"

Jack looked directly at him and replied, "Give us a year or so to recoup, then ask us, Professor. We might be more inclined to agree by then."

Noel was quiet for a moment then she said, "I'll be going back at some point to see Jacqueline." She looked at Carson and asked, "Will I be going alone?"

"No way," he said, "especially if it's not during basketball season. I definitely want to meet your sister and see the canyon so I can get some sense of what you and your group experienced. Right now though, you and I both have committed to a team so once summer gets here it shouldn't be a problem. What do you think?"

"The summer sounds good to me, Carson, I'll just keep in touch with Jacqueline via the phone and face time." She looked at the others and said, "I hope you guys will come watch some of our games."

Jack said, "Send us each a schedule and I know Lila and I will be coming to as many as we can."

Jennings and Angela agreed they would as well. Hollingsworth said, "Splendid, it'll give me something to look forward to in the evenings. I'll most likely bring a pillow for my backside though, those bloody bleachers are always hard, you know."

That comment produced more than a few chuckles. There were individual and group hugs all around. Then as they were leaving a certain amount of sadness could be seen on each face. Before they were all out of the building Jennings turned and said, "There's always going to be more adventures down the road, my friends, be safe and God bless."

Three months passed and the basketball season was winding down. Both Carson's and Noel's teams had made it to the playoffs and both teams advanced to the championship round.

Carson's team managed to win the final game and he was glad

Noel was there to see him play. Her final game was only a few days away and she made sure all the members of the expedition were reminded.

Noel had had more than one conversation with Professor Jennings about how she struggled to keep her abilities in check. His advice was to pick a scripture to repeat over and over again before each game. It'd helped her all season long but this game was for the championship and she was feeling the pressure.

Before she entered the building she asked Jack and Lila to pray for her while they were still in the parking lot. Just as he was about to start Jennings and Angela pulled up and got out.

Jennings looked at Noel and could see the uncertainty written all over her face. "Butterflies, Noel?"

"Yes," she replied, "My adrenaline is pumping at an unusually high rate."

Jennings said, "Let's all join hands." He looked at Jack. "Were you going to do the honors?"

Jack nodded and said, "Let's bow. Lord, all of us here have come to love Noel, in different ways certainly, but You Father love her more than we could ever imagine. So we ask right now that you would calm her spirit and body so that every move she makes tonight will be directed by you and your spirit. And we thank you ahead of time that in the spiritual realm our petitions have already been answered, in Christ's name, Amen." He smiled at Noel and said, "Now you're all set."

The gym was packed that night and from the first tip off to the last buzzer Noel played a brilliant but perfectly human game. Carson's voice was hoarse by games end from yelling and Noel's team had won the final game by one basket just as the clock ran out.

10

The flight back/ The wedding.

Three weeks after the final game summer had officially arrived and with the exception of those attending summer school, everyone was free for the next three months.

The expedition bug had bitten Jennings bad as well as Hollingsworth. Jennings did a group text asking if they might be interested in taking another trip that summer. Hollingsworth sent a thumbs up emoji and Angela sent him a check mark emoji.

Jack, however, called the professor. "Hey, Jack, what do you think, up for another trip?"

"The trip, yes, another expedition, not sure. You know that two-year plan I told you about last year?"

"Yes, I remember."

"We decided to get married this summer. We both have part time jobs now that our bosses have assured us we'll transition into full-time once we've graduated."

"That's great news, Jack, any plans as to where you'll be tying the knot?"

"Yes, we're thinking about a canyon wedding, Professor."

"As in the Grand Canyon?"

"The very same.

"Okay, sounds like a hoot, is that what year grandpa would've said?"

"Exactly, Professor and we'd like for you and Angela to be there and Hollingsworth too. Carson's going to be my best man and Jacqueline and Noel will be Lila's maids of honor."

"That's very appropriate, given the circumstances of last summer."

"Yes, I totally agree Professor, we'll talk later."

"Sounds amazing, Jack, I wouldn't miss it, just tell me when and I'll let Angela know."

"Already taken care of Professor, Lila called Angela a few minutes ago and she was as excited as you are."

"Jennings thought he'd have to do some major convincing to get everyone to agree on going back to the canyons but now they'd not only be going back but they'd have a very good reason to do so.

"Oh, wait Jack, what about Lila's mother, what did she have to say about the trip?"

"Well, she had plenty to say, but Lila told her she was an adult and that it was her decision to make, no one else's, and that was that. Frankly I thought her mother took it rather well."

"Did her mother ever find out that her daughter was the one Noel and Jacqueline saved?" "She did, and she was horrified, but then she eventually calmed down and wrote a letter to Noel and Jacqueline expressing her undying gratitude for having saved their daughter. I think that was somewhat cathartic for her, so obviously her parents are coming I just hope she keeps her suggestions to a minimum. Lila's dad will be fine; he and I are quite a bit alike. I'll call you after we've made the reservations and booked the flight; and hopefully we can all go together."

"Sounds good Jack."

"We'll talk later, Professor."

When Professor Jennings and Angela got together that evening Angela said, "I think I'd like to have a special place like that to get married, Marvin."

"I'll keep that in mind, Ms. Drake. Are you upset she didn't ask you to be her maid of honor?"

"No, not at all, the Danvers sisters deserve that honor, without a doubt. I'll just be glad to be present. Lila and I really bonded on the trip though and I saw her practically every day at the college."

"Yeah, those two are quite something. They're super intelligent, well except for math but tutoring them again gave me a chance to see them twice a week this year and we're always bumping into each other at the Museum."

He'd no sooner finished his sentence when his phone rang. "Professor?"

"Yes Jack, I didn't expect to hear from you so soon, what's up?"

"Is Angela with you?"

"Yes, she is."

"Okay, good. Lila and I have booked a flight for two weeks from now and I've already told Professor Hollingsworth and Noel. I'm sure she'll tell Carson. They said they'd call the airline ASAP. You and Angela should call soon too."

"Right, I'll call now, Jack, and thanks for the heads up."

"Sure, Professor."

The two weeks went by quickly and Lila's mother was being her usual self. "It'll be fine Mom, the man in charge of this wedding assured me we'd be at least 50 feet away from the edge of the canyon wall at all times and that there wasn't any chance of rockslides where they'd be conducting the ceremony."

"Okay, fine, but I for one am going to be as far away from any ledge as possible and only be as close to the ceremony as is necessary to hear it."

Noel had already contacted Jacqueline and told her the time the flight would be landing. Jacqueline said, "What, no double wedding.? What about you and Carson?"

"I'm believing it will happen eventually, Sis. I told you about the engagement ring didn't I?"

"Yeah, you did, you didn't say how big it was though."

"It's big enough, I think he said it cost two thousand dollars. I'd have been satisfied with anything really."

"Okay then, how am I supposed to try on the maid of honor dress exactly; and how are you going to find a dress long enough for you?"

"Lila knows a seamstress and she's positive she can pull it off. You and I have the same body measurements she just needs to make mine 5 inches longer than yours. I am all legs you know."

"Okay, I was just checking, you and I aren't the norm after all."

"It'll be fine, Sis, we'll talk later, love you, bye."

"Right back at ya, Noel."

The day of the flight came and everyone except Jack and Lila were waiting at the boarding gate. His and her parents were anxious as well. The seats were extremely uncomfortable and Hollingsworth said, "I knew I should've brought my pillow. They must not want anyone to be too comfortable while they're waiting to board. My backside is positively numb. I wonder what's taking the betrothed couple so long getting here?"

"I'm sure they'll be here in time, old friend," Jennings said. "We won't be boarding for another thirty minutes or so, then we'll most likely be another twenty minutes on the plane before it takes off."

"I hope you're right, dear boy."

Practically everyone that walked by the group stared at Noel and Carson. One passenger even asked if they were famous. They laughed and Carson looked at Noel and said, "She's famous to me." The woman just smiled and walked on.

"It's just because we're tall," Noel said.

"Because you look like a movie star, Noel." She gently nudged him with her elbow and said, "Hello…, it was a woman and she was looking at you, Carson."

Noel's phone rang just then. It was Jack on the line. "Hey Jack, where are you?"

"We just pulled into the parking lot so we should be there at the gate in about twenty minutes."

"Cutting it a little close aren't you?" She looked at the departure time board. We're loading in twenty minutes."

"It'll be okay, Noel, you know they'll make you wait on the plane."

"I know, see you in a bit."

She told the others who looked relieved to say the least. "It simply wouldn't do for them to miss the flight," Hollingsworth muttered. The call came for them to board and still no sign of Jack or Lila. The rest were seated and an unsettled anticipation ran through the group.

"I should go and check on them," Noel said."

"I'm sure they'll be here in a minute," Jennings responded, "Jack's resourceful he'll get them here on time somehow."

Just then Jack appeared at the door of the plane with two bags in hand and Lila not far behind. He made his way toward the others and five steps away he tripped over the outstretched legs of another passenger already seated. Noel got up quickly, caught him complete with bags just before hitting the floor; lifted him complete with bags like they were nothing then looked around quickly to make sure no one else saw it.

Jack and Lila put their luggage in the overhead compartments and as soon as Noel sat back down she said, "No one noticed that, right?"

"Jennings gave her a look and replied, "We all did and I believe that old lady just across the aisle saw it also. Her eyes got really big; she shook her head a bit then went back to looking at her phone."

Jennings turned around and said, "A memory lapse, Noel?"

"She gave him a look that said, sorry, then replied, "It won't happen again, I hope."

Jack leaned over toward Noel and whispered a thank you to which she gave a tentative nod. Halfway there the old lady sitting next to him leaned in toward Noel just as Jack had and said, "You must be one of those lady weightlifters, deary, that was quite a save you made, wish I had gotten it on my phone."

Noel grinned at her and said under her breath, "I'm glad you didn't."

Carson overheard the conversation and whispered to Noel, "Can you imagine how that would've gone viral in no time."

"Thank God for small favors, Carson,?"

The flight took a little over four hours and thankfully was uneventful for the remainder of the trip. Jacqueline was waiting for everyone when they got there. Noel introduced Carson to her sister first thing.

"Well, tall and handsome, Noel." They shook hands and Jacqueline helped with the luggage. She brought the company van which seated twelve people easily even though the space was still a little lacking. Carson toughed it out with his head slightly bent.

When they reached the hotel Lila and her parents checked in first, then Jack and his mother. Jennings and Angela had separate rooms as did Hollingsworth. After they were all settled in they met in the dining area. Jacqueline had a three-bedroom home her aunt left her so Noel and Carson were going with her but stayed with the others before going so they could go over their itinerary together.

Jack stood up and thanked everyone for coming. He said, "As you all know there are only two days left before the wedding. The only group thing we have planned of course is a trip to the Canyon tomorrow. There won't be any mule rides but there is a spot at the northern rim that overlooks a large portion of the canyon. I thought since that's where the ceremony will take place it would be good to go there and check it out."

Noel raised her hand.

"Go ahead, Noel."

"Who's going to perform the ceremony?" Jack pointed to Jennings and said," I thought everyone knew."

"No," Angela remarked. Then she looked at Jennings and said, "I didn't know you were a licensed minister."

He grinned and replied, "I'm not, but anyone can perform the ceremony as long as there is a licensed minister present and signs the marriage certificate."

"So, where is the minister?" Carson asked. Jack smiled and replied, "The hotel retains the service of one at all times." The hotel manager said they have at least fifty marriages a year performed at or near the canyon."

"Well," Angela remarked, "I'm glad someone's on the ball."

Everyone could tell Lila's mother had been kept in the dark about the particulars by her furrowed eyebrows and disgusted look but her father never blinked.

"I know everybody must be tired from the trip," Jennings said, "so we should probably get something to eat and rest up for tomorrow.

Noel, Jacqueline, and Carson stayed up most of the evening talking. Jack and his mother went to bed early as did Lila and her parents while Jennings, Angela and Hollingsworth checked out the recently renovated museum then turned in for the evening.

Jacqueline picked all of them up the next morning after they'd had breakfast. Before they got in the van Carson started to ask Jacqueline about her and Noel's amazing save. He said, "Has anyone ever fallen to their death?" Noel gave him a quick albeit controlled jab to the ribs, leaned in close and whispered, "Xnay on the accident."

He whispered back, "Oh, yes, of course, sorry."

Fortunately Lila's parents weren't close enough to hear and once they were all aboard Jacqueline said, "Keep your eyes open and rotating folks, there's a lot of beautiful scenery between here and the actual canyon."

When they got to the northern rim she stopped, looked back and said, "This is it people, my advice is to not get too close to the actual rim, there's a lookout point at the top of those chiseled out stairs that has the best view and there's a place to sit if you'd like."

Once they reached the top of the steps and looked out everyone was oohing and aahing. They read the plaque telling about the canyon's history and how the trails were cut from rock. Lila's mother said, "I can't see how you or anyone could be foolish enough to ride on those narrow trails."

"It's perfectly safe, Mrs. Harper, I assure you," Jacqueline commented.

"So you say." She whispered under her breath. They stayed for a while enjoying the scenery until it was time to go back. Jacqueline said, "I'll drive by the stables so you all can see the mules the expedition used to go and explore the caves."

When they got there Carson exited the van with Noel and she showed him the mule she always rode. He noticed her mule was larger than the rest and after he mentioned it she said, "I can't very well have my feet dragging the ground now can I?"

The others in the expedition were petting the mules but Lila's mother was standing back in the distance. She looked at Lila and Jack and said, "I can't fathom how you could stand the smell of these animals, it's atrocious."

"Oh Mom, stop, you just get used to it and it's not so bad once you're out on the trail."

"Okay people," Jacqueline yelled, "let's load up and head back."

Just as they got there Jacqueline's phone vibrated. "Yes, what? Okay Cal, what did you say? Right, I'll be there as soon as I can."

She turned and looked at the others and said, "You folks need to get off and head to the hotel, one of the tour groups is in need of assistance." She looked at Noel and asked her to come with her.

Carson looked at both of them and said," I'm coming too." Jack and Jennings said almost simultaneously, "Can we help?"

"No," Jacqueline said firmly, "we should be able to handle it; you folks enjoy the rest of the day." Come on Noel, Carson, let's go."

When they reached the tour group they could see six of Cal's group setting with their backs against the wall that ran along the trail. Jacqueline looked at one of the men and asked, "Where's Cal and the others?"

He pointed down, as in over the ledge. She got on her stomach and looked over the edge to see Cal beside two others on a narrow ledge about 15 feet down. Carson walked as close to the edge as he dared then step back quickly with a wide-eyed expression.

Cal yelled up and said, "Tie off one of the ropes to my mule and slide it over the edge carefully. Once I'm up we can get those two." It only took twenty minutes after they pulled Cal up for him and the girls to get the other two men back onto the trail.

Noel and Jacqueline took Cal aside and asked him how it happened. He gave them a somewhat sheepish look and said, "We were dismounting to use the porta potty and they dismounted on the wrong side of the mule and slipped over the edge. I explained to them that they should dismount on the left going down and on the right coming back but I guess they must not have been listening. The rope I had fastened onto the saddle slipped loose as I was climbing over the edge to retrieve them. It's a good thing they weren't 5 feet to the left or to the right or they would have fallen to their deaths. Thanks for coming so quickly."

"Glad we could help," Jacqueline said.

Noel was giving Cal the evil eye. Then she looked at him and Jacqueline and asked, "How's my replacement doing you two?"

"She's a real overachiever and careful to a fault." Cal replied. "Honestly I guess I need to be more like her from now on, I assumed they were listening when I said always dismount on your left going down and you're right coming up. I think I can take it from here, ladies, thanks again."

He hugged Noel and said, "It's good to see you cousin." He chuckled a bit then said, "I really can't wait to see you two tomboys in your bridesmaids dresses."

"Yeah, Jacqueline remarked, "that should be a real treat for everyone, see you tomorrow."

Cal shook hands with Carson and said, "I'm glad to see Noel found someone her own size." Carson grinned and replied, "Not as glad as I am, I assure you."

The ones at the hotel were terribly worried and two hours after they left Jack got a call. "Everyone is fine, Jack, tell the others we should be back in time for lunch." "That's good news Noel, see you guys in a bit."

The others gave him a questioning look. Jack understood the look and said, "No detail folks but everything's good, and everyone's safe."

Those from the expedition were accustomed to things going wrong but Lila's parents were beside themselves wondering whether or not the venue their daughter and her fiancé had chosen might be too dangerous. Lila's mother said," Had I known how dangerous those trails were I'd never have let you go, it's a miracle you all made it back; I wish this ordeal were over with."

Lila's father put his arm around his wife and said, "There, there dear, we'll be heading home day after tomorrow."

"Small consolation," she quipped. After Jacqueline, Noel and

Carson got back they met in the dining room area. Jennings asked if they were eating with them.

No," Noel replied, I want Carson to meet my parents and Gramma Rose, you guys go ahead and we'll grab something on the way."

Needless to say Carson was more than a little impressed with Gramma Rose and he and Noel had a good visit with her parents. Just as they were leaving Noel's mother pulled her aside and said, "Does he know about you and your sister?"

"He does know, and he's okay with it, no drama from him, Mother. You and dad are picking up Gramma Rose tomorrow aren't you ?"

"Yes of course, you know she loves weddings, we'll be there."

"Have you and Jacqueline tried on your dresses yet?"

"I have, Mother, but she hasn't. She's going to do that now."

They gave their parents a hug and Carson shook hands with them both and said, "It's so nice to meet the ones who raised this amazing woman."

Noel smiled at Carson, looked at Jacqueline and said, "We'd better go, you have a dress to try on."

On their way there Jacqueline asked Noel what the dresses looked like.

"Not your usual plain jane color, Sis. They're a deep burgundy red, which is our color."

"Really," Carson remarked, "I thought it was tradition for the bridesmaids dresses to look drab so the bride really shines."

"Lila isn't like that, Carson, she's a very humble person."

Once they were dressed they both walked out to show Carson. He took one look and said, "Wow." He paused momentarily then continued. "I never use that word but it seems appropriate here. You two look amazing. I only hope Lila's dress is as equally impressive."

The day was winding down and the rest of the group spent the afternoon at the amphitheater watching slides taken from the helicopter of the entire canyon. "A very impressive show: without the danger," Lila's mother remarked.

Afterwards they decided to eat an early dinner and turn in, in anticipation of the big day tomorrow. Early the next morning Jack was trying to track down the minister who was supposed to make an appearance and sign the marriage certificate and he wasn't having any luck.

When he finally got in touch with him the minister said he'd come down with the flu and couldn't make it. When he told Lila and her mother Lila almost broke into tears.

"What now, Jack?"

"I don't have a clue, Lila, I wish I did." He'd no sooner said that than his phone vibrated. It was Jack's grandfather.

"Grandpa, we need you."

"Well grandson, I'm only about 40 feet away." Jack turned around immediately then ran over and hugged him. His grandpa wasn't a small man but his gray hair, mustache and wrinkles pretty much gave his age away.

"Someone told me you needed a minister to put his John Henry Hancock on the license. Well, I'm ready willing and able, Grandson. By then the others were there and more than a little pleased to see Jack's grandpa.

Hollingsworth shook his hand and said, "It's good to meet the individual that mentored this brilliant young man. He was a godsend on our expedition, Sir."

"Yes, Professor, Jack kept me informed every step of the way with texts, it must have been an exciting journey. I wish I could have come, but I'm afraid these old bones are a bit too feeble to be riding a mule into the canyon. But I lived vicariously through all of Jack's communiqués."

He shook hands with all of the others then said, "I must say I haven't seen this many lovely ladies since my days at the University." He looked at Jacqueline and Noel and said, "Jack didn't exaggerate one little bit about you two. Well, let's get this wedding started, where's our ride?"

"Right, to the canyon then, shall we?" Jacqueline said, "follow me, the van will only hold twelve comfortably but if Jack can hold his bride to be on his lap and two others double up there should be just enough room. Any volunteers?"

Jack's parents said simultaneously, "We'll be happy to double up, folks."

"Great," Jacqueline replied, "let's get on board."

The sun was high in the sky with just enough clouds to stave off the heat. Everyone got out and took their places and Jennings stood behind a small rock formation that was just wide enough to hold his Bible. The rest were seated on folding chairs with the exception of Jack and Lila who were facing each other hand-in-hand.

Jennings said, "It's been my pleasure to know these two young people for a while now and if I started to talk about them and how special they are it would take more time than would be appropriate here. I'd like to ask everyone to bow with me if you would. Lord of heaven and earth we stand in awe this day of the beauty that surrounds us and we give thanks for all the many blessings You've allowed us to enjoy. Now."

He tried to stave off the emotions he was feeling, cleared his throat and said, "Jack, do you take Lila to be your lawfully wedded wife, to have and to hold, in plenty and in want, in sickness and in health, as long as you both shall live?"

"He smiled and said, "I absolutely do."

"And do you Lila take Jack to have and to hold, in plenty and in want, in sickness and in health, as long as you both shall live?"

She smiled and said, "Absolutely."

"Seeing that you both have pledged your lives to each other before God and these witnesses I now pronounce you husband and wife, and you know what comes next."

Jack kissed Lila and all of those in attendance clapped and cheered. Jack looked at Carson and said, "You being the tallest and also having the best vantage point would you be willing to take a group photo?"

"Sure, everyone line up and say cheese." They put down chairs for Gramma Rose and Grandpa Jack in front with everyone else lined up shortest in the front and tallest in the back with a panoramic view of the canyon in the background.

Carson smiled and said, "This is going to be a beautiful wedding photo." snap, snap. "Now just the bride and groom, please." snap, snap. "That's it, now the parents with the bride and groom." snap, snap. "That's good, now let's get a photo of Gramma Rose and Grandpa Jack with the newlyweds."

Jack and Lila knelt down in front of the two grandparents who placed a hand on their shoulders and Carson said, "Say cheese." snap, snap. "Great, that's going to be an amazing picture."

Before everyone got back in the van they just stood around talking and enjoying the view for what seemed like a very long time. Grandpa Jack signed the wedding license, handed it to Jack and said, "You're all legal now namesake."

Jennings and Angela walked over to Carson and Noel who were in a tight embrace and Jennings said, "How about a double wedding here this time next year?"

Carson replied, "I'm game," he looked at Noel smiled and said, "How about you, Amazon princess?"

"A double wedding sounds good to me, now if we can just find my beautiful sister a mate between now and then it could be a triple wedding."

Jacqueline smiled and replied," Hey, find me a man and I'm all for it."

Carson said, "I know a lot of tall guys, I'll see what I can do to make that triple happen."

They all laughed and Hollingsworth quipped, "Smashing, simply smashing, I wouldn't have missed this for the world, I do so hope I'll be invited in the event there is a triple."

"Absolutely, old friend," Jennings replied, "We may even let you officiate."

Printed in the United States
by Baker & Taylor Publisher Services